At the Sign of the Clove and Hoof

ZOË JOHNSON

 Moonstone Press

This edition published in 2023 by Moonstone Press
www.moonstonepress.co.uk

Introduction © 2023 Moonstone Press

Originally published in 1937 by Geoffrey Bles

At the Sign of the Clove and Hoof © the Estate of Zoë Johnson

ISBN 978-1-899000-56-2
eISBN 978-1-899000-57-9

A CIP catalogue record for this book is available from the British Library

Text designed and typeset by Tetragon, London
Cover illustration by Jason Anscomb
Printed and bound by CPI Group (UK) Ltd, Croydon, CRO 4YY

Contents

INTRODUCTION

"This has come straight from the murderer, don't you realize that? Hot from his bloody hand. Don't stand there dithering, man. Don't you realize you hold the key to everything? All unwitting, you've stumbled on the villain's secret! Quick, quick, what is it you've seen, heard, felt, smelled, dreamed?"

Christian Peascod in *At the Sign of the Clove and Hoof*

At the Sign of the Clove and Hoof was first issued in 1937 by British publisher Geoffrey Bles, who had a reputation for spotting new talent. It was author Zoë Johnson's first book and gathered good reviews: the *Evening News* cited "an admirably complicated but clear plot, with first-class characters". *Truth* magazine devoted a lengthy review to the novel, highlighting its "clever character drawing and good atmosphere", summarizing the book as "a first-rate detective yarn, with thrills and excitement throughout" and naming Zoë Johnson as a new author to be reckoned with. Johnson followed with a second detective novel, *Mourning After*, in 1939, that also garnered favourable reviews. But like other Golden Age of Detection examples, she stopped writing novels and the books fell out of print and were forgotten.

In 2021, vintage crime historian John Norris discovered the book and gave it a glowing review in his Pretty Sinister blog, praising the novel for its offbeat sense of humour and colourful characters, a world of "kooks, oddballs and eccentrics galore". He applauded the way Johnson "dared to flout the tacit and written rules of detective fiction and come up with a solution that defies all those conventions". Interested in seeing the book back in print, John went looking for biographical information on Zoë Johnson and initially found nothing, which suggested the name might be a pseudonym. The book's largely male cast of characters, hard-edged satirical humour, emphasis on men gathering in a local pub and knowledge about the life of a fisherman seemed likely to be the work of a man, and there were other male writers published by Geoffrey Bles with similar styles who used nom de plumes. However, further digging revealed an online update to Allen J. Hubin's *Crime Fiction, 1749–1980: A Comprehensive Bibliography* that referenced the possible author (with caveats) as Zoë Grey Johnson (1913–92).

At this point John passed the baton and we took up the hunt for Ms. Johnson. Mining the publisher records was not fruit-ful: Geoffrey Bles had sold to William Collins & Co. in 1953, and they in turn were eventually absorbed into the behemoth HarperCollins—the available archives did not contain any ref-erence to a Zoë Johnson. We then went down the genealogical rabbit hole and made the mistake of doubting Hubin's reference to the middle name Grey, thinking it must be one of several options. And surely that Zoë was a bit young for such an accomplished first effort? Dear Reader, we paid for that hubris—research on Ancestry.com revealed nine potential Zoë Johnsons whose age and location made them the possible author. Searching the databases became an evening pastime and ever so slowly the list condensed. (One candidate looked particularly promising until we found the record of admission to a religious order in 1937, which made her unlikely to be writing novels with "clove and hoof " in the title.) Eventually the real author was found: Zoë (née Grey Turner) Johnson. Hubin had the correct name (or at least part of it) from the start.

Zoë Grey Turner was born on 24 April 1914 in Northumberland, England. Her father, George, was a distinguished surgeon (after whom 'Grey Turner's sign', a rare form of abdominal bruising, is named). Initially, she was educated at home by a series of French, German, Italian and Spanish-speaking governesses. She was then sent to a boarding school, Queen Ethelburga's in Harrogate. From there, she went to St. Hugh's College, University of Oxford, which she attended between 1932 and 1935, graduating with a degree in Modern Languages. She married Vernon Johnson (a contemporary of hers at Oxford) on 28 September 1939, so technically "Zoë Johnson" was a pseudonym for her first book and perhaps for her second as well, depending on its date of publication. At the time of her marriage, she was living at Rycote Park, Milton Common, Oxford, and her marriage certificate listed her profession as author. After the Second World War, the couple moved to St. Austell, Cornwall, and by all accounts lived a quiet life. Vernon died in 1987 and Zoë died on 19 October 1992.

Moonstone Press is delighted to reissue *At the Sign of the Clove and Hoof* for new audiences to enjoy.

At the Sign of the
Clove and Hoof

FIRST DEATH AND SECOND DEATH

"And so, in conclusion, I would urge those of you whose faith has been so lukewarm in the past as not to play a prominent, nay, a paramount rôle in the life of every day, to turn afresh and lift…"

The Vicar of Larcombe always read his sermons, but as a concession to such members of his flock as looked for more spontaneity and direct inspiration in his teaching, he was in the habit of raising his eyes from his book at intervals of about three minutes, to show that his congregation was not entirely out of his mind. At the word "lift," he shot one of his customary glances into the body of the little church and in doing so, his eye, his watery eye, took on an expression of, at once, great surprise and indignation; surprise that there should be a stranger present and indignation that the stranger should be asleep.

In the second pew from the back was a man; a very big, broad man with a square, pink face; he was wearing a dirty raincoat and his face was happy as he slumbered.

The Vicar frowned and proceeded, "… your faces to the Lord, seeking the Light."

The choirboys hurriedly stopped their Noughts and Crosses. With a sharp click of her false teeth, Mrs. Busby the butcher's wife shut her mouth which she invariably kept open throughout the sermon, and nudged her husband for no reason at all. Under the schoolmistress's inexpert, podgy fingers the ancient organ gave its preliminary cough and set about wheezing the final hymn.

As the Vicar stepped down from the pulpit, the whole church seemed to rustle in anticipation, and it was this rustle that woke the sleeper in the second pew from the back. Evensong was at an end. The handful of glum worshippers, uncomfortable in their Sunday starch and polish, shuffled out with whispering and creaking into the bleak September drizzle.

The little vestry of Holy Trinity was ill-lit and cold and damp, and it reeked of the carbolic soap which Mrs. Fitzroy lavished on its bare boards. With his mind on the remaining blank spaces in Torquemada's Cross-Word Puzzle and the outstanding half of a bottle of whiskey, the Rev. Ernest Pratt swiftly unvested and hurried out into the rain. But a little old man with the voice and cheeks of a child was waiting for him; it was Sam Bowle; he doffed his hat and said, "Beg pardon, sir, I was wondering if you could spare a minute for our poor Dick. He thinks he's going to die and he wants to see you bad. Would you mind, sir?"

The Vicar made very little effort to conceal his disappointment. "Is it as serious as all that?"

"Well, you can't rightly say, sir, with our Dick being like what he is. Dr. Girdwood has been saying he might pop off any minute for these last three years. But he wants to see you bad, sir; he does, indeed, sir."

"Oh, very well." The Vicar pulled his blue raincoat tightly round his throat, pushed the brim of his clerical pork-pie low over his eyes, and strode off down the hill, his trouser-legs flapping, his shoulders hunched, while poor Sam, almost at a trot, tried to keep up with him and to draw him out with talk of Alan Charnock's new boat and the forthcoming marriage of his own cousin Lil at

Setterham. But the Rev. Pratt maintained an ungracious silence all the way down the hill and seemed to find solace only in squinting down the long length of his rheumy nose.

Before his unfortunate illness, the invalid Dick Bowle had been remarkable in Larcombe for two things; the excellence of his private blends of tobacco (especially his justly-popular "Rich and Strong" at 6½d.) and his extreme sensitiveness as to the baldness that had come upon him with such suddenness. For his seven hairless years he had worn a bowler hat every minute of the day; there were rumours, even then, that he wore it in bed— but now that he was bedridden, Larcombe *knew* that it was so. Practically everyone in the village had been to visit him at some time or other, and they had seen it, this ripe old bowler perched on his long, flat head, and they were, in a way, proud of their tobacconist who had thus distinguished himself. The clergyman frowned and pursed his lips as he came into the sickroom. Old Dick was sitting propped up against soiled pillows on his crude, brass-knobbed bedstead and wearing a seaman's blue sweater for a bed-jacket; between his teeth was a short-stemmed clay and the air was blue with the smoke of thick-twist; the patchwork quilt was littered with sheets of a sporting, sensational Sunday newspaper. The old man removed his clay and waggled it in welcome, indicating a rush-bottomed chair from which brother Sam hastened to remove a teapot and a tin of sardines. Pratt sat down on the very edge of this chair, locked his fingers together and cracked his knuckle-joints.

He always performed his visiting-duties perfunctorily and unsympathetically, and he ministered to the incongruous Dick with especially bad grace. This time, however, he was shaken out of his uninterested mumbling.

"Did you notice that big, red-faced man in church to-day, sir?" enquired Sam during a lull in the Vicar's drone.

"Yes, I did. The wretched fellow was asleep. Who is he?"

"I dunno proper," replied the tobacconist's brother. "He only come this morning. But they were saying at the Cloven that he were a detective from London."

If Sam had announced that the Vicarage was on fire, he could not have surprised and distressed the clergyman more. For a moment, Pratt sank back on his chair without saying anything, his watery eyes dilating and his thin, knobbly throat giving out pitiful clucking sounds. Then he got to his feet and muttering something about a letter to get to the post, shot out of the house. A very surprised Sam watched him round the quay and set off up the hill towards the Vicarage, half walking, half running.

Sam went back to the bedroom.

"I never could abide that man," he said.

Old Dick cackled. "Now, now, you mustn't be saying these things. He's a minister, ain't he? Ministers, I reckon, is not like other folk. Ministers 'as their own ways of doing. And I must say, Sam boy, yon's done me a power of good. Yes."

"You'm be a bit better then?"

"Surely. Them Bible-things is fine stuff."

Dick's clay was drawing again and he reached for a sheet of his newspaper. But his brother shook his head.

"He's a crabbid old bouncer. I've always said so and I always will. What's he want to go galumping off for like that?"

"Brew a cup o' tea, Sam boy," said Dick, deep in the report of a divorce case.

*

At this time, so early in the evening, things were pretty quiet at the Clove and Hoof, but the six or seven who were in the Bar at the front were having their money's worth and no mistake. The big man in the dirty raincoat came up for breath from the depths of his pot and repeated for the third time in a quarter of an hour: "I can't tell you nothing definite about my business here."

Then he peered closely and fiercely at his audience, one by one, so that they started, even the immovable Bert Yeo behind the bar, and gulped their cider in concert.

"But if any of you knows of anything suspicious that's going on round here, or has been going on, you'd best tell me. If you don't—"

He said no more, but ordered another pint instead.

There was a silence and then everyone started talking at once.

"Horrel, up to Corfield, he's lost three sheep and a heifer."

"My boy Joe found a skull in the sand."

"There's been lights on the Head more than once in the middle of the night."

"There used to be a woman as they say had the Eye—good with the warts she was, too."

"One at a time, one at a time!" shouted the big man, taking out a notebook. "Now then," he said in his Cockney voice, "let's have it systematic. Now who was it as said they found a skull?"

Sam, the Lobster Man, was shaping up for a reply when the Bar's attention was taken by the sound of hurrying footsteps on the road outside. Alan Charnock was sitting by the window and he peered out into the dusk.

"'Tis the Vicar," he said, "and he's going like he had wind under his tail."

"What's his hurry, then?" enquired the landlord. "If he runs up the hill like that once or twice, he'll be popping."

"He takes too much spirit, does *he*," said Sam the Lobster Man.

"Drinks whiskey for pastime," grunted a farm-hand from up the valley.

But they were all much more interested in the detective than in their Vicar and they turned to him once more, only to find to their quick surprise that he was hurriedly draining his pot. He replaced his notebook, muttered a "Good night all" and bustled from the room, buttoning up his coat as he went.

The men in the Bar looked at one another. Alan Charnock gave a low whistle of incredulity. They crowded to the door. They looked up the road, and sure enough, the detective was taking the hill to the Vicarage. They came back slowly, like a puzzled jury returning to the box: some rubbed their ears, some shook their heads, some licked their lips and ordered more cider, all talked.

"The Vicar!"

"I knew'd all along!"

"The Vicar!"

"He's emptied yon Church of decent folk!"

"The Vicar!"

"Handcuffs—I saw 'em with me own eyes!"

"The Vicar!"

"I never could abide that man!"

"The Vicar!"

"The Church funds!"

"What's he done?"

"What *can* he have done?"

"The VICAR!!!"

The Clove and Hoof was filling up now, and there'd never been such a hubbub over one topic since 1918. Surprisingly enough, Bert Yeo was the only man who had no theory to offer and nothing to say; he served the drinks dully, not at all like his usual effervescent self; he wore a puzzled frown and his eye was constantly on the door.

The Vicar was so preoccupied as he hurried up the hill that he never noticed the footsteps behind him until he came to the absolute quiet of the little stretch of road separating the Vicarage from the last cottage in Larcombe. But before he turned round to look, he knew very well who was following him. It was almost dark by this time, but there was no mistaking the looming bulk of the big man with the square, pink face. If he had dared, Ernest Pratt would have run the rest of the way to his house; but he did not dare.

His housekeeper let him in, and he nearly knocked her down as he brushed past her to collapse in an arm-chair. He looked half-crazed as he sat there under the suspense of listening for a slow crunching on the gravel-drive; but the dead silence remained unbroken except for the heavy, indignant breathing of Mrs. Fitzroy whose ear was glued to the study door.

After a time, he went up to a bedroom giving on to the road and cautiously looked out; for about ten minutes he stood by the window becoming less and less hysterical, for there was no movement of any kind down below. Then suddenly a match flared out in the dark, lighting up a face that was both pink and square. The Stranger lit his pipe and made himself as comfortable as possible with his back to a stout tree; seemingly he was settling down to a long vigil. But judging by the lack of interest in his face and in his bearing and by the number of times he unguardedly struck matches for his pipe, his heart was not in his work.

The Vicar left his evening meal untouched; the slippers by the study fire got warmer and warmer, but he stuck to his damp, black boots. "16 Down" in Torquemada, "Soil a basket-swing with Neapolitan quartz for a pettifogging fustilarian," remained unsolved, though earlier in the day he had had glimmerings of what the twister was up to. Only the whiskey received its due and customary attention.

Every quarter of an hour or so, he creaked upstairs to the front bedroom and looked out into the road. Sometimes a match was struck almost at once, sometimes he had to wait quite a long time for it; but sooner or later the Stranger's pipe would go out and require re-lighting.

About midnight, Pratt unlocked a little drawer at the back of his desk, took out some papers and after some hesitation, threw them on the fire without reading them. He knelt down in the hearth to see to it that each sheet burned properly, and though he was very close to the fire, he was shivering. When the papers were charred, he raked the ashes with the poker. Getting to his feet, he locked his fingers together, cracked his knuckle-joints and looked about him. His study was neat and clean; even the books on the many shelves were clean, but it was due to his fanatically tidy housekeeper that they were not laden with dust: it was not due to him, for he never read books other than books of reference for his cross-words. There was a pile of Parish Magazines on a side-table. There was an unlovely engraving of Keble College over the mantelpiece. There was an empty soda syphon, a whiskey bottle and a tumbler on a tray by the leather arm-chair. There was an aspidistra on a stand by the window. There was a brown stain, strangely like a map of Australia, on the ceiling. The Rev. Ernest Pratt looked about him and cracked his knuckle-joints. He was still shivering.

It was about this time that the Stranger left his post after striking the last of a full box of matches. He was cold, but he seemed not unhappy as he strolled down towards the village, for he was humming a little tune to himself. The wind was freshening from the West.

Larcombe awoke on the Monday morning fully expecting to find its Vicar in chains. Instead, it found him dead.

The driver of the early mail-van coming along the Setterham road had stopped to investigate the matter of a small car, stationary, abandoned and with its front wheels within a few feet of the unguarded edge of the cliff. Suspecting an accident of some kind, he had looked down over the edge and sure enough, he had been able to make out a crumpled black heap on the rocks far below. He had rasped the stubble on his chin with one hand and pushed back his peaked cap from his forehead with the other while he debated with himself whether or not he should try and climb down to the sea without further delay. But he did not climb down to the sea: he returned to his car and drove as fast as his cautious nature would permit down into Larcombe.

A quarter of an hour later he was telling his tale to Police Constable Jack Marsden in the latter's whitewashed, green-tiled cottage.

"And I'm damned if I don't think it's a man or summat," he said.

Jack, who was in the middle of his breakfast, fastened the last button of his tunic and helped himself to a final gulp of thick tea.

"Eh?" he squeaked in his inquisitive falsetto. "A man or summat? Thank you, Alf, I'm much obliged."

Jack Marsden was not stolid, nor was he fat or lazy or supercilious towards his fellow-bumpkins. He was thin and scraggy and big-eyed; something of an acrobat and tap-dancer; and had he not suffered from heartburn, brought on, as any Harley Street man could have told him, by his inveterate habit of bolting his food and drinking too much stewed tea, he would have been very happy in his work, which was chiefly concerned with dog licences and the helping home of drunken men on Saturday nights.

Knowing that the bottom of Crale Cliff was difficult of access from the road and knowing that the tide was right for putting a boat out, he very properly commandeered Alan Charnock's new craft and gave the owner orders to let her go flat out.

There was something rather fine about him as he crouched in the prow of the *Daisy*, shading his eyes with his hand, the better, as he thought, to make out the car at the top of Crale Cliff. He was like a dyspeptic, but none the less eager greyhound. Tragedy was a bit of all right.

The crumpled black heap on the rocks was a man sure enough. More, it was the Vicar.

The enthusiastic light in Marsden's eye dimmed when he drew near to the broken conglomeration of protruding bones, clerical grey and blood, but it returned for a moment when he looked up the cliff…

"Poor old Vicar," he was murmuring. "Poor old chap. Fancy a thing like that happening to him, just fancy." And then his voice rose even beyond its customary shrillness as he turned to Charnock who was looking uneasy and vaguely sick. "Hey, Alan, wait a minute though. He—he couldn't have *fallen* out of that there car, could he? Could he hell though. What's all this? Not the Vicar, surely! A clergyman wouldn't *chuck* himself over, would he? Surely not?"

Charnock, who was a shy youngish man with ginger hair, was looking uneasier than ever. "It's a proper mess," he said.

Jack pulled out his notebook and pencil for want of something better to do, but he could think of nothing to write in it except "Rev. Ernest Pratt."

"Tell you what, Alan," he said at last. "I'll stay here and keep watch and you scoot back and ring up Dr. Girdwood. That'll be best, won't it?"

"I suppose so," said Charnock. "What will his number be?"

"Bert Yeo'll know."

Charnock pushed off and Jack watched the boat as long as he could so as to be able to keep his eyes off what remained of the Minister of Religion.

On principle, Dr. Girdwood from Corfield detested all clergymen—and all his life he had detested the Vicar of Larcombe more than most. When, therefore, he arrived on the scene and knelt down to turn the corpse over on to its back, his first feeling was not, as it usually was in such cases, one of melancholy disgust at the essential ugliness of every form of death, but rather of sardonic relish. He had hated Pratt. Pratt had died. Pratt had died an unpleasant death. Good. Dr. Girdwood was like that. He was a hard, childish man. But his relish gave way to surprise, shocked incredulous surprise, when he shifted his gaze from the dead man's face to the dead man's chest. There was a little hole in the waistcoat where there should have been no hole, and there was blood round the edges of it. Dr. Girdwood wrenched the jacket and waistcoat off the corpse and bared the breast which he probed with instruments from his black bag. When he had done, he growled at Jack. "This is most extraordinary, Marsden. The man's got a bullet in his lung. You'd better get on to headquarters. I don't like the look of this."

Back at his cottage, poor Jack had to repeat many of his words three and four times over the telephone. Excitement had made his voice shriller than ever. "Bailiff? No, sir, not bailiff. No, no, no. Crale Cliff, sir, that's right, that's right; your side of Larcombe."

"Keep everyone away from the body," grumbled the important voice, the impatient voice, from the other end, "and from the car. You understand? And watch what you do with your own fat feet. I'll be right over."

Jack would have banged the receiver down hard, only he wasn't sure whether his gesture wouldn't be noticed. He wasn't very handy with telephones. He looked down at his feet, feet that could tap out the Yankee Eight Reverse with any in Devon. "Fat feet," he said. "Ahhrr."

When Inspector Blutton arrived at the Crale Cliff he did not have as much time to consider the corpse, its immediate surroundings and its position relative to the car as he could have wished, for the tide was nosing up only three or four yards away. A brief examination taught him nothing new. The neighbouring rocks were like any other rocks. There were no helpful strands of cloth or incriminating buttons clenched in the dead clergyman's fingers. His face was not contorted in any terrible grimace.

Blutton, conscious of the handful of spectators surveying him from the road above and of his subordinates studying his methods at closer quarters, strutted up and down looking, in knowing fashion, now to left and now to right. After some minutes of this play, he gave orders for the remains to be conveyed to Setterham. Then he turned to Marsden. "Is there no easier way of getting up to the road?"

"No, sir, not with the tide being in, you see," said Jack, who was fidgety in the presence of this famous martinet.

The Inspector grunted "Huh!" and nerved himself for yet another fearsome and slippery clamber up the crazy track that zig-zagged across the face of the cliff about fifty yards from where the Vicar lay.

The rain of the previous evening had left the earth round the car beautifully soft and in the way of footprints, there was everything that a good detective could desire. There was an almost embarrassing plethora of well-defined tracks.

"What did I tell you about keeping people away from the car?" barked Blutton in his best bully manner.

"Nobody's been near to this car, sir," piped the indignant Jack, "before you came. And Jipps has been here since."

"There's been nobody," affirmed P.C. Jipps.

Blutton said, "You're *positive* of that?"

Jack and Jipps were positive and the Inspector duly set to work. He was painstaking and skilful and in half an hour he had learned a great deal. There had obviously been a struggle, and judging by the marks on the ground, it looked very much as if the Vicar had had to do with two, possibly three men. Blutton was on his hands and knees when Jack surprised him with a very sensible suggestion. "The G.P.O. man was here this morning; it was him saw it first."

"Good," grunted Blutton: one set of prints was sensibly fresher than the others. "Very good. That lets *them* out. So we've got two to reckon with. Come here, you—Marsden." Jack came. "Pratt hadn't a wooden leg, had he?"

Jack shook a startled head.

"And I don't think he'd be wearing hobnail boots, either, do you?"

Again Jack shook his head. Blutton, apparently satisfied with the constable's silent expressions of opinion, took measurements and impressions from the soft earth. Then he examined the car itself. The hand-brake was on, the door was open and suitcases were piled high on the back seat. The only sign of disorder that presented itself was the jumbled packing or unpacking of the suit-cases—of whose contents Blutton made a summary examination. The clergyman had obviously intended to be away from home for some little time. There were many changes of linen and hose, black shoes and slippers, a silk dressing-gown and a woollen one, hats, sets of studs, four night-shirts, two overcoats and a large wallet containing share certificates and vouchers, a cheque-book and passport. Conspicuous by their absence were Bibles and prayer-books, ecclesiastical raiment and clerical dickies. This last fact, however, escaped Blutton's notice, so intent was he on searching for traces of theft. That he found no traces of theft puzzled him considerably.

Still pondering and assailed by an uneasy feeling that the case was not going to turn out to straightforward pattern, he went up to Corfield to get his first-hand medical evidence from Dr. Girdwood. The latter was pretty confident that death had taken place between three and four o'clock that morning. "He wasn't shot at very close range, say two or three yards. Here's the bullet; came from an old Service revolver if you ask me. Not the slightest possibility of suicide, I'm afraid. Nasty business, Blutton. Odd for this part of the world. I can sympathize with anyone wanting to exterminate the Church and all its works, but I'm blowed if I don't think this is a queer way of starting. And why start with potty Pratt, anyhow? Now if the Suffragan had been put away quietly in his sleep…"

Blutton, who was not a Nonconformist for nothing, showed his fierce disapproval of such talk by frowning and making his mouth a thin, straight line. The sour little doctor coughed and broke off. "You're quite *sure* it wasn't robbery?"

"They didn't touch his money, his cheque-book, or his gold cuff-links or watch. The stuff in his bags is all higgledy-piggledy, but if they did take anything they were polite enough to lock the cases up again and put the bunch of keys back in the poor chap's trouser pocket. No, I don't think it was robbery."

"Then what was it all about?"

"I'm blowed if I know," grunted the policeman, reaching for his hat.

P.C. Jipps was driving the police car.

"The Vicarage," said Blutton, "and quick about it."

"O.K., sir," said Jipps patiently.

Mrs. Fitzroy at the Vicarage disliked Blutton very much indeed. To begin with, he had told her that her snuffling and nose-blowing made it difficult for him to understand what she said. She was a Christian widow, was Mrs. Fitzroy, and it shocked her to the very soul that a man should fail to be impressed by her parade of grief for a departed master and a Reverend at that: moreover, he didn't show a proper respect for the dead; nor for her proper place in the household.

"Give me the keys," he had said, and, "You stay where you are till I've finished my business." But his final shot as he left the room had been the worst of all. "I shall want a word with you, later." There had been insolence, suspicion, menace in his voice.

While the policeman went about his business, Mrs. Fitzroy sat in her kitchen, rocking her chair backwards and forwards in a most agitated way, clasping and unclasping her hands, sucking in her lips: she could hear him clumping about upstairs and she wished she'd thought to throw away those empty whiskey bottles. People had no right to burst in unexpected like that.

But he was a little less rude and alarming when he eventually settled down to serious talk with her. "You say you didn't hear the Vicar go out last night, Mrs. Fitzroy," he began. "Surely you must have heard the car?"

"I certainly did not. My room's at the back, and anyhow, when I goes to bed to sleep, I sleeps."

"He was still up when you went to bed then?"

"Yes, he was. He was doing a cross-word puzzle and he had his boots on, if you really want to know."

"Did he usually do cross-word puzzles in his bare feet?" When Blutton poked fun he poked as with a battering-ram.

Mrs. Fitzroy reddened. Blutton laughed. "What time did you go to bed?"

"I never been up a minute later than ten for the last seven years; never since Fitzroy died."

"Was he drunk?"

"Really! Really! I don't know what you mean."

Blutton stood up to repeat his question slowly. "Was he drunk?"

Mrs. Fitzroy began to snuffle.

"You're not going to sit there and tell me you don't know about his drinking?" His voice had risen. "When was that case delivered?"

"A fortnight ago to-day."

Blutton whistled. Twelve bottles of whiskey in fourteen days. Not bad going, at least for a clergyman. Once more he said, "Was he drunk?"

"He... he finished off half a bottle. But you see, he was a bit upset last night. He come in like a house on fire, he wouldn't touch his supper, he kept his boots on and he kept going up to his bedroom, up and down he was, up and down and up and down. I don't know *what* was the matter with him."

Blutton leaned forward and licked his lips. "Oh, he was, was he? And you've no idea what made him like that?"

Mrs. Fitzroy shook her head with conviction.

"Did he by any chance behave in a similar way last Monday?"

A look of surprise came into the woman's face. "Now you come to mention it, sir, he did. He didn't do any running up and down stairs, but he was in a horrible temper and snapped at me something awful. He drank a whole bottle, too, a whole bottle! And he never went out all day. He sent Jem, that's the boy who cleans the car, over to Corfield to tell them he was ill. There was a christening on, you see."

The policeman suddenly produced an envelope and thrust it under her nose. "Ever seen this before?" The words were rapped out.

"I should just think I have. Oh!" she gasped. "Oh, I see what you mean. Good gracious, yes. D'you know, I never thought that might have had anything to do with it. When I put it by his plate on the Monday morning, I said to myself: 'That's funny. Fancy *painting* the name and address on an envelope.' I thought it must be an advert, or something."

"Did you see what was inside it?"

"No. No, sir, I didn't. I didn't even see the envelope again, not till just this minute."

Blutton seemed disappointed and he changed the subject. "Did the Vicar have many visitors?"

"Well," she pursed her lips in thought, "let me see now. There's the Mothers' Knitting Guild officers and Annie Scoutey who does the Cubs and Brownies."

"No, I don't mean people like that. I mean private visitors."

"Oh, I see. Oh, no. Nobody like that. The Vicar, poor man, kept himself very much to himself. Oh, no. Nobody ever came to see him, friendly like."

Blutton did not know what line to pursue with Mrs. Fitzroy. He had, as yet, no theory to work on and that hampered him. He put a few more routine questions and then left her.

Jack Marsden, bursting with excitement, was waiting for him outside.

"There's been a Scotland Yard man here, sir!"

"What!" The Inspector almost laid hands on him as he yelled his surprise. The village constable told him what he had heard.

A big fat man had arrived by the morning bus from Setterham on Sunday. He had taken lodgings with one Jeremiah Scoutey. He had attended evensong at the church. He had drunk beer at the Clove and Hoof. He had spoken mysteriously and yet had made it abundantly clear that he was going to arrest the Vicar. He had followed the latter up the hill to the Vicarage. And that was the last that had been seen or heard of him.

"Take me to this Scoutey," cried the Inspector, startled for once in his upper-dog life.

Marsden led him to a little shop in the Orchard—a square of thatched cottages standing back from the quay.

"Hey," grumbled Jeremiah, the moment he set eyes on his uni-formed visitors, "I'm about sick of this, I am. And who wouldn't be? Didn't I sit up till past one o'clock last night, waiting to let this fellow in? whoever he is. And did he come? No! He damn well didn't. And he didn't pay me any rent, either. It isn't as if he'd left any luggage, either, there's only a cheap cut-throat and an old soft-collar. No, it isn't the game, that sort of stuff—even if he is a London detective. And d'you think it does a respectable barber and greengrocer any good to have the police at his shop? Look at them," he expostulated. "Look at them!" There was an interested housewife at every cottage door; there was a pop-eyed grubbage of children three yards away; the loungers at the near-by quay were looking towards the barber-greengrocer's shop.

In the ordinary way, Blutton would have told him to shut up the moment he had opened his mouth, but Blutton's head was in such a whirl that he let him run on. "What name did he give?" he asked, at length.

"He didn't say un's name."

"And he didn't say when he'd be back?"

"No, he did not."

"What did he look like?"

"He looked," growled the irate tradesman, "like a big fat cow. He had a red face and a mackintosh. He was about as tall as you, I should say... and a good bit fatter."

"Clean shaven?"

"Yes. Clean shaven, yes, I'm sure he was. And he talked like one of they Cockney chaps."

"Did he tell *you* he was a detective?"

"No, he didn't tell me nothing about his business. But at the Cloven they're saying..."

"I see," interrupted Blutton. "Well, listen to me, Mr. Scoutey. If he turns up again, you let Constable Marsden know at once. You understand? At once!"

"If he's a detective, why doesn't he do that himself?"

"You heard what I said," barked Blutton and strode from the shop.

His next move was to telephone to Setterham. Setterham immediately put a call through to New Scotland Yard and while he waited for the reply to this call, he listened to Marsden's report of what stray information he had picked up in the village. "I know for a fact, sir, that there's only one man with a wooden leg in Larcombe and that's the Cap'n—John-Thomas. He's out to sea though. Has been for a bit. And from what I can find out about hobnail boots, it's a funny thing, sir, but it looks like there weren't hardly any. Week-days, you see, the chaps here wears their rubbers, and Sundays, of course, they have their best, and no hobnails, sir, you see. Mind you, I don't doubt you'll find a tidy few big boots on the farms to Corfield and Poridge. They all have them there, all the farm chaps like. About the other thing— nobody in the cottages on the road heard the car last night, but old Hannabus says he did hear *something*. Mr. Peascod's the only one I didn't ask about that. You see, he isn't up yet, sir, or else he's away. I couldn't get no reply when I knocked."

The telephone-bell rang and Blutton learned that Scotland Yard had no officer operating in Devonshire; they suggested that the man might be from some Private Detective Agency; enquiries would be made. Blutton put down the receiver. "I'll talk to this Hanaby or whatever he calls himself, the chap who says he heard something. And we'll have a look at Peascod. You go in for pretty funny names down here, don't you, pretty funny?"

Jack smiled and said he supposed they did.

Old Hannabus, who had a shop on the road that led to the Vicarage, was a taxidermist, an antique-dealer, a rabbit-trapper, a clock-mender, a photographer, a herbalist, and he'd pull out a bad tooth for sixpence. His Christian name was Sebastian, he wore a beard and thick spectacles, and he did not wash over-much. He was very nervous in front of the Inspector. "Well, I heard a little noise all right, but I wouldn't like to say it was a motor. More like something slithering on the gravel."

"About what time would that be?"

"Well, I'd been in bed a long time. I woke up because my gumboil was worse and I thought it would be a good thing if I sucked a piece of alum, so I went downstairs to fetch some and it was then I heard this little noise."

Blutton regarded the man with ill favour. Blutton hated dirt—and there was no denying that his face and beard and hands and finger-nails and clothes were dirty. He loved orderliness and decency—and there was no denying that the shop was insanitary, with its poky, cobwebbed window, its strange smell composed of numberless dusty, decaying ingredients ranging from acid drops to old tarred rope, and its fantastic jumble of junk. Looking at his own boots to avoid seeing the stains of nicotine and food on Hannabus's moustache and beard, he said, "And I take it you didn't look out to see what was making this little noise—as you call it?"

Old Sebastian shook his head. "I only wish I had, sir."

"What d'you mean by that? You wish you had, eh?"

Old Sebastian began to stammer. "Only, sir—I mean, sir—If I had looked out, sir—I'd—I'd be able to tell you what I saw, sir—wouldn't I, sir?"

Blutton snorted and took his leave. When he got outside he wiped the back of his hand across his mouth and took in several very deep breaths of the good sea air.

Next door to Hannabus was a tumbledown cottage called "The Nook": it was, probably, the smallest in Larcombe and it was certainly the most extraordinary to behold. The bulging, sloping walls which leaned upon the shop as upon an old, old friend were covered with a pink wash glaringly at variance with the white of the other cottages; the woodwork round the minute windows was painted a harsh blue, the door was green and on it was an enormous brass knocker that would not have looked out of place in Belgrave Square.

"If you'd be wanting to talk to the Mr. Peascod I was telling you about, sir, this is where he lives."

"I'll see him," said Blutton.

They interrupted Mr. Peascod while he was boiling his midday breakfast—an egg. He turned out to be a young man with a shock of straw-coloured hair, bright blue eyes, a very gentle voice and long, thin hands; he was dressed in a flowered dressing-gown and he refused to open his door more than a couple of feet. He was also very uncommunicative, declaring that he had heard nothing and that he knew nothing likely to interest his visitors—and was surly in his ignorance. "You ought to know, officer, that I am a stranger here. I stand aloof from village politics."

"But," cried Blutton. But the door was shut in his face.

"Is this fellow barmy?" he asked Marsden.

"Oh, I dunno, sir. I don't know nothing about him except he paints pictures and plays the piano."

The Inspector went on his way, puzzled and more than suspicious of everything and everyone in the little fishing village of Larcombe.

Late in the afternoon, he talked matters over with his chief. He made no secret of the fact that he was far from seeing daylight in the case. "This is all I know so far; or at least, this is what I think *happened*. The Vicar, Pratt, came home after evening service in something of a state. He was very fidgety. He wouldn't eat his supper. He drank a lot of whiskey. Some time in the early hours he packed four suit-cases with clothes, underwear, etc., and most of his valuables. He left the Vicarage quietly, *pushed* his car out into the road—he must have done that or his housekeeper would have heard him—and free-wheeled down the hill through Larcombe as far as the quay. Then he drove round the quay and up along the cliffs on the Setterham road. *And someone stopped him after about a mile.* There is every indication that he struggled with two men—a man with a wooden leg and another wearing size 10 hobnail boots. There are marks on the ground that make this practically certain. He was shot at fairly close range with a revolver and he was pushed or he fell over the cliff."

"I see," said the light-hearted Chief Constable. "So all you want now is the cripple and the beetle-crusher."

Blutton forced himself to smile and went on solemnly. "There have been no reports of any suspicious vagrants in the neighbourhood, and Larcombe itself is full of pudding-faced oafs who think of murder as just something you read about in the newspapers. There's only one chap with a wooden leg and he's at sea. His name's Ridd—they all call him the Captain and he seems to be a bit of a card. I'm pretty sure it wasn't robbery, as I've already told you, and I have a feeling it wasn't accidental. To be honest, sir, I'd feel a lot happier in my mind if I knew why the Vicar was running away."

"Running away? You really think he was?"

"Well, it certainly looks like it."

"But why should a Vicar bolt? Injudicious rape? The Parish Funds? There's not much else you can think of, is there?"

"I don't know about that, sir. I've got Hardy and Kettle's to send a man to go through his books to check up on the financial side."

"Good."

Blutton rubbed his ear. "And now, sir, I don't want you to think I've gone all sensational or anything, but what d'you think of this?"

He handed over the envelope he had taken away from the Vicarage. The Chief Constable's eyebrows went up as he examined it: on an ordinary envelope, plain and of cheap quality, someone had painted in block capitals: "Rev. Pratt. The Vicarage. Larcombe. S. Devon," in blue water-colour. It had been posted in Larcombe on the previous Sunday. He laughed. "The real Penny Dreadful touch, what? On the other hand, maybe someone had run out of pens and pencils."

"When he got that letter, sir, he behaved very queer. He shut himself up in his room all day and drank a bottle of whiskey, a bottle at least."

"Did he now, Blutton? A remarkable cleric."

"And I'm going to suggest that that letter wasn't an ordinary one, quite apart from its painted address. People don't do things like that for just nothing at all."

The Chief Constable shifted in his seat. "What are you getting at, eh, blackmail or something?"

"I'm not at all sure, sir. But I do know there's more in this case than…"

"Than meets the eye. Quite, Blutton, quite."

"And when I know who wrote that letter, and when I know who this so-called detective is, perhaps I won't be in the dark quite as much as I am at present."

"Very likely not. I shall be very surprised indeed if you are; and now, my dear fellow, if you'll excuse me, I must go and take wine with our dear Mayor—the Radical bounder."

Blutton departed to his own office and had been there not more than five minutes when a report came in from London stating that as far as could be ascertained no recognized Private Detective Agency had sent a man to South Devonshire within the last three months. The Inspector smiled grimly as he read it. "London detective!" he muttered to himself. "Pah—the besotted dolts!" Then he picked up the telephone and gave orders for extra men to be drafted to the Larcombe area. An immediate and general hue-and-cry for Jeremiah Scoutey's lodger was to be set up.

This done, he himself returned to the scene of operations. Driving down the hill into the village from the Crale Cliff side of the Creek, he noticed, despite the dusk, that there was something different about the place. Something odd which he could not place at first. It was a ship, a dirty little tramp tied up at the jetty; ugly amid such picture post card beauty, for however insanitary and unstable the Larcombe cottages might be, they looked very pretty from the outside, sloped together along the creek with their backs to the wooded cliff; thatch, whitewash, blue smoke, nothing was wanting. The unsightly cargo-boat struck an incongruous note. It had certainly not been there in the morning or early afternoon.

He paid another call on Scoutey, this time to examine his erstwhile lodger's bedroom and the scant luggage he had left behind him. But there was nothing to help him. There was only the razor, which was of a well-known make and many years old, and the soft-collar—old too and of a type that was turned out by the thousand every year; moreover, the latter bore no laundry mark. The man, whoever he was, was certainly travelling light. Blutton couldn't help wondering if his dentures were artificial or whether he carried a toothbrush in some fairly clean pocket. Surely people didn't come to the seaside without a toothbrush.

Blutton was for ever plaguing himself with questions like that, for Blutton was a man of very cleanly habits. He sighed and made a note that Jipps should go over the place for finger-prints: not that he had much hope that this manœuvre would yield any valuable results. Then he sought out Jack Marsden for news of the one-legged sailor.

There was noise in the Clove and Hoof and one man was making it. John-Thomas Ridd, the mariner home from the sea. You had only to look at him to know that he was drunk on rum. He had a wooden leg, a black patch over his left eye and his dress was cut in an out-moded, sea-faring mould. Summer visitors to Larcombe distrusted him. He looked too good to be true, and he mocked them. He would sit at the trestle table outside the inn and if any visitor did come his way, he would plunge at once into an account of the most ludicrous adventures which he gravely swore had befallen him; fantasies on the hard-worked theme of Sea Serpents, pirates, treasure-trove, sharks, smugglers, octopuses and duels with cutlasses were his chief stock-in-trade. He was like an illustrated joke in *Punch*. The visitors knew he was laughing at them and they were uneasy in his presence. In their embarrassment they would ask him to have a drink. "A little tot o' rum, thankee," the true legendary touch. But however much strangers disliked his extravagant mockery and his solemn buffoonery, Larcombe loved him. He was the "Cap'n." He was the Oracle. He was the arbiter of political discussions, religious bickerings and family disputes. He was the Bar. And his homecomings were always an event.

And so there was noise in the Clove and Hoof that evening. John-Thomas was in the middle of an enormously improbable story of how, in China, he had once seen six parsons—not a niggardly *one*—shot in the stomach with arrows, half-roasted and then thrown to a pit of lions just before life was extinct, when Marsden came into the Bar.

"Would you mind, Cap'n?" he said diffidently; "the Inspector would like a word with you."

"Delighted, Jack me boy. You know that any friend of yours is a friend of mine." The Bar laughed loudly. "Ask the gentleman to step up."

"Maybe he's signed the pledge," croaked old Hannabus. The Bar laughed loudly.

Jack blushed. "He'd be obliged if you'd come into the Parlour."

The Captain put on a mock-mournful face and voice. "Perhaps you'd rather put the bracelets on here and now, sonny."

The Bar laughed loudly and raised a cheer as he stumped out.

Jack was uneasy, he wished he'd explained more fully to the Inspector the privileged and unique position which John-Thomas held in Larcombe, especially when the former refused the old salt's jovial handshake.

Blutton wasted no time. "When did you get in?"

"At five o'clock as near as makes no matter," said John-Thomas, eyeing him curiously.

"From Symouth, I understand."

"Correct, mister."

"And you left there at what time?"

"Soon after half-past one."

"Where did you spend last night?"

"In the *Saucy Sue* off Number 3 Steps in Symouth Pool." John-Thomas over-emphasized a belch. "And by your leave, sir, may I ask why the hell you're so bloody inquisitive?"

Jack Marsden looked very unhappy, but Blutton ignored the question, rose, and as he made his way out, he spoke over his shoulder in an intentionally quiet voice: "I shouldn't let it worry you too much."

Outside, the two policemen listened to a great roar of laughter that was obviously occasioned by Ridd's description of the adventure that had just befallen him. It was a safe bet that from thenceforth Blutton would receive little but derision from the people of the Larcombe Creek. But he gripped the constable's arm as if in excitement. "I want a map!"

"Yes, sir, in my cottage."

As he hurried away, the Inspector thought fast. It was a possibility, a distinct possibility considering the geography of the district. Larcombe stood on an isolated promontory: to the west was the port of Symouth, to the east, Setterham—with the big Symouth-Setterham Road making the base of the triangle. There was no direct road from Larcombe to Symouth, but there was no lack of winding country lanes between the two points. Given a fast car and a knowledge of the country you could make the double journey from Number 3 Steps in Symouth Pool to Crale Cliff and back in a little over two hours, even at night. There were the unmistakable traces of a wooden leg at the scene of the crime and John-Thomas Ridd had an unmistakable wooden leg.

Blutton checked his surmises on the Ordnance Map. They were bad, twisty little country lanes, the ones to the west of Larcombe, but even so, it could be done.

Blutton's eyes were shining as he carefully folded up the map: and as he did so, Marsden surprised him very much by breaking into his thoughts with the melancholy remark, "They say the Cap'n was expected back this morning."

The Inspector laughed almost good-naturedly. The idea was fantastic. This ridiculous old salt rushing from Symouth through the night to shoot a country parson who happened to be making a bolt for it because he'd received a painted envelope, and with the mysterious "detective" lurking in the background. It was rich. But rich as it was, it was the first workable theory that had cropped up. "And," said Blutton to himself, "I'm going to get my teeth into it and I'm going to hang on." Cheerfully he rubbed his hands together. There was no getting away from the wooden leg.

"He sent a post card to Bert Yeo at the Cloven, sir, saying he'd be back some time this morning. He always lets the chaps know when to expect him."

"You wait for me here. I'm going back to have another talk to our one-legged friend." Blutton slammed the cottage door behind him and Jack reached down his big, cracked teapot from the shelf, speculating simply and sombrely on the awful predicament in which his beloved Cap'n was shortly to find himself. In his heart, the Cap'n yielded first place only to his sweetheart Jane McQueen, who kept house for the Cap'n and was own sister to Rosa—barmaid of the Clove and Hoof and a bit of a flibberty-gibbet into the bargain.

"Bert," said Norman the Lobster Man, "you'm looking a bit brighter like."

For answer, Mr. Yeo smiled his enormous smile. Yes, he was feeling himself again; his smile stretched across his face like the ponderous gold chain that spanned his belly. "Have one, John-Thomas," he beamed.

"Don't interrupt," cried the Captain. "Thanks very much. Now what was I saying? Yes. Is this Peascod a Bolshie? Does he wear a red tie? Has he got long hair? Yes, he has. Does he go to church? Does he drink Christian Beer? or celestial Rum? No, he don't. Which only goes to show that—what shall I say?—that you've got to be careful, very careful. Once the Bolshies run this country, we'll all be killed in our beds. I'm a travelled man, I am, and I know what idolatrous the Bolshies are. Once they used to bow down to ikons and now they're iconaclisms."

He roared with laughter and, after a little hesitation, the Bar laughed with him. "It's as clear as a pikestaff," he went on, "that the Bolshies are at the bottom of all this. You tell me that this fat fellow who came here was a detective, huh! Did he show you his badge of office and his warrant? Eh? 'Course he didn't. He's no detective, he's a Bolshie and it's him and you-know-who that's done it between them. And now that I've settled that little point for you, let's have a song. Let's have the Ram of Derby:

> And if you don't believe me, sir,
> And if you think it's a lie…"

Inspector Blutton came in. The ballad stopped. But the Inspector was smiling. "Don't mind me," he said. He walked straight up to John-Thomas. Awkwardly, a teetotaller, he did his best to be pleasant. "Would you like a drink?"

John-Thomas looked him up and down slowly before he replied, touching his cap. "Thankee, mister, a little tot o' rum."

The Bar was an embarrassingly silent audience. Blutton cleared his throat. "Would you mind coming into the Parlour? I'd like another little talk with you."

John-Thomas grinned and leered with his one good eye. "A pleasure, mister, as the fly said to the handsome spider."

Blutton thought it best to laugh with the howling Bar.

When they were in the Parlour, he said, "Now, Captain Ridd, I'm sorry to have to trouble you like this, but murder's a nasty thing and you can't blame me if I have to go very carefully. I'm going to be very frank with you. The point is this—we have reason to believe that a man with a wooden leg was somewhere about Larcombe last night."

Ridd laid a hand on his arm. "Just a minute, officer. I'm not as drunk as I look, see? Let's get this straight. Now are you telling me that you think I've had something to do with this murder? because by cripes, if you are—!"

"I never said anything of the sort, Captain. All I want is an assurance that you were nowhere near Larcombe last night."

"But cripes, man, I've told you once I was in my bunk at Symouth. D'you think I'm a bloody flying ghost or something?"

Blutton lowered his voice. "Now keep your hair on. I've already said I can't afford to neglect any possibility, however slight. It so happens that Symouth isn't a thousand miles from Larcombe and there are such things as motor-cars. Do you follow me? Now you tell me the names of three or four people who can prove you were in your bunk between one o'clock and six o'clock this morning and I promise you I'll trouble you no further."

John-Thomas tossed off his rum, scratched his poll and swore an extravagant oath. "Let me see. Little Jimmy was aboard all right, but he was fast asleep, and me two hands were with their uncle who keeps the Penny Whistle; they're brothers, you see, and I'd given 'em the night off, seeing as there was nothing doing."

"I see." The policeman was silent for a moment. "And how was it you didn't get back here this morning as you'd intended?"

"Oh, that was funny, that was. You see, I'd reckoned on using the flood about ten and that would have got me in round about one o'clock, but just as I was set, who should blow along but old Simon Rope from the Customs? He said that they wanted to see me up at the Office. And what d'you think they wanted?" Ridd slapped his wooden leg and laughed a trifle bitterly. "This," he said. "This—me old rolling pin. Now I ask you, skipper, take a look at me. Take a good look. Do I look as if I'd ever stoop to trying me hand at contraband, as the Opera says? 'Course I don't. Well, believe it or not, the Customs was suspicious. 'There's been a lot of funny business going on,' says old Simon, 'and we've had orders to keep our eyes open. No offence meant, Captain Ridd,' he says, just like you, he says, 'but what about this piece of timber of yours?' The long and short of it was, they wanted to know if it was hollow or not. Can you beat it? Some of the drug people have been up to such flipperty dodges lately that they had to make sure. 'Course, I didn't take offence, it isn't my nature as anyone in Larcombe will tell you, so I offs with me leg and plonks it on the table. 'If that's hollow,' says I, 'you can clout me over the head with it.' Well, we had a good laugh and Simon brought out something that had come all the way from Jamaica, and before I knew where I was, it was midday. And that's how I came to be late."

And Blutton had to be satisfied with that.

After giving Marsden special instructions to obtain, by fair means or foul, an accurate impression of Ridd's wooden leg for future reference, he drove back to Setterham.

The Chief Constable was drinking fairly good port, his legs stretched out to a log fire. It was a sharp early-Autumn night and the wind was in the right quarter to allow the chimney not to smoke. He was very happy, as, indeed, he always was: he was enjoying the luxury of a fire for the first time for months, he was drinking fairly good port, his mind was a comfortable blank, and he was fiddling with the ears of his sprawling spaniel.

And then Inspector Blutton apologized his way into the room. The Chief Constable sighed, put his glass down and abandoned the ears of his dog. His hearth had suffered from the Inspector's zeal before this.

"Have some of my wife's Turkish Delight, Blutton, she assures me it is exquisite."

Blutton stuffed his mouth; then when his teeth were free from the sickly muck, he said, "What am I to do about this man Ridd, sir?"

"What's he been up to now?"

"I've just been given a 'phone message from Marsden. Here it is, sir. 'Leg and shoe fit like a glove.'"

"Eh," said the Chief Constable, sitting up in his chair.

"I left him the impressions I took of the prints this morning and told him to compare them with Ridd's own marks, and I take it the message means he's done it."

The Chief Constable showed rather more interest.

"That's one thing, sir. Now a quarter of an hour ago I rang up the Customs Office at Symouth and discovered that this beauty has been telling me a whole pack of lies! When I asked him why he was late in getting to Larcombe this morning, he pitched some yarn about being held up because the Customs had wanted to know if his wooden leg was hollow, and I even believed him when he was telling me."

The Chief Constable laughed. "Well, if he can take *you* in, Blutton, he must be either cracked or clever. But have you really got your eye on him?"

"That's what I've come to see you about, sir. I honestly can't make up my mind. On the one hand, you see, there's no doubt Ridd could have got from Symouth to Larcombe by car, done this business and got back to his ship in time to sail this morning. He hasn't got a ghost of an alibi for the early hours and for some reason best known to himself he pitches me a lot of lies about the Customs; on top of all that, he has a wooden leg which is identically the same pattern as the one that made the prints round the Vicar's car. On the other hand—" he ticked off the points on his thick fingers—"on the other hand. Point One: there isn't a glimmer of a motive. Point Two: he must have had previous knowledge that the Vicar was going to bolt at the very minute he did—which is unlikely—and he must have had an accomplice to drive the car because I discovered he's never handled one in his life. Point Three: if two of them arrive to meet the Vicar, that's all right, we've got two sets of prints. But where does the fake detective come in? I'm sure *he's* mixed up in it somewhere. You see, sir, from the time he followed Pratt up to the Vicarage, no one has seen or heard anything of him. And apart from Mrs. Fitzroy, the housekeeper, he was the last person in Larcombe to see the Vicar alive."

The Chief Constable bit the end of a cigar. "He might be in with Ridd. He might have gone back to Symouth in the car."

"Making three of them?"

"Um. And you can't find a motive?"

Blutton made a gesture of hopeless speculation. "It wasn't robbery. Passion? revenge? hate? jealousy? none of the *normal* things seem to fit the killing of a country parson."

"But how normal was your parson, Blutton? I thought you said he was bolting."

"So I did, sir. And yet I don't know. All his accounts are in order and—what's more—he'd over four thousand pounds worth of Gilt Edged with his bank."

There was a long silence. The spaniel yawned and scratched itself. The Inspector surreptitiously scraped a piece of Turkish Delight from the cavity of a molar with his finger-nail.

"You'll agree, sir, there's something odd about friend Ridd, something very odd—but I doubt if we have enough to touch him yet."

The Chief Constable shook his head. "I agree with you entirely. Keep an eye on him for a day or two; the Mysterious Stranger may have turned up by then and Ridd may have done something sillier than spin yarns. Then we'll see what's what."

"Right, sir; and I'll get on to Symouth to see if they can help at all."

They said good night and the Chief Constable returned to his dog's ears, his fire and his happy anæsthesis.

The next day, Blutton was very busy. With the help of Marsden and one of his own sergeants, he went the rounds of every house, cottage and bungalow in the village, requesting chance information relative to the tragedy and checking the whereabouts of all inhabitants during the night and early morning in question. He did not learn very much. To set up a satisfactory alibi for the middle of the night is, for the ordinary man, not an easy business. Those who had wives had least difficulty; but the statements of several of the younger large-footed men were neither entirely conclusive nor yet inconclusive.

Nor could he unearth any pair of hobnail boots large enough either at Larcombe, at Corfield or at Poridge to coincide with the prints left behind by the assailants of Ernest Pratt. The only lethal arms in Larcombe itself turned out to be several airguns and one ancient cannon, a relic of the Crimean War.

One highly important fact, however, did emerge. John-Thomas Ridd was able to establish an alibi.

When, on the previous evening, Jack had set out to obey his Inspector's orders to compare the Captain's footprint and wooden leg with the impressions taken from the muddy ground on the cliff, he had screwed up all his courage and tackled the old man as he was stepping round to the side of the Clove and Hoof for a purpose not unconnected with his potations. Now Jack was a favourite of his and when the old man had been given to understand that "the bloody Setterham bobby" had gone back to his kennel, he was quite willing to oblige. They had gone back to the Parlour to get the business over and Jack had felt sorely hypocritical and guilty as he drank his victim's health in new cider. There could be no doubt about it, however. The shoe and the stump were identical with the impressions—and it was with a heavy heart that he had telephoned the news to Setterham.

The next day, Blutton, confident that he had got hold of something, went up to Ridd's bungalow, the "Moorings," on the Crale Cliff side of the creek, to re-question and to caution him. But John-Thomas showed fight.

"I warn you," he roared in real anger, "if you come pestering me again, I'll dot you one on the nose. You think you're clever, don't you? with your footsteps and your tape-measures and your God-knows-what? Well, listen to me, mister; you've got to get up a bit earlier in the morning to catch an old sailor like me." And he proceeded, with great bluster and imprecation, to state a case that impressed even the biased Blutton. The two hands and Jim, the boy, off the *Saucy Sue*, and Jane McQueen who kept house for him were there to give it substance and support.

It seemed that John-Thomas had gone up to the "Moorings" as soon as his boat was safely tied up. He had had his bath, changed into his land clothes and taken from the hands of Jane herself his newly-polished buckled shoe which the girl swore had stood on the boot-rack for the ten days her master had been at sea.

"And that," roared Ridd in full-gulleted triumph, "is the shoe young Jack was a-measuring up off and a-messing about with last night in the old Cloven! Why, you poor galoot you, I was wearing me *sea-boot* when this 'ere murder of yours was going on! And now get out. You go and try to hang somebody else."

Blutton blew out his cheeks and turned on his heel; but as he was opening the garden gate, John-Thomas came stumping out after him. "Hey, mister," he bellowed, "just you wait a minute." His anger was gone, and its place, on his face and in his voice, was take by something approaching apprehension. "You're—you're not making any mistake about these footsteps of yours, they really are like what you say?"

"They are," said Blutton, "and I'm not making an mistake. That shoe and that wooden leg—or the very spit of them, the very spit of them to within a hundredth of an inch—were on Crale Cliff the night the Vicar was murdered."

Ridd stared him fiercely in the eye, and his stare was returned.

"Oh, they were, were they?" he said, and without another word swivelled on his stump and hurried back into the house.

Blutton walked down to the quay with a very glum face. He had no real wish to hang an innocent man, but he felt that he had been cheated. He felt angry that Ridd had established an alibi; not so much because he had a grudge against him but because he represented the one tangible starting-point for police action in this business. He was the man upon whom the Inspector had day-dreamed of founding a neat, quick case that would have redounded to his efficient energy, his unsparing devotion to routine enquiry, his common sense, his… The Inspector blew his nose on a big handkerchief and the noise he made caused a family of rabbits in the gorse above him to streak for home. He took out his notebook and ran his finger down a long list of names; the finger stopped at "Peascod." Blutton hadn't liked what little he had seen of Peascod and Peascod had given no satisfactory account of his movements. He pocketed his notebook, gave the pocket a determined slap and turned his red face towards "The Nook."

Mr. Peascod was still in his dressing-gown when he received his second visit from the police and, to begin with, he would only open his door just sufficiently for him to stick his head round. He spoke in monosyllables.

"Good afternoon," began Blutton with as much politeness as he could muster. "Might I have a word with you?"

"No," said Mr. Peascod.

"But I'm afraid it's rather important."

"Oh."

"I'm anxious to account for everybody's movements in Larcombe on Sunday night and early Monday morning. Could you—?"

"Trance."

The Inspector frowned. "France?" he growled.

Peascod shook his head. "*Trance.*"

But he wasn't understood. "Look here!" said Blutton.

Then the man behind the door did a strange thing; he flung it wide open so suddenly that Blutton took a step backwards;

he groaned, pulled a very wry face and said, "I should not have believed that the Flesh could have been so weak. Oh dear, oh dear. My very good sir, you are witness of a weak-kneed surrender. But come in, come in, do. I won't take no for an answer!"

Blutton, mentally blinking and rubbing his eyes, found himself ushered into a room bare of furniture and bare as to the walls and floor. Murmuring that he might as well go the whole hog, Peascod shuffled out, to return with two chairs and, after a second journey, with a bottle of champagne and two filigree-stemmed glasses. Blutton accepted a chair and refused the wine. But he had to wait until the cork had popped and the goblet was frothy before his host explained himself. He apologized for his rudeness on the Inspector's previous visit and for his lack of politeness at the door—and offered Yamasjhi as his excuse. It appeared that on Sunday he had begun to practise the Discipline laid down by the eastern Sage. This consisted in a five years' silence in a denuded chamber; a diet of eggs; sitting naked with the knees drawn up to the chin on a narrow plank—alternating with recumbence on the same; and occasional self-inflicted lacerations of the flesh.

"You see, Yamasjhi claimed that this Discipline induces trances which bring with them vivid visions and divine inspiration. I imagined that my painting and my poetry might benefit."

Blutton's right foot was tapping the bare boards. "And you're telling me you were going to sit like that for five years?"

"Oh dear me, no. Just for a week. But as you see, my friend, I've only been able to last two days. It's a pity—but nether callosity proved my undoing. I think my rump would have turned gangrenous if I'd stayed on that board a minute longer. Perhaps there is something about the Occidental cuticle that…"

"Have you anything further to add to the statement you made yesterday?"

"My statement? Oh— of course, yes, I was meaning to ask you. You are a policeman, aren't you? Yes, of course you are. Enlighten me, please. Why are you so anxious to know my movements?"

Blutton was impatient and sarcastic. "It so happens," he said, "that the Vicar of Larcombe was murdered early on Monday morning."

Peascod refilled his glass and held it before his eyes to watch the bubbles. "Was he now? That's news to me—but I must say I'm not a bit surprised. He was a bad man."

Blutton raised a fierce eyebrow.

"…Yes, a bad man. He reads Bishop Craeper's Sermons from the pulpit, and from what I gather, he's been reading them without respite for nigh on twenty years. My own holy uncle did the very same thing and he ended up by falling out of an aeroplane. Little wonder that the Vicar was held in universal abhorrence. Little wonder, indeed! Tell me, was he despatched in some appropriate manner?"

"He was found shot at the bottom of Crale Cliff."

"A pity. I was hoping they might have stoned him in proper Old Testament style… or something fitting like that."

"They?"

"Yes, the whole village."

Blutton was angrily interested; he leaned forward. "Was he *really* as unpopular as all that?"

"He was abominated," said Peascod. "No child ever smiled on him, no dog would wag its tail at his approach, no buttercup…"

Champagne works fast on an empty stomach and the poet-painter was growing spry. Blutton, whose gorge always rose at sprightliness, took his leave—his mind full of conflicting doubts and suspicions.

He next visited the man most nearly approximating to the local Squire, Mr. Lionel Gedling who lived in the big dilapidated house high up behind the village on Larcombe Head.

This gentleman turned out to be an old eccentric curmudgeon with bloodshot eyes, a strawberry nose and shattered nerves, who was very short with Blutton and who gave every sign of resenting his intrusion intensely. He said that he had heard and seen nothing out of the ordinary on Sunday night. He said that he could throw no light on the tragedy. And he said that, having other more important things to think about, he was not in the slightest degree interested in it. As to his movements, he had played cribbage with his factotum, Costigan, until two o'clock on the Monday morning.

The servant Costigan testified to the truth of this latter statement.

As the Inspector talked to this odd pair and listened to what little they had to say, he covertly examined their feet. And his scrutiny taught him that neither of them could possibly have trampled the soft ground round about the Vicar's car, for both Master and Man were possessors of a small neatly-turned foot.

A weary Blutton returned to his office in Fore Street, Setterham, to consider what information his colleagues and subordinates had acquired during the day. It was almost exclusively negative information. The Symouth police knew nothing to the detriment of John-Thomas Ridd nor had any car driving at high speed westwards in the early hours of Monday morning come under their notice.

No news relative to Jeremiah Scoutey's lodger, the soi-disant detective, had come to hand from the specially drafted search-party or from any station in the West Country. The one meagre shred of positive evidence was that a ticket-collector at Setterham remembered the arrival of a big, red-faced, clean-shaven, rain-coated, luggageless man by the slow up-train on Sunday morning. Beyond that—nothing.

Starehole Gap was a beauty spot. Not a commercial and official Beauty Spot with Tea Rooms run by languid, rapacious gen-teelwomen and with Period Car Parks for chars-a-banc. No; it was just a pretty, unnoticed place, the private property of Lionel Gedling and part of his small estate on Larcombe Head. The Gap itself was a steep little glade sloping down to the sea, whose chief attractions were a delicate waterfall and a deep, green pool. People said that had Lionel Gedling not been so thick-skulled and simple and crazy, he could have made money out of it simply by changing its name to the Faery Grotto, hanging lanterns in the trees and opening it to the holiday public at a shilling or more per head.

As it was, Larcombe lads fished the pool for jack-sharps, min-nows and tiddlers, Larcombe lovers hugged one another under the trees and, once or twice a year, Professor Harrod came there to wave his net at moths and butterflies. Otherwise, its pretty peace was undisturbed.

On the Tuesday after the murder of the Vicar, a pair of lovers—or rather, a sort of lover and a barmaid—were lying side by side on their stomachs, staring at their reflections in the green pool. Spray from the waterfall rippled the surface a little and made their mirrored faces wobble and boggle, but to them it didn't seem to matter very much. The man was making this phenomenon the text of an amatory address.

"Instability of countenance, my beloved," he was saying, "has nothing to do with stability of heart. Were you afflicted with the Twitch or the St. Vitus's dance, do you imagine I should love you a whit the less? No, Rosa, it is your noble spirit, the hallowed flame within you, that has touched my heart! Were you a blackamoor or a pock-marked beldame, your spirit, your flame would shine undimmed from your eyes and my heart would be natheless ravished."

"Oh, go on, Mr. Peascod," smirked Rosa McQueen, "you do say such things!"

"Oh, dear—why must you always use my surname? You know I dislike it."

"But your other name, it makes you feel sort of funny to say it, it's like swearing."

"My dear Rosa, what absurdity! Mine is a very beautiful name and I insist that you use it."

"Oh, all right, Christian!"

"Thank you. Thank you, Rosa. And now I shall kiss your pictured, your watery lips. Behold a heterosexual Narcissus!"

"Oh, go on with you. You'll only wet your tie, and besides, I don't like you using words like that to me."

But Christian had already stuck his face into the water. And he only came up for air when Rosa the barmaid screamed, screamed as though she were a sow and her throat were about to be slit, and went on screaming.

The young man scrambled to his knees and regarded her in open-mouthed amazement. Water was dripping from the end of his nose, from his chin and from his hair. His wet locks made him look more ludicrous than ever, for as vermicelli is to macaroni, so was Christian Peascod's hair to straw; thin, wet straw makes a sorry sight. Rosa's screams continued for a few more seconds and then, just before she fainted, she pointed a shivering finger at the pool.

He turned and saw, to his great surprise, a human head bobbing up and down in the water, turning slowly as it bobbed and thus revealing that it was no longer attached to a human body or to any body at all. He rose slowly to his feet and glared fascinated and puzzled at this unusual object; he took a step forward as if to retrieve it from the water, thought better of it and turned his attentions to his stricken sweetheart. Love had prior place in his heart, even to curiosity. Automatically he fumbled with her dress to gain access to her stays which he realized, quite properly, ought to be loosened in such an emergency. But despite careful investigation, he could find no trace of either stays, corsets or bodices. Not at all dismayed, he plucked a feather from her hat and took out his cigarette-lighter. But the machine would only spark and the feather would not kindle from sparks alone.

Peascod squatted happily on the grass and applied his thoughts and energies exclusively to this new problem. The head continued to float and twirl. Rosa's long thin nose was, for that time at least, preserved from a pungent smoking, for she came to while he was still twitching the little bevelled wheel.

Her first words on regaining consciousness were: "Well? What have you done about it? Oh! Oh! It's still there." She screamed violently again. "Can't you show your manhood?"

"My manhood?"

"Yes. Go and get Jack Marsden or something."

"Oh—you mean the policeman. Yes, of course. But I'm afraid I don't know where he lives."

"Well, I never thought, Mr. Peascod, that any man could be such a coward. Yes, a coward! Here's a dastardly murder been done under your very nose and you just sit and play with your cigarette-lighter. It's disgraceful! It's inhuman, and I'll never speak to you again. I'll do my duty—if you won't. And don't you dare follow me!" With that, she ran off towards the village as fast as she could go, leaving her disconsolate swain behind her to mutter, "Oh, Rosa! Rosa! You little know my singleness of purpose."

If he had known how to swim, he would have plunged into the pool and brought the severed head ashore; but he could not swim. All that was left for him to do was to throw stones at it in the hope that it would drift to the side. And this is what he was doing while Rosa scrambled through the bushes and gorse on Larcombe Head, slithered down the bank on to the road and trotted as fast as her skirt would let her down to the village. Her heart was thumping uncomfortably and her stomach was queasy, but the itch to glory, the glory of bearing momentous news, kept her going, and as she went she yelled blue murder. Down the hill trotted Rosa, past the Vicarage, on and on past "The Nook", Hannabus's shop, the Clove and Hoof, Frisby's the butcher, on past the Orchard and round to the quay with half Larcombe rushing to doors and windows to watch and marvel at this epic trot.

Blutton and Jack Marsden were down among the boats at the quay, prying about, questioning, meddling, irritating the fishermen. They heard Rosa from afar off and went forth to meet her.

"What's all this?" said the Inspector, taking a step backwards as the barmaid tried to collapse into his arms.

"Oh," she gulped, scarlet in the face and battling for breath. "Oh, oh, sir, come quick! Horrible things are going on! Oh, terrible! You'll never guess! There's been a murder. Oh, come quick, please."

By a happy chance, Dr. Girdwood was just at this moment backing his car out of the Orchard after a visit to poor Dick Bowle. Blutton hailed him, acquainted him with the meagre facts of the new catastrophe, and bustled Rosa and Marsden into the back seat.

When the party arrived at the Gap, they found Peascod standing by the pool, pensively flicking stones at the still floating, still twirling head. On the way up, Rosa had spoken to Blutton on the subject of her swain in such a way that the former now addressed him brusquely, even disdainfully. "Clear off now, young man— you can't do any good here. But I shall want to have another talk to you later on."

Christian was only too pleased to go. He had already got the first two couplets of an Ode on the Bloodiness of Man, and he knew he would forget them if he tarried much longer.

With the aid of a branch of a tree and the doctor's walking-stick, Jack Marsden managed to fish out the gruesome Thing. Floating on the pool, it had been a macabre enough sight, but there had also been something playful, something almost coy about it. The green, sunlit water had robbed it of its sickening aspect of detachment. On dry land, it was naked and revolting; even the doctor was none too happy about it. As for the village constable, his face was very white as he conducted Rosa to a suitable distance.

Girdwood covered it with a large handkerchief when he had finished his inspection. "It's been dead some considerable time. About forty-eight hours: maybe a bit longer. But it's only just been severed; can't be more than an hour ago. With a saw or something like that."

Blutton did not fail to catch the implication underlying the doctor's last remarks, but two murders in as many days were more than enough even for a County Inspector. He stood irresolute, sucking his pencil; irresolute and rather shaken. That the person who played at executioner had been in these woods within the hour was obvious enough; that this same person would not hang about these woods just on the off-chance of being discovered by the police, was an equally sound argument. Even if he were there still, Marsden and himself would not make a very efficient search-party over this wooded headland. On the other hand, they might possibly find the headless trunk.

He took his pencil out of his mouth. "I suppose you don't know who this is, do you?"

Girdwood shook his head.

"Well, would you do me the favour of getting back to Larcombe as quick as you can and ringing up headquarters for some spare men to help me out here?"

"Certainly," replied the doctor, "and I'll take this pretty piece back with me. I'll be able to tell you more about it later."

"You might take this girl along with you too."

But Rosa McQueen was not to be moved before she'd had her say for the second time that day. "Mr. Peascod and I were simply sitting here, chatting nicely and so on—when all of a sudden there was a splash and that dreadful thing popped up from nowhere. Oh, it *was* dramatic, you've no idea!"

"Popped down you mean," said Blutton, nodding towards the waterfall. "By the way, how long had you been here?"

"About quarter of an hour."

"And you say you didn't hear or see anything peculiar?"

Rosa was sincerely sorry to say that she did not.

"D'you come here often with this Peascod?"

"I've been here before, of course, but it's the first time I've ever been with *him*, and the last," she added with considerable warmth.

The Inspector found the body—without the assistance of a search-party.

He and Marsden had clambered up to the stream above the waterfall and had followed its course, searching the bushes on either side as they went. An hour's careful work brought them in sight of Gedling's house, Old Barton. The wood had given way to thicket and the thicket ended when the stream curved away to skirt the stretch of dishevelled lawn that lay in front of the house. It was in this last sheltered yard of stream that they found the body; a man's naked body with a great, red gash between the shoulder blades.

Four hours later, Blutton stood awkwardly before his Chief Constable and confessed himself beaten. "We'll have to call the Yard in, sir," he said. "I haven't liked this case from the very beginning. I wouldn't ask you to do this if I thought I could get to the bottom of these two crimes in a month, or in two months even. But they're not routine jobs. There's something very fishy about them. I've hardly had any sleep since Sunday night, I've been at it every minute, and I'm just not getting anywhere."

The Chief Constable stopped drawing circles on his blotting-pad, looked up and said, "I'm sorry it has to happen, Blutton—but don't let it worry you. You've worked damned hard and you've nothing to reproach yourself with. I'll ask the Yard to send someone down right away. In any case I expect their man will want you with him. I'm as sorry as you are—I really am. But cheer up. It's not your fault. Here, have a cigarette!" He held out a silver box, but Blutton shook his head ruefully.

"No, thank you, sir. I don't smoke."

"Oh—I'm so sorry. So stupid of me to forget."

Blutton turned and slunk out of the room, questing for some subordinate upon whom to vent his bile.

THIRD DEATH

A letter from the Commissioner concerning the C.I.D. man arrived in Setterham a few hours before he himself did.

The Chief Constable frowned in a worried way as he read this letter, and in the middle of reading it a second time he rang for Blutton.

"I just wanted to talk to you about—er—your new—er—colleague," he said when the Inspector came in.

"Oh, yes, sir." He was on the defensive immediately.

"Yes. It seems he's a bit out of the ordinary. The Yard have their hands full just at the moment, what with the Royal Visit, the Peace Conference and the Oswaldthwistle affair, and so they're sending us a man from their Special List. Detective-Sergeant Plumper's the name—ever heard of him?"

"No, sir," said Blutton without hesitation.

"Nor have I, as a matter of fact. Anyhow—he's described as 'a very promising young officer though somewhat unorthodox in manner and method.' He was transferred from the Intelligence Department. M'Lord Harry's been pumping in new blood and this chap seems to be a sample. So go careful, Blutton, and humour him. Don't let him get your back up."

"I don't think there's any fear of that," said the Inspector, smiling with his mouth. "I flatter myself I know how to handle most types of men."

The Chief Constable coughed. "Of course you do, and I'm certain you'll get on fine together. Still… don't forget that you and I are a couple of old war horses, Blutton, and we don't always take too kindly to the ways of the youngsters. It's only natural, you know."

"I've always done my best to keep abreast with the times."

"Quite. Well, anyhow, this Plumper will be here by midday, so I think you'd better meet him."

"As you say, sir."

The Chief Constable sighed as Blutton stalked from the room with his shoulders set and his head high; the man looked as if he were going out to meet his Doom.

Det.-Sergt. Plumper had just finished growing a moustache—and he was very proud of it. He loved to stroke and smooth and twiddle the ends of it; long, silky and black they were, like a mandarin's. This habit of his infuriated Blutton. When you spoke to the man, he would lean his chin on his hand, run his first finger and thumb down and up, down and up the left side of his growth, leer at you, positively leer at you with his little pig-eyes and say hardly anything but "Ah" and "Um." But the Inspector was very careful not to allow himself to be put out. He held himself in rigid check.

The two men were sitting together in the latter's office—a room that was as cheerful as a Workhouse, as spotless as an Isolation Ward and as chill as a Police-woman. Blutton bit his lip, avoided Plumper's eye and went on with his story. "Well, we found the body in the stream right by the lawn in front of this Gedling's house—not fifty yards from the windows. It had a knife wound in the back, deep and downwards, and according to Dr. Girdwood—that's the local G.P.—it had been dead for forty-eight hours or longer. The head had been sawn off not an hour before I found it; the jagged edges were quite fresh. Think of it, Sergeant… broad daylight and a chap and a girl in the same wood! Not only does he lay the body in full sight of the house." Blutton broke off, abnormally excited. "I tell you, this is a mad-man—a madman or else somebody who doesn't care a—a dash for anything or anybody. It's weird, I tell you."

Plumper half smiled through his leer, but said nothing.

Blutton blew his nose and continued in a minor key. "Identification was not an easy job, though I must say I had an idea when I saw how big the body and the feet were. It was as much as I could do to get anyone in Larcombe to look at the head—they're a nasty lot down there, dead set against helping me, and I feel sure there's some of them know more than they'll tell. However, in the end, I made Scoutey, that's the chap he lodged with, and Bert Yeo from the Public, see if they could recognize it. They did, both of them. Yeo—he's a huge fat fellow—took it badly and I thought he was going to faint; actually, he was as sick as a dog outside. It wasn't pretty, I can tell you."

"I don't suppose it was," murmured Plumper. "And what about this Gedling?"

"Ah, Gedling. Now that was funny. Gedling who doesn't leave his house for weeks on end, mind you, had come into Setterham that very afternoon with his man Costigan, to go to a matinée at the pictures! They left Larcombe immediately after lunch and didn't get back till the evening."

Plumper looked down his nose. "What was on at the cinema?" he said in his hoarse voice.

It was Blutton's turn to sneer. "I'm sure I've no idea. I never waste time at the pictures." He waited for more questions. No more questions were forthcoming. The man from London seemed more intent on trying to gnaw the end of his moustache than on the matter in hand; not that he took his eyes off the Inspector for one instant.

The latter fidgeted. "Well, I suppose you'll be wanting to get on to Larcombe. If you're sure there's nothing else you want to know? I'll get Jipps to drive you over." Blutton stood up. Plumper stood up. Neither spoke. Plumper followed Blutton out of the room.

When Plumper had left Paddington that morning, it had been raining hard, the air had been harshly cold and the station had smelt more than ever of decomposed cabbage and leaky gasometers. But on the Setterham cliff-road the sun was beaming as Jipps drove him down to Larcombe. The sea was as quiet as a child and remarkably blue, the air was soft, seagulls were wheeling and screaming, the cliffs were red and brown and benevolent, and smooth fields sloped away from their tops. Plumper was not impressed by what he saw; in any case, he had seen it so often before on railway posters. He was thinking about the honeymoon from which he had so lately returned; he was remembering it very carefully.

"This," said Jipps, jerking his thumb, "is where they done it."

"Really," said Plumper.

Ten minutes later he was depositing his beautiful pigskin Gladstone on the step of the Clove and Hoof. He raised his hand to the heavy door-knocker and brought it down with quite unnecessary violence.

Jipps, behind him, let out the clutch and made a grimace in his direction.

An upper window of the inn was flung open and Bert Yeo stuck his angry sleepy head out. "What the hell's the matter—

banging like that?" he bellowed. "It's after hours. What is it you want?"

Plumper slowly tilted his head. "You," he croaked.

Bert came down and opened the door. Serving drinks behind the bar in his shirt-sleeves and fancy waistcoat, with his great watch-chain and great smile, his ruddy face and his jolly word for everybody, Bert Yeo looked very much ye olde Landlord; at this moment he did not look quite so pretty; he was collarless and the folds of his neck hung down like dewlaps, his eyes were sticky with sleep, his oily hair was rumpled and hanging about his head in rats'-tails, his cheeks were pasty and not so much ruddy as grey. "I was just having me nap," he said. "Now then, what is it?"

"I want to stay in this house."

Bert didn't like the look of him; a queer bird, and with all this trouble about. But he couldn't very well refuse him. "Just for the one night, is it?"

"I don't know about that. Maybe a week, maybe longer," said Plumper.

"I see." Bert stared hard at him for a second or two. "Oh, all right. I'll take your bag."

"No, you won't." Plumper stroked his moustache.

Again Bert stared at him. And then he turned and led the way upstairs, muttering to himself as he went.

The bedroom was old and low and good and its window gave on to the creek and the sea beyond. There was room to move about, there was a comfortable chair, a table to write at, and the bed, though it creaked abysmally, seemed soft enough.

When Bert brought up the book, Plumper wrote "Amos Plumper," hesitated over the address and finally put down, "21 Cresswall Place, S.W.10." He described himself as "Agent."

Then Rosa came in, giggling, to ask if there was anything he'd be wanting. He looked her up and down very deliberately before he spoke.

"I want a telescope, a detailed map of the district, pens, paper, ink, another blanket on the bed, a pot of very weak Chinese tea and the name of a man who has trustworthy boats for hire."

Rosa made eyes like pennies and fled.

Plumper chuckled, sat down to scribble a quick love-letter to his bride, and was re-reading it for the fourth time when the barmaid returned to bring him everything he had asked for except the telescope.

"Mr. Hannabus might have one," she said in a faint voice. "He keeps the shop just next door."

Old Sebastian Hannabus was busy disembowelling a cormorant and chatting to Peascod when Plumper stepped into his shop. Both looked up in considerable surprise at the stranger: the old man wiped his hands on his handkerchief and shuffled forward down the gangway between the antique furniture on the one side and the oil-lamps, seines, rolls of linoleum and gingham, stuffed birds and basque berets on the other.

"Yes, sir?"

"I was wanting a telescope."

"A telescope? Well, let me see, sir, I think I have three. Yes, indeed. Now this one here is not only a particularly fine instrument, it has historical value also. It came from the wreck of the French schooner *Marie-Alix* that broke up on the Garl Rocks over fifty years agone."

Plumper took it to the door and focused it on the other side of the creek—on, to be exact, John-Thomas Ridd's bungalow.

"D'you do any cobbling?" he said without turning round or taking the glass from his eye.

"No, sir, Sam Bowle's the cobbler. He lives in the Orchard—that's the square of cottages on the left by the quay. But if ever you need the services of a mole-catcher…"

Plumper decided to take the telescope, and while Hannabus was getting him his change, he wandered round the shop. As he seemed to show some interest in a rather oddly-carved chair, Peascod, who had been eyeing him with undisguised curiosity from the lobster-pot on which he was seated, saw fit to inform him that the piece was a poor middle-Victorian imitation of Chippendale's Chinese Style.

Plumper bowed slightly and said: "It's a pity, don't you think, that Chippendale's Chinese Style is so essentially un-Oriental? He knew nothing of the East. Chinese and Indian were synonymous terms to him."

Peascod approached him eagerly. "Are you a visitor to Larcombe? Are you staying here?"

Plumper nodded.

"My dear sir, how splendid! It's weeks, weeks since I heard a polysyllabic word. Synonymous! Synonymous! It made music in my ears. You must talk to me frequently. You must dine with me to-night—to-night in my little cottage next door, the cottage called 'The Nook.' You will?"

Plumper nodded briefly, collected his change and walked out of the shop with the telescope under his arm.

"*What* a nice man!" cried Peascod.

Hannabus, who had resumed his taxidermy, shrugged. "Funny time of year to come visiting down here. And fancy a stranger like him not mentioning the murders, or the weather, for that matter. Can't say as I liked the looks of him."

Once Jack Marsden had accustomed himself to Plumper's peculiar mannerisms, the two got on like a house on fire.

Immediately after buying his telescope, the detective had strolled up to his cottage, which was beyond the quay and a little way up the valley towards Corfield, and Jack had bid him welcome very timidly. But in a very few minutes he found himself—for the first time in his official life—talking to a superior as he would have talked to a sympathetic ally. The Scotland Yard man sat in the arm-chair in front of his fire, put his feet up on the mantelpiece and asked him if he could oblige with a fill of plug. He was the first officer Jack had ever met who would allow him to talk and who, moreover, seemed interested in what he said. He was the first officer he had ever met who had taken him into his confidence. Such things had never happened to Jack before; and they hadn't seemed quite right, at first—not quite natural. But only at first. Very soon he came to rejoice in Plumper and to be his doting slave. Had Blutton condescended to ask him what he—the man on the spot, as it were—thought of the murders? No! Did Plumper? Yes, and he couched his questions in highly flattering style. Little wonder that Jack opened his heart.

"It's difficult for me, sir, but I have a feeling there's some jiggery-pokery going on in Larcombe—among the Larcombe men, I mean. And that's just the trouble. You see, sir, some of 'em I respect, some I like and some likes me, so it's hard for me to treat them as suspects, as you might say. Call it Christian feeling if you like."

"How exactly do you mean—jiggery-pokery?" grunted Plumper.

"I mean, look at Mr. Gedling there, for instance. Who but a Larcombe man would know that he was going off to Setterham, leaving the coast nice and clear for dumping that poor fellow's body and head? And take Cap'n Ridd. Somebody here was trying to make it look like he had a hand in killing the Vicar. You're not going to tell me that footprint and wooden-leg business was a coincidence! And the Cap'n knows it wasn't too. Oh, he knows all right. He's proper smart—and he hasn't been down to the Cloven since it all came out. Believe me, Mr. Plumper, sir, he suspects something. He's already had a row with Bert Yeo!"

"Perhaps he's got a guilty conscience?"

Jack cackled his shrill laugh. "Cap'n Ridd? Ha! You don't know him, sir. He's one of the nicest men who ever trod. He wouldn't harm a fly."

"Oh, wouldn't he? Half an hour ago, I saw him trying to— shall I say harm?—a young woman who was hanging out washing in his garden."

Jack jumped to his feet, and then sat down again. "You're joking, sir."

"No," said Plumper, "I just happened to be focusing my telescope."

The constable looked as if he were going to burst into tears. "That's Jane McQueen," he gulped, "the girl I'm supposed to be courting. She keeps house for him when he's at home."

But Plumper showed no interest in or sympathy with this sad remark.

"Tell me more about this Gedling person who so conveniently and so contrary to custom leaves his house on the very day the decapitated body is placed in full view of his windows. Tell me, for example, why he lives in a large house, alone with one manservant."

Jack did his best to banish the subject of Jane McQueen from his mind, but his voice was still muted with melancholy. "Oh, he's just an old gentleman, sir, and people say he's rather soft in the head. Jane thinks he was crossed in love, but I dare say he's shy and keeps himself to himself because of his nose."

"His nose?"

"Yes, sir. Poor man, he had it frost-bit once and it's grown all funny and spread too, you know."

Plumper nodded. "And this servant of his?"

"Costigan? A stranger, sir. Very close. We hardly ever see him down in the village."

"What's on at the cinema at Setterham?"

"Well, there are two, sir, you know, the Tivoli and the Electric Kinema."

Jack consulted a pamphlet: "Monday, Tuesday, Wednesday, Tivoli—'Stained Saints.' Electric Kinema, 'Sex Unmasked— Adults Only.'"

Plumper smiled. "I want you to do something for me. Go up to this Gedling's house, innocent like—sell tickets for the Police Sports or ask to see the dog licence. Talk to Costigan and ask him how he liked the pictures; find out what he thought of the Staining or the Unmasking. And don't let him go till you've found out!"

The detective rose to go soon after that, and Jack, having escorted him very fussily to the garden gate, was all for walking home with him. But the former waved a restraining hand. "No. Don't do that—thank you all the same. And remember, I don't want people to know who I am, for a little while yet."

"I won't forget, sir," cried Jack.

Back in his cottage, he reached for his cracked teapot and settled down to a pensive brew. How nice to be a gentleman; how nice to be a Detective-Sergeant; how nice to be able to live in London. And how nice to be wed with Jane McQueen. Jane McQueen! What had Mr. Plumper said? "I saw him trying to— shall I say harm? a young woman." Jack tried desperately hard to reconcile in his mind the John-Thomas and the Jane he knew with the Ridd and the McQueen that Plumper had seen through his telescope.

Plumper returned to his inn to find the Bar hostilely curious. It was already known of him that he had arrived at the Cloven in a police-car, that his name was Plumper, that he wanted a boat, that he was going to dine that very night with Peascod, that he had bought a telescope, that his shoes needed repairing, that he had been closeted with Jack Marsden. What exactly an agent might be had been the subject under discussion just before he came in. "Some sort of detective," Jeremiah Scoutey had said cheerfully. "And you know what happened to the last one like him!"

"Maybe a traveller in handcuffs, whistles and truncheons!" suggested old Hannabus.

Amid dead silence, Plumper walked up to the bar and ordered a quart of ale. Greengrocer Scoutey, taxidermist Hannabus, cobbler Bowle, boatman Charnock, the two hands from the *Saucy Sue*, the brothers Turner, and Sam the Lobster Man were seated on the benches round the walls of the little room. Yeo, saturninely drunk but carrying it very creditably indeed, was behind the bar. Sam the Lobster Man spat on the floor. The younger Turner turned his face away, laughed suddenly and as suddenly stopped laughing. Alan Charnock scratched his chin and kept his eyes on the ceiling. Hannabus nervously tried to break the general embarrassment. "Glass all right, sir?"

Plumper was leaning against the far corner of the bar and unconcernedly making an entry in his diary with one hand and straining the beer out of his moustache with the other. "Tolerably," he said without looking up.

Bert helped himself to another large whiskey. Alan Charnock drained his can hurriedly, mumbled a "good night all" and went out. Scoutey got up and made a pretence of playing shove-ha'penny. But the Bar—and nowhere else is silence so damnable—was still.

Then Plumper spoke. "Your name's Hannabus, isn't it?"

In a very relieved voice, the taxidermist admitted that it was. Scoutey strolled over to the bar and began, in a very loud voice, to discuss with an apathetic Yeo the current prospects of Symouth Albion's ever getting out of the Second Division. Sam the Lobster Man edged nearer to Hannabus so as to be in the running for a pint from the stranger should a conversation develop. The Turners started to talk in undertones.

Plumper continued, "A name I've never met before."

"Really, sir? It's West country. You go to Tiverton for example, and you'll find any amount of Hannabuses."

Sam the Lobster Man broke in: "Me wife's cousin's a Hannabus. Lives at Tiverton too. Keeps a grocer's shop, West-Exe side of the bridge." He spat on the floor.

"You must be a sort of cousin of mine then," laughed Sebastian.

The Bar was itself again.

It was even suitably impressed by Plumper's treatment of his yellow double-handled mug and ventured on a "good night" as he went out to keep his engagement at "The Nook." But the greeting was not returned.

Peascod, with his own skilful hands, had built a dinner round a cock-a-leekie: a fine dinner. Indeed, cookery seemed to be the only real talent of this pensioned-off, gently-lunatic product of a much-divorced mother and a much-bankrupt father. Gently-lunatic but not corybantic or daft; his mania was self-expression—and he had a truly embarrassing enthusiasm for all forms of painting, music, the written and spoken word and alcohol, though he could neither paint well, sing or play well, write well, speak well or drink deep. But for some strange reason, he could cook well.

Plumper interrupted an attempted rendering on the piano of Medtner's "Fairy Tale in F Minor"—an attempted rendering which had been going on almost continuously for four hours.

He was still wearing his apron and tall chef's cap when he came to the door to admit his guest. "Ah, there you are, my dear fellow! Come in, do. Let me see now, you're the detective from Scotland Yard, aren't you?"

Plumper was surprised and chagrined, but he contrived to look sinister.

"Eh—? What are you talking about?"

"Oh, never mind," cried his host as he filled two very large glasses with Amontillado. "Never mind. Only you see, as you arrived here in a police-car and as you have held a conference with the village constable, no to speak of the Inspector forsaking us and you spying out the land with telescopes and looking as if you were pretending to be somebody else, is it surprising? Is it? But here's to your very good health."

Plumper said nothing.

"But in any case—now you're in Larcombe, you must give a little thought to our fascinating crimes, you really must. They've already had a remarkable effect on me. It was I, you know, who found the head in Starehole Gap. You can have no idea how the discovery amazed me. I was struck dumb. I could do nothing.

The afternoon sun had turned to black and the marrow of my bones had become as water. The song of the birds was a hellish cacophony and the silly noise of children was an abomination in my ears. The earth I trod was unstable and perverse. It was most extraordinary, I can assure you. But my mind has come to life again. From to-morrow onwards I am going to do some very serious thinking on the question. I am going to devote three hours of every day to the solution of the two problems."

"What do you do with the rest of your time?" smiled Plumper, who was prepared to forgive the boy anything for the sake of his wine.

"Oh, I have a very definite programme. I rise at six. Until nine o'clock I write verse or Critical Essays in the manner of T. Earle Welby. From nine to twelve I play the piano. From two till five I paint. From five till seven I drink alcohol and meditate. From nine until midnight I read."

"But you were playing the piano just now."

"Ah, yes. I draw no hard and fast lines."

"You have no other hobbies?"

"Hobbies, my good sir? Hobbies! I would have you know that these things form the very essence of my life."

"Not really?" said Plumper. "And do you never relax?"

"Never! Relaxation is the curse of this age and generation. We are for ever trying to relax, to escape, to escape from heaven knows what. A thousand cinemas and one crematorium, that is the sum total of our life—"

"Quite," murmured Plumper hurriedly. "And what period of your day will you devote to the detection of crime?"

"That will depend entirely on circumstances."

"Of course."

Peascod refilled the very large glasses. "I am passionately interested in criminology. I have here all the works of Bailey, Doyle, Van Dine, Roger East, Freeman, Wills and Croft, and the Misses Sayers and Christie. This interest, combined with the training in Speculative Philosophy I received during my four terms at Oxford, should make my reflections on the cases most interesting and valuable."

Plumper stared him very hard in the eyes, bowed slightly and sneered.

"Yes, indeed. And have you by any chance arrived at any theories yet?"

"Not any co-ordinated or well-developed theories. As I say, I haven't as yet systematized my thinking. But I may say that I believe that I have a feeling that there might be *two* very useful theoretical approaches to these crimes. One geographical and the other antiquarian. Or rather, *one* approach, the geographico-antiquarian. But I will explain as we eat."

And over the savoury cock-a-leekie he did.

"You will have noticed that Larcombe stands at the head of a lonely promontory. Communication with the outside world is not easy. To reach Setterham, you must go by the difficult cliff road. Between us and Symouth stand more cliffs, a moor and a few devious and ill-kept country lanes. We are, in a word, off the beaten track. And what you may not have noticed is the valley that runs parallel to the coast on the other side of the hills at Corfield and Poridge. Now what does that suggest? Nothing, perhaps, to you. But to me it suggests that the Larcombe promontory was once an island and that the Larcombe people are the descendants of primitive, isolated islanders! Observe how pagan and unsympathetic they are. Few of them ever go to church, none of them except perhaps dear old Sebastian Hannabus ever makes friends with strangers, and they intermarry in a shocking way. Now it is quite possible that in the subconscious minds of some of these villagers, there should linger some of the primitive urges, the behaviour-motives that were their ancestors' many hundreds of years ago."

Plumper's beady eyes had never left Peascod's face; he interrupted, rasping, "Do you work in oils exclusively?"

Peascod was impatient. "No, no, no. I frequently use water colours for rough sketches. And so I have been debating with myself whether or not the Vicar could have been killed because he was a Christian Priest—arch-enemy of the prehistoric island Cults, and the 'Detective' because he was a stranger, a sinister, dangerous interloper, a man supposedly representing the forces of the Outside World!"

Again Plumper broke in. "I paint a little myself. Can I get colours in the village?"

"Eh? Oh, yes. Hannabus stocks them. So that these murders become sacrificial rites—though I dare say the actual slayers did not recognize them as such. And then there is the Sea. The Sea! I am sure that the Inspector has not taken the Sea into account nearly as much as he ought to have done. This, remember, is a fishing village and…"

He rambled on for some little time before Plumper spoke again. "D'you know a man called Costigan?"

"Costigan? Costigan? No, I don't think I do."

"Gedling's servant."

"Oh, him. Is he called Costigan? Yes, I've seen him about the place once or twice. He came into the Clove and Hoof while I was there on Tuesday morning; he wanted to know what time the buses run into Setterham. Small, silent man."

"Pardon my curiosity, but do you remember who else was in the Bar on Tuesday morning?"

"Oh, the customary crowd, you know. Charnock, Captain Ridd, Scoutey, Bowle, Hannabus and two others, I think they were off the *Saucy Sue*—that' Ridd's boat."

"Is that all?"

"I think so, unless you count Yeo."

Peascod seemed surprised at these questions, but Plumper gave him no time to voice it. "Show me some of your pictures," he said.

"Ah, no, I couldn't do that. I've only shown my pictures once—and I shall never show them again. My mother gave me what she styled 'a nice little exhibition' at Cheltenham as a twenty-first birthday present. I remember it well. Several old ladies came to the tea-party on the opening day and several more to the sherry-party on the last. On the five intervening days, eleven people visited the gallery. Eleven precisely. I know, because I counted them. I sat at a little table where the piles of catalogues were and I ticked down my visitors on a piece of paper as they came in. And the only adult male was a lame old gentleman in white spats who sniggered at the one and only nude there! I was very disappointed that I didn't quite make up the dozen, but I took heart from the fact that this number in some way symbolized the philistine heartiness of the town. The Cheltenham XI, pah! So now I merely paint for myself and posterity."

"Very wise of you," said Plumper and turned the conversation into other channels by abruptly asking him if he could in any way account for the sudden apparition of the severed head in the Starehole pool.

"Ah, that!" said Christian Peascod. "Now if you come to me to-morrow and ask me that same question, I don't doubt that

I shall have a few very interesting theories to put forward. But at the moment, as I said before, my detective work has not yet begun. To-morrow—work. To-night—play. Come, sir, let us drink to the successful outcome of my endeavours and to our better acquaintance!"

And drink they did.

Nevertheless, Plumper was up early next morning and paid a call on Constable Marsden to hear the result of his visit to Old Barton.

"Oh, good morning, sir," piped Jack, grinning gladly and largely despite the fact that his mouth was crammed with hot sausage.

"Well," said Plumper, "and how did you get on?"

"Well, sir, I went up like you told me—as a matter of fact I haven't been up to the house not for donkey's years and I must say it's a lot more tumbledown than it used to be. Anyhow, I went up like you said, sir, and when Costigan came to the door, I give it out I was collecting for the Police Orphanage. He wasn't monstrous pleased to see me and I can tell you he had no wish to stand there chatting with me like. But anyhow, I managed to get him to tell me that him and Mr. Gedling had been to Setterham all right, but they *didn't* go to no pictures, sir!"

"No?" said Plumper.

"No," said Jack.

"Where did they go then?"

"That, sir, is what I couldn't find out. That's what Costigan wouldn't tell, though I tried my hardest—I did honestly, sir. It was very awkward not being able to ask him straight like. I did my best, sir."

"You've done very nicely," smiled Plumper.

"Have I really, sir? Oh, *thank* you, sir," cried Jack *voce di testa* and rubbed the back of his left boot against his right trouser-leg.

"You didn't see Mr. Gedling, I take it?"

"No, sir. There was no chance of that."

"I see," said Plumper. "Well—I'll be seeing you very soon."

When the detective arrived back at the Clove and Hoof, Yeo was waiting for him with a long and suspicious face. "Inspector's here for you."

"Bring another coffee-cup," said Plumper and leered at the mystified innkeeper as hard as he could.

When Blutton appeared, he did not trouble to greet his colleague or to ask how he had slept; instead, he held out a letter addressed to himself. It was from Lionel Gedling and it was written in pencil on a grubby scrap of lined paper torn from some notebook. "Dear Sir," it ran, "Come at once to my house. Important. Yrs. L. Gedling."

"Came this morning," said Blutton shortly. "Hadn't you better come with me?"

Plumper gnawed his whisker and nodded. "Have some coffee," he murmured.

"There's no time like the present, you know."

"I know that, Inspector. And so does my stomach."

Blutton sat by with very bad grace while Plumper made an enormous breakfast.

The entrance to the drive that led to Old Barton was about fifty yards higher up the hill than the Vicarage. As the two policemen walked down this drive, the sun was shining and the air was sharp, but there was not the exhilaration about the place that should come from sharp air and morning sun. The woods bordering the drive had been allowed to run wild; there was much rot, much dankness and the shadows cast by the trees were cold. At Old Barton itself there were many cracked and broken windows. But it was not a sinister or mysterious house, it was just big, ugly, dirty and in a dreadful state of disrepair. It was a Victorian monstrosity—too tough ever to run to seed and too tough ever to borrow any graces from Time. Empty milk-bottles lay about the rococo porch and a teeming dustbin stood a few yards away. When Blutton pressed the door-bell nothing happened.

"Nice place," said Plumper, looking about him.

Then the Inspector banged hard with the knocker. Almost immediately a curtain was drawn back at a side-window and a face peered out at them. A few seconds later, the man Costigan let them in. "Come this way," he said.

They found the master of the house in a big room at the back that overlooked a lawn and Starehole Gap beyond. The air in the room was stale and as foul as the floor; there were cigarette-ends and cigarette ashes everywhere; old stains, dirty glasses, empty bottles of whiskey, crumbs and scraps of old food, holes in the carpet, dust, a pack of cards and a cribbage board, a new shotgun standing in a corner.

Gedling himself was small and thin with a big head. His nose was very big and very red; unnaturally big and unnaturally red; it was diseased. His hand shook so much that he could only with difficulty raise his glass to his lips without spilling the whiskey. He was dressed in dirty white pyjamas, a thick, faded dressing-gown, an old-fashioned velvet smoking-cap and black, unlaced boots; the ends of his pyjama trousers were tucked into the top of these boots. He looked drawn and tired and he had a very soft voice which would have been pleasant had he been able to control it better.

"Forgive all this mess," he said as they came in. "I'm an old man and I don't like fuss." As he spoke he looked doubtfully at Plumper. Blutton explained that he was a colleague and assured him that he could speak freely.

When they had seated themselves and refused whiskey, the old man made it clear why he had written asking the Inspector to come and see him.

"It's nothing to do with your murders," he began. "It's to do with *me*. It's persecution!" His voice rose unsteadily. "It's some damned hanky-panky! Somebody's up to mischief and you've got to stop it."

Blutton looked at Plumper, but Plumper's eyes were on the old man.

"Exactly what d'you mean, Mr. Gedling?" he said.

The latter pointed a trembling finger at the big window. "Look at that," he cried. "It was done last night." There were three neat small holes in the glass. "An airgun—I'll swear it was! I was sitting here at about midnight, playing cards with Costigan, when we heard the glass break. We heard no shot, we just heard the glass break. He drew the curtain back and two more shots came. I wouldn't let him go out. He wanted to go out to see what was going on, but I wouldn't let him, it wasn't safe. But funnier things than that have happened. A lot funnier. I always stay up late I do, and I'm always tired when I go to bed. Now a week ago last night, it must have been getting on for three o'clock before I turned in and I was so tired I could hardly keep my eyes open as I pulled back the bedclothes, and what d'you think I found when I did pull 'em back? I found a mess of rotten, stinking fish—that's what I found."

Blutton smiled despite himself. Plumper's face was very grave.

"Ah, yes, I knew you'd laugh," snorted the old man. "But it didn't make me laugh, I can tell you. Another time I woke up in the middle of the night with a maddening slow ticking in my ears. It was like a death-watch beetle or something. It went on and on and on, and I thought I should go mad. I called for Costigan in the end, and what d'you think he found? One of those music things, what d'you call it?—a metronome! Yes, a metronome. That's funny too, isn't it. Very funny indeed. But what about the body that someone left outside my windows? That wasn't particularly funny, was it? And what about this?" He fumbled among the litter on the mantelpiece and handed over an envelope. Blutton took it and immediately his eyebrows shot up and his jaw dropped. On the envelope, in block capitals, there had been painted in blue water-colour—"Mr. L. Gedling, Old Barton, Larcombe." Inside the envelope was a sheet of plain paper on which was written in an identical medium: "Somebody knows something. I would not be in your shoes for anything. You watch your food."

Blutton handed it to his colleague without a word. Plumper showed no surprise. "May I keep this?" he said.

The old man was impatient. "Yes, yes. It came last Friday and on Saturday morning the bottle of milk was all curdled and green—yet the milkman swears it was perfectly fresh when he left it on the doorstep. I tell you it's driving me mad. Someone's up to something. I hardly dare eat anything except out of tins. It's driving me mad I tell you, and you've got to do something about it. It's your duty. That's what you're paid for."

Plumper looked at Mr. Gedling in a kindly, rather whimsical way and said, "Tell me, sir—have you any idea what this 'something,' referred to by your reticent correspondent, may be? You know—the something that somebody is supposed to know?"

"How many more times," cried Gedling petulantly, striking the arm of his chair with a tight-closed fist, "have I to tell you that I know nothing whatsoever about it!"

"You haven't told us once, yet."

"Well, then—I'm telling you now. *Now*, once and for all!"

"I see. Thank you very much, sir." Plumper was remarkably bland.

There was a silence—which Blutton seemed to find awkward and Lionel Gedling exasperating. The Inspector looked at the Sergeant, but the Sergeant kept his mouth shut; so he coughed and said, "Why didn't you come to us when it first started?"

Gedling seemed to hesitate. "I thought it was just some practical joke at first, and anyhow, I don't like the police about the place."

"I see. Well, I'd like to have a look at the milk in that bottle you were talking about, if you don't mind."

"I'm afraid we threw it away."

"A pity you did that, Mr. Gedling. What about the metronome, then?"

Gedling helped himself to more whiskey and laughed uneasily. "That's another funny thing. It's disappeared completely. Costigan can't find it anywhere." He ended rather lamely. "But the holes in the window are there right enough, and the letter. And that body didn't disappear, did it?"

Blutton was anxious to go. The atmosphere of the room was sickening him and Gedling's nose was an abomination. "I'll make enquiries and I'll get Marsden to keep an eye on the house and grounds. If anything else happens, let me know at *once*. It's probably only some silly practical joker. And you might have another look for that metronome; I should very much like to see it."

Gedling was obviously disappointed; the visit of the policemen had not given him that feeling of protection, that measure of security for which he seemed so angrily anxious.

At the door, Plumper spoke over his shoulder and indicated the shotgun standing in a corner. "Did you buy *that* in Setterham on Tuesday?"

For answer, the old man seized it and brandished it furiously. "Yes, by God!" he shouted. "And I mean to use it too. D'you hear that? I'm not going to sit here and be…"

Plumper shut the door firmly behind him.

"Well?" said Blutton as they walked away down the bedraggled drive.

"Well?" replied Plumper with his customary leer.

The Inspector was anxious for information. The Inspector wanted to know how he, Plumper, had known about the gun, what he intended doing with the painted letter, whether he thought the finding of a headless body in his garden had unhinged the old toper and made him imagine things, or whether something was seriously and dangerously afoot. Whether he thought that this business had any possible connection with the two murders or not.

Blutton wanted Plumper to talk—but he was disappointed. All Plumper would say was "Ah" and "Um" and, as they came to the drive gates: "Is anyone living in the Vicarage?"

"No. It's locked up. But Marsden's been told to keep his eye on it."

"D'you mind if I have a look round?"

"Not a bit," said Blutton who minded a great deal. He had already given Plumper a very detailed report of his very detailed investigations in and around the Vicarage and he saw no reason why they should waste time going over old ground when new and more promising ground had been opened up to them.

But as soon as he got the front door open the Inspector swore for the first time for many years. "Damn!" he cried. The house had been ransacked. The contents of every drawer, cupboard and box had been scattered on the floor. Someone had been through the place with, as they say, a fine toothcomb.

Blutton rushed from room to room, looking for he knew not quite what. Plumper sat down in the study arm-chair and looked about him—at the engraving of Keble College over the mantelpiece, at the aspidistra, at the neat rows of books, at the antipodean stain on the ceiling; and he looked especially at a pair of worn black slippers sitting disconsolate against the fender of the empty grate.

Eventually Blutton found what he least expected to find—a clue! In the middle of the kitchen floor lay a handkerchief, a bloodstained handkerchief, with a laundry-mark neatly sewn on one corner with red thread. The kitchen window was open and upon the woodwork were unmistakable signs that a jemmy had lately been applied there. "Ha!" grunted Blutton hardly above his breath, "burglarious entry or I'm a cuckoo."

It was with triumph and a slightly theatrical gesture that he demonstrated his find. "Something at last!" he shouted.

Plumper twiddled his moustache and seemed to sneer.

Blutton lost his temper; his lips tightened and a little colour came to his cheeks and ears. "I know you people think—" he burst out. But he said no more, he bit his lip and held his peace.

Plumper got to his feet. "Well, sir," he said, "this is an interesting find and no mistake."

Blutton looked at him very suspiciously. He always mistrusted compliments and friendliness.

"Looks as if someone had cut their hand or something, doesn't it?"

"It does," said Blutton coldly.

"Cut their hand a long, long time ago." Plumper gave him a sidelong glance.

"What d'you mean, eh?"

"Only that this blood's very old blood."

"Oh," muttered Blutton. "Yes, I suppose it is."

"In which case, if our burglar dropped this on his way in or out of the kitchen window, he must be quite an odd sort of a chap. Chaps don't usually go about for weeks on end with blood-soaked handkerchiefs in their pockets—not clean chaps who blow their noses. Do they?"

Blutton shrugged and said nothing.

"But our man's certainly a colourful humorist. Like friend Peascod, he's read his detective novels. The Clue of the Wooden Leg. The Clue of the Headless Body. The Clue of the Painted Letter, and now the Clue of the Bloody Handkerchief. Rich—very rich. Too rich."

"You're definitely linking all these up, then?"

"Oh, I think so, Inspector. I don't see any harm in that, do you?"

"Not yet, I don't," said the Inspector.

They found nothing more of any particular interest at the Vicarage and it was decided that Blutton should return to Setterham to do what he could about identifying the handkerchief among the several laundries there and that he should send out men to go over the house for finger-prints.

As Blutton stepped into the car waiting for him outside the Clove and Hoof, Plumper said, "If I were you, I'd get your analyst to have a guess at the age of that blood, when the handkerchief's been identified, of course."

"I was going to do that, anyway," grunted Blutton.

An hour later, the man from Scotland Yard was rowing a dinghy down the creek and out to sea. It was a lovely day. The sun was bright and the sea calm and as soft as the russet of the cliffs. But Plumper was scowling. He was angry and he was worried because he had a strong feeling now that he was up against a maniac of some sort; one who was treating crime as a game, taking fantastic risks because he was too crazy to care about personal danger, playing mysterious tricks because it amused him to do so, acting from inconsistently abnormal motives. The whole business was too theatrical, too Grand Guignol. A sane man out to murder a vicar and a Stranger would have shot them or knifed them or poisoned them, and had done with it; he would have sat back in his chair with a thumping heart and hoped for the best. But this lunatic with his rotten fish and his metronome, his painted correspondence, his faked footprints, his beheading, his bloody handkerchief. Plumper felt sure that one man was behind it all; his hallmark was on everything. But that was the only thing Plumper felt sure about.

He was very unsure, first of all, about the Stranger, the "Detective." Why had he come to Larcombe? Was his coming partly or wholly responsible for the Vicar's death? If so—did someone in Larcombe know of his coming and warn the Vicar against him by means of an anonymous letter? If so—was this sane person warning Lionel Gedling in the same way? If so—what was he warning him against now that the Stranger was lying in two pieces on a mortuary slab? And why was the Stranger killed? Was it because he had killed the Vicar? Why was his head cut off? Where was his body between the time of the Vicar's death and Tuesday afternoon?

And the Vicar—why on earth was he running away? Why on earth was he killed?

And Ridd—had someone really tried to plant a murder on him, and yet tried in such a half-hearted, unsubtle, innocent way? Why did he lie in such a fatuous manner to Blutton over the question of his late arrival at Larcombe?

And Gedling?

Plumper rested on his oars and looked back up the creek. A pretty fishing village. It seemed ludicrous that a madman should be sitting and chuckling to himself in one among that handful of cottages, or in that bungalow, or in that big neglected house.

The boat drifted and bobbed. Plumper gnawed his whiskers fiercely and dismissed these hydra-questions from his mind. He had come on this little boating expedition simply to get the lie of the land from a different angle. He didn't need his glass to see Old Barton sitting up above the surrounding trees on Larcombe Head; and as he got farther out to sea, he could make out roughly the spot on Crale Cliff where the Vicar had fallen. There was the zig-zag path and—Plumper became stiffly alert and reached for his telescope—there was a man, a lanky young man with long hair. It was Peascod—the sleuth a-sleuthing, magnifying glass and all. Plumper smiled and rowed over towards him.

Peascod hailed him joyfully and excitedly as he grounded the boat.

"I say, I say!" he shouted. "I have a most brilliant suggestion to make. Have you by any chance, my friend, a diary with you?"

Plumper nodded as he scrambled ashore.

"How very fortunate! And does it mark the phases of the moon?"

"It does."

"I really ought to know, but I'm afraid I haven't been out at night lately. Tell me, was there a fullish moon on Sunday night?"

Plumper was able to and did inform him, without reference to his diary, that the moon had been almost at the full. Peascod fairly capered with delight. "Bon bonissimo! What did I tell you. The Sea! The Sea!" Plumper's scowl sobered him a little.

"Forgive me—but I'm so excited. I never expected such quick results. I must collect my wits and marshal my arguments." He sat down on a rock and Plumper obliged him with a cigarette. "As I told you, sir, I've given myself over to detection. I've been very busy and I've come to some remarkable conclusions, so perpend, sir, perpend! Now I'm going to assume that two men had a hand in the Vicar's death, and I'm also going to assume—stop me if you think that my assumptions are ill-founded—that one of these two was the Stranger whose head I found. Very well. I know, by the medical evidence published in the newspapers, that the Stranger was despatched at pretty well the same time as the clergyman; and according to my assumption, he spent his last hour or so on earth at this very spot where now we sit, or at least, within a stone's throw. All well and good. We next meet him in the neighbourhood of Starehole Gap. Now I put it to you, Mr. Plumper, if you wish to convey a carcass from this very spot to the neighbourhood of Starehole Gap with the least discomfort and inconvenience to yourself and with the least risk of being observed by the prying eyes of Larcombe, what method would suggest itself to you?"

Plumper jumped to his feet, looked hard at his companion, swore softly and snapped his fingers. "A boat," he croaked. "That rock out there would be the ideal place for the body from Sunday night till Tuesday afternoon… What a damn fool I am!"

Peascod beamed. "Exactly."

"Tell me, no, that's absurd, the tide doesn't cover it, does it?"

"What, the rock? Oh, no, not by a long chalk."…

Plumper started clambering back into the boat. "Come on," he chuckled. "There may be a chance, just a little chance."

Very inexpertly, Peascod pushed off and soaked his trousers in doing so.

The bare rock lay in the middle of the creek at the point where the latter met the open sea. At first sight it seemed inaccessible; but when they had circumnavigated it, they discovered a flat shelf that enabled them to make a fairly easy landing. The tiny island offered little in the way of cover and it did not take them long to assure themselves that what they sought was not there. If the man who had killed the "detective" had really used the rock as a temporary hiding place for the corpse, he had not stripped it and left the clothes behind him in that place; nor had he left behind him any useful pieces of evidence in the way of weapons and such like. But Peascod was able to lend weight to his theorizing, for on some small boulders, facing out to sea and well out of reach of the tide, he found traces of what looked very much like dried blood.

Plumper marked his satisfaction by using both hands on his moustache, Peascod his jubilation by beating his chest and proclaiming himself a genius.

They took to their boat again, Plumper rowing and Peascod piloting him round Larcombe Head towards the place, the narrow gap in the cliff, where the Starehole stream burbled its way to sea. The latter talked very fast and at great length. "Up to a point, it's obvious, elementary, autoptical!"

"Oh?" said Plumper.

"Oh, yes. My dear fellow, of course it is. Our conspirators slay the Vicar on the cliff and then, as murderers will when blood is on their hands, they fall to quarrelling. There is heated bickering aboard their frail craft as it rides the glittering sea, bickering born of guilt shared, bickering that grows to open strife. Then what is that I see? Ah! A wicked blade flashes in the cold moonlight, a muffled groan, a bulky and now, alas, lifeless body slumps with a sickening thud to the bottom of the boat. One conspirator is no more! Dead men tell no tales! His erstwhile friend, as a precaution against identification, strips the corpse, weights the clothes and drops them overboard. Then instead of giving him a watery grave, he casts him on the inhospitable rock, covers him with sacking which, by the greatest of good fortune, he discovers in the boat's locker—and then slips back to harbour, home and bed, proud of a good night's work! All that is simplicity itself. But here it is that doubt creeps in. Now why didn't he make identification well-nigh impossible by dropping his chum in the sea along with his clothes? Why did he, under the cover of darkness, transfer the body from the rock to Mr. Gedling's wood? And why, why, why did he spend Tuesday afternoon butchering about with a hack-saw? Perhaps he hated him *enormously*. Perhaps murder pure and simple didn't satisfy him. Or, again, perhaps he felt spiteful towards Mr. Gedling and hoped that the police would think *he* had done the deed. Mind you, Mr. Plumper, I must say I think—if I were the police—I think I should have apprehended the villain by this time. All you need to do is to line up every man, woman and child in Larcombe and make 'em damn well explain exactly where they were on Sunday night and Tuesday afternoon."

"Inspector Blutton has been actively engaged on that selfsame task."

"With any success?"

Plumper put on a solemn face and said: "I'm sure he is the only one to be able to tell you that." As he spoke, he drove the boat's nose up on to the narrow strip of sand that ran between the gap in the cliff.

This gap was of a peculiar formation. It was very narrow and the great height of the cliff made it seem narrower still. The wall of brown rock, on your right as you entered the Gap, rose up almost perpendicular; the other wall was not nearly so high and it sloped away. There must have been some sudden fault in this part of the rock, for after sloping gradually for about a mile and a half in the Symouth direction, it ceased to be a cliff at all and degenerated into the smooth Thurlebury Sands.

Together they splashed through the little stream into the gloom and chill of the Gap, until the sand gave way to rock and they began to climb. In five minutes, they were at the Starehole pool.

"You see how simple it is," said Peascod with a wave of his hand. "This little bit is his only portage. He dumps the body in the wood above the pool on Monday night. On Tuesday afternoon, when the coast is clear, but wait a minute. How did he know the coast was clear?" And then he smiled. "Ha ha, ha ha, you old fox, you sly rogue you, you knew all the time. That's why you were pumping me about the Bar on Tuesday morning. Costigan, of course! Of cou—" He broke off and his mouth fell open. "Mr. Plumper, do you know, I honestly believe I'm gifted. I have a sort of second sight, or so it seems. Light is bursting upon me from all sides! Congratulate me, my dear fellow. Congratulate me. I can lay my finger on your man within a quarter of an hour!"

But Plumper was not impressed. "Really?" he said.

"Yes, don't you see? The criminal must be someone who was in the Cloven when Costigan came in to ask about the buses!"

"If I remember rightly, you said there were nine people in the Bar at the time."

Peascod reflected. "Eight," he insisted.

"Nine—with yourself."

"My dear fellow!"

Sergt. Plumper sighed and folded his arms. "I said, including yourself. Now, as you would say, *assuming* that Costigan did not meet and talk with anyone else on his journey to and from the pub—we have nine suspects of whom three—the Captain and his two men—would seem to be the least suspicious by virtue of their supposed presence in Symouth on the night of the murders. Right?"

"Right," said Peascod.

"Then who remain? *You* have an alibi for Tuesday because you were making violent love to a barmaid at the time, and for Sunday night because you say you were in a trance. Hannabus's alibi is even weaker; he claims a gumboil on Sunday night and uninterrupted taxidermy on Tuesday. Yeo protests that he was sleeping in his widowed bed on both occasions. Bowle like-wise. For Tuesday afternoon, Charnock says that he was out fishing and Scoutey that he was tending his allotment which lies, I am given to understand, on a waste piece of ground behind the Vicarage. There you are, Maestro, take your choice. Six suspects, not one of them with cast-iron alibis and with no scrap of definite evidence against any of them. You mentioned a quarter of an hour, I think."

Far from being cast down, Peascod laughed out loud and proposed that they should go home and split a bottle of champagne to celebrate the startling brilliance of his deductions.

He himself took the oars this time. His suggestions were not yet exhausted. "Look here, if our man knifed his comrade in a boat, wouldn't there be some gore about the place? He might have washed it off, of course, but even the greatest criminals make small mistakes. That's axiomatic. I shall make it my business to examine all the small craft in the creek. And what about his own clothes? Is it feasible that he should have stabbed his man and come out immaculate? I must consider my cronies' garb with an eagle eye. Mustn't I?"

"The only trouble with you," said Plumper, "is that you're as noisy in honest doubt as was Arthur Hugh Clough himself."

When they had returned to "The Nook," Plumper said, as if à propos of nothing at all, "You wouldn't possess such a thing as a metronome, by any chance?"

"A metronome, Mr. Plumper? As a matter of fact, I do. And what, pray, would you be wanting with a thing like that?"

"Oh," said Plumper airily, "I just want to make one or two experiments in Time, you know. I'd be very grateful if you'd lend it me for a few days—if you won't be using it yourself, that is."

Peascod replied that he would lend the instrument with great pleasure, that he himself had not used it for several months and that he would start looking for it immediately. As good as his word, he set about opening cupboards, shifting furniture, groping behind the piano and in dark corners, and lifting all his music out of its big oaken chest; he even looked under his bed and inside the grandfather clock—but he could not find the metronome.

Just as he was beginning to lose his temper after declaring
a dozen times that "It must be *somewhere*," and waving aside
Plumper's suggestion that it didn't really matter as much as all
that, someone came to the door and knocked.

It was Blutton. Peascod was delighted. "How splendid,
Inspector! Now our party is complete. The three investigators
gathered together under one roof. We can put our heads together
in comfort. Come in, do."

Blutton gave him a stony stare. "Mr. Plumper is here, I believe.
I would like to speak to him. I'll wait outside."

When Plumper came out into the street, Blutton jerked his
head in the direction of "The Nook." "That handkerchief," he
said. "It's his."

The other replied in a low, soft voice, "Gedling's metronome
was his too."

"Oh, it was, was it? Well, what are we going to do about it?"

Plumper was silent.

They paced slowly down towards the quay and there was a
face at every window they passed. "I think," said Plumper after a
while, "that it's very much of a piece with your faked footprints,
or a piece of preposterous bluff. We're obviously expected to
look with suspicion on this apparently shatterpated young man.
God knows why! Just as we were supposed to look with suspicion
on John-Thomas. The only troublesome thing about Peascod is
that he's young."

"I don't follow you." The Inspector detested Plumper and,
as he told his spinster sister who kept house for him, wished to
goodness he'd had the courage not to call the Yard in.

Plumper shrugged impatiently. "Everybody in Larcombe connected with this game—the Vicar, the Captain, Gedling—they're

all men well over the middle age. Peascod's young; he doesn't fit; he's a stranger here."

Blutton coughed. "So was the 'detective.' I've been wondering," he went on, "if we haven't been overrating the criminal intelligence. There have been so many clues which we've chosen to ignore, treating them as things purposely left to put us off the track: the footprints on the cliff, those things up at Gedling's, this handkerchief—even that head. You don't think we may be falling into the habit of looking for complicated cleverness and red herrings where they don't exist? I know burglars don't go dropping laundry-marked handkerchiefs with blood several weeks old on 'em—but if Peascod *did* go in for burglary I can't see him being very efficient or careful."

"You get him to cook you a dinner some time—you won't say he can't be careful then."

Blutton ignored the interruption. "And you say the metronome's his. Don't forget, either, that he was on the spot when the head so mysteriously appeared."

Plumper smiled in his slow, aggravating way.

"All right! All right!" cried the other. "I *feel* as sure as you do that this nincompoop has had nothing to do with it. The only point I'm trying to make is that there must be a limit to all this artificial evidence. It's childish, pointless."

"Did I ever say that I felt that Peascod has had nothing to do with it?"

"Oh, never mind that now. Let's get clear what we're going to do about this handkerchief. We can't just do nothing."

"I suggest," said Plumper, "that you go and talk to him and find out if he's any explanation to offer—though I shouldn't tell him about the burglary yet. I'll be at the Cloven if you want me.

Oh, and by the way, before I forget, sir. If you could possibly spare an odd man to come down here to give Marsden a little moral support I think it would be a good thing. There's so very much for him to keep his eye on."

"All right. I'll see to it and I'll pick you up at the public when I've finished with Peascod." He turned and went back up the hill at a brisk pace.

An hour later, Plumper was taking his ease on the bench outside the Clove and Hoof. A quart beer-mug, a few breadcrumbs and the remains of a thick hunk of tolerable cheddar were before him on the table; the telescope was by his side.

The Inspector had been and gone: he had aired his ill-humour at the young artist's expense—but that was the only satisfaction he got from the interview. The latter had admitted haughtily that the handkerchief might well be his, but at the same time he swore that the blood on it was not from his veins. "Why!" he had exclaimed, "the last time I bled to any extent was when I walked into a wall in the dark: my nose didn't stop bleeding for two hours on that occasion and I must have lost over a pint of gore. But that was three years ago in Carcassonne—they have a very stout wall there, you know." And Blutton had had to be satisfied with that.

Peascod had been and gone too: he had come to protest in a spirited way against the Inspector's bullying of him as a near-suspect. "Am I am not sacrificing Poetry, Music, Painting in the interests of this boor's very cause?" he had said.

Plumper had dealt with both in a patient, non-committal way.

And now he took his ease and pondered in stout comfort which was only disturbed when, on the stroke of time, Rosa came out to clear away. She was still shy in the presence of the detective, for she could make of him neither head nor tail; he was so brusque and cold when he spoke to her and yet she was sure that, in his eyes, he was making fun of her: he liked his drop of drink and yet he seemed to have all the cankered qualities of the abstainer: he had a very handsome face and yet he chose to disfigure it with a most peculiar moustache: people said he was a policeman and yet he had never said so himself and, in any case, he didn't look like one. Rosa was at a loss.

She gathered the plates on to a tray, avoiding his eye very carefully and was just about to say, "It's keeping quite fine, isn't it?—considering," when he spoke abruptly. "Where's Mr. Yeo?"

Rosa coloured. "I think he's taking his nap, sir. We're very quiet at this time of year, you see, so I'm able to do most what's needed—except at night. But I don't think he's been feeling too well to-day."

"What's the matter with him?"

"Oh, sir, I'm sure I don't know. But he's been a bit off his feed. I think these horrible murders has been getting on his mind a bit. And I don't blame him. It's horrible, and if anybody ought to know, I ought to know, didn't I?"

Plumper did not take the proffered bait. "Has Captain Ridd been in this morning?" he said.

"He most certainly hasn't, sir, and I wouldn't be surprised if he was never to come near us again, not after what was said."

"Yes, I heard there was a bit of a row. Was it a good one?"

Rosa giggled; she was feeling more at home now. "I should just think it was. There was nearly blows."

"Was it about anything in particular? Or were they just drunk?"

She looked up apprehensively towards Bert's bedroom window. It was tight shut, but nevertheless she dropped her voice.

"Mr. Yeo was a teeny-weeny bit, and the Cap'n very. Nobody knows what it was about proper. They'd been by themselves in the Parlour for nearly an hour, and when they came out, Mr. Yeo had a long face and the Cap'n was swearing awful."

"At Yeo?"

"Yes and no. He was swearing sort of at everything in general. Mr. Yeo told him to go easy a bit, and *that* did it! I thought there'd be a fight then, I really did. The Cap'n raised his stick like he was going to strike Mr. Yeo—and then I screamed. That did the trick all right. That stopped him all right. He stamped to the door and just as he was going out he said, 'All right, Bert Yeo, you so-and-so so-and-so,' he said, 'I'll show you. You're just a so-and-so coward, that's what you are.' Those were his very words, sir. Yes, it'll be a long time before we see *him* again!"

"Have they ever quarrelled before?"

"Not to my knowledge, sir, they haven't. They've always been very close ever since I can remember."

"They've always been great friends, have they?"

"Oh, yes, sir, always."

Plumper leaned back against the wall and said no more. Rosa hesitated for a moment or two as if expecting more chat and then, with a return of her old feeling of uneasy mistrust towards him, scurried off indoors with her tray.

For no particular reason, he picked up his telescope and trained it on to the "Moorings" across the creek. What he saw brought a smile to his lips. John-Thomas Ridd was there with his good eye to a glass of his own—and the glass seemed to be pointing straight at the Clove and Hoof! Plumper was not of an oversensitive disposition, but he felt slightly embarrassed. The sensation of being scrutinized minutely and suspiciously at close quarters even by a potential friend is seldom a pleasant one; the sensation of being so scrutinized at long range by a potential enemy, never.

Tucking his telescope under his arm, he strolled away up the hill, eventually taking the cliff-path to Larcombe Head. His sense of embarrassment was still with him. Impatiently, and angry with himself, he took another sight of the "Moorings." John-Thomas, larger than life, was still sitting there on a white, iron garden-chair in front of the verandah as he had been sitting ten minutes before; the only thing that had changed was the direction of the telescope. It had shifted its line from the Clove and Hoof to the cliff-path leading round to Larcombe Head.

Plumper shrugged his shoulders and walked on, resigned to the rôle of cynosure. He had not yet met the Captain, but he already felt acquainted. Before he had taken a dozen steps, a fairly strange thing happened. A man's head and shoulders popped up almost under his feet. It was Hannabus. With abnormal agility, the old man hoisted himself over the seemingly treacherous lip of the cliff and scrambled to his feet in front of the detective. A brace of dead rabbits was strung round his neck, his cheeks were puffed out and his face was contorted by a desire to utter a greeting and an inability to do so.

"Are you trying to break your neck?" said Plumper.

Hannabus carefully removed two large bird's eggs from his mouth.

"Good afternoon, sir. Break my neck? Good lord, no. It's not as bad as all that when you're used to it."

Plumper looked over the edge. Admittedly, the cliff was scored with a few grassy gullies at 45 degrees and an occasional scree at 60; there were even a few ledges, crannies and fissures; but there were also many overhangs, and in most places—after about twenty-five yards of smooth slope—sheer drops. "Very nice," he growled.

Hannabus chuckled in his beard. "I reckon I can go wherever the bunnies can, old as I am. You interested in eggs, sir?"

"Only hens' and plovers'."

"Ah! Fascinating study, birds' eggs. And profitable, I might tell you. I've nearly fifty clients I collect for, all over England. Now these. I suppose you wouldn't recognize these? Not one in ten would, as a matter of fact. They're rare. This one's a Grag and this one, look at those green markings now, this one's a Prillet. Both rare and both late layers. I had a ticklish five minutes with the Grag. I—"

"I'd rather talk about water-colours." Plumper's manner was abrupt and unsympathetic to ornithology.

The old man was disconcerted. "Pictures, sir?"

"No. Boxes of paint."

"Oh, yes, yes, paint-boxes, for painting with."

"Precisely."

Without realizing it, Sebastian found himself being walked back down the hill. "Excuse me, sir, but they were saying in the Bar that you're a sort of policeman. Are you really down here because of the… of the businesses?"

"Partly," said Plumper.

Sebastian grew more nervous and ill at ease with every step.

"You sell paint-boxes, don't you?" barked the detective.

"Yes, sir, one or two, now and again. Mr. Peascod mostly. Summer visitors sometimes."

"Now think carefully. This is important. Who else in Larcombe, besides Peascod, have you sold any paints to within the last few months?"

The old man pondered. "Well, let me see. Young Annie Scoutey, that's the barber's girl, she looks after the Cubs and Brownies, she bought a box a few weeks back. And wait a minute—there's somebody else. Now who was it? Lord, oh lord! I've got a memory like a sieve. Just about the same time, it was, that I sold another one. I remember two went in the same week. Ah, yes! Yes it was. It was Alan Charnock, sir; yes, so it was. That's right, Alan Charnock, him whose boat you had out this morning. For little Georgie's birthday. I knew there was somebody else."

"Is that all?"

"Yes, I think so, sir, not counting the two-three I sold to visitors. Might I ask why—?"

"You're quite sure of that? Peascod, Charnock and Miss Scoutey—those are the only ones?"

"Quite sure, sir. Quite sure."

"Good afternoon," said Plumper and, without further ado, left him at the door of his shop and walked on past the quay, down the Corfield road towards Jack Marsden's cottage. About a hundred yards from his destination, he stopped and turned and brought his telescope into play, and discovered, to his vast amusement, that the eye of the mariner was still upon him.

The village constable was delighted to see him. He was in the act of adjusting his trouser-clips preparatory to cycling out to Corfield on his afternoon patrol, and he was only too glad of an excuse to postpone the long uphill climb.

"Has the Inspector told you about keeping a watch on Gedling's grounds at night?"

"Yes, sir. My relief man comes to-morrow. He's going to take over for a few hours in the daytime so I can get some sleep."

"Good," said Plumper. "Now look. You must stick close to the house for an hour or two *after* one o'clock. That's the important time, I think. Keep your eyes and ears open, but don't show yourself. I shall be very surprised if there's any more monkey-business, but we've got to make sure. Oh, and there's one other thing. Have you ever put the fear of God into anybody?"

Jack looked doubtful.

"It's very easy. All you've got to do is to pretend to know something and yet say nothing. Look fierce and do a lot of shouting. Frown and stick your chest out. And what *you*'ve got to be particularly careful of is not to blush."

Jack blushed.

"Anyhow, I want you to call on two friends of yours, Mr. Scoutey and Mr. Charnock, and demand of them the two paint boxes and the paint brushes that are kept in their houses. Tell them you aren't at liberty, just at present, to say why the police want to examine them. Stare them hard in the eyes as you put the boxes in your pocket—and slam the door as you go out. Can you do that?"

In a very perplexed voice, Jack said that he would do his best.

Back at Setterham, Blutton was giving an insincere opinion to the Chief Constable. "I think things are narrowing themselves down, sir. Plumper seems to think—and as a matter of fact, I agree with him—that our man is still up to some sort of tricks and that it's just a question of waiting for him to put a foot wrong."

The Chief Constable said, "Good—so long as we don't have to wait too long." And then gave, for the sixth time, his considered verdict on the criminal. "He's bughouse—bats. He must be!"

Blutton hazarded a pleasantry. "I only wish, sir," he said, "that he'd go about with straw in his hair—we might be able to pick him out then."

"Ha ha," said the Chief Constable quickly.

When Blutton returned to his office, a report was handed to him informing him, in effect, that an elderly gentleman with a diseased nose had, on the previous Tuesday, purchased from Messrs. Barson and Meredith of 27 Fore St., Setterham, not only one shotgun but also one sporting rifle, one automatic pistol and a considerable quantity of ammunition. The Inspector whistled softly to himself and then scratched his head. He had been inclined to regard old Gedling as a drink-sodden neurotic unbalanced by the gruesome discovery in his garden: but he began to modify his views when he remembered that these armaments had been bought *before* the discovery—bought on the very afternoon, indeed, that the truncated body had come to light. Was this, mused the Inspector, Gedling's reply to the anonymous painted letter—as flight had been the Vicar's? It seemed a more sensible reply, anyhow.

At the very moment that Blutton was giving his closest attention to the new issues raised by Lionel Gedling's disquieting purchases, Plumper was taking a last curious look at Ridd's bungalow, "The Moorings." To his relief, the telescope, the tripod and the Captain had disappeared: the latter had been watching his movements for getting on for five hours!

It was about half an hour before dusk and the tide was out. Plumper crossed the road from the Clove and Hoof and climbed down the steep stone steps (called, curiously enough, Pilchard Cellars) that led to the water. His own dinghy and one other were made fast to rings at the bottom of these steps, but the tide had left them high and dry, at the same time uncovering a line of broken rocks running along the foot of the cliffs.

Plumper proceeded to clamber over these rocks in the direction of Larcombe Head—and he was making the journey with a set purpose. It had occurred to him that it might be possible for a man to work his way round these rocks at low tide and reach Starehole Gap unobserved, even in broad daylight, by anyone in Larcombe who did not happen to be leaning over the cliff and looking down. He would be exposed only to the view of somebody out in a boat or to somebody armed with a telescope on the Crale Cliff side of the creek. That would be one solution to the problem presented by the fact that whoever had sawn off the "detective's" head in the wood above the pool on the Tuesday afternoon had made his journey to and from that place without being seen by man, woman or child; or at least, according to the testimony of every man, woman and child in Larcombe. The normal way of reaching the Gap was, of course, to go up the hill past the Vicarage and then cut through the woods bordering the Old Barton drive. This would have been the ideal route for the criminal in so far as the Vicarage and Old Barton itself were empty on that afternoon and, with any luck, there would have been no one at all on the Vicarage hill. *But* Jeremiah Scoutey claimed to have been tending his allotment (which was in a position to give him a clear view of the hill and the drive) from two till four—and he maintained that he'd seen "nothing nor nobody but that there Peascod and Rosa." A fairly recent landslip had very effectively blocked the other approach—the cliff-path round the Head. The sea route was always possible, but only one man admitted to having been in a boat at the material time—and that man was the doltish, tongue-tied Alan Charnock. And to take out a boat unobserved in a place like Larcombe, where there was always somebody or other lounging against the quay wall and staring vaguely out to sea, would be no easy matter.

Plumper had a confident feeling that he was on the right track. But this was by no means the easiest way to Starehole Gap, as he soon realized after he had been splashing for five minutes through beautiful rock-pools, stubbing his toes on flinty crags and barking his shins and elbows on boulders of jagged rock-slate.

Eventually, he sat down to regain his breath after a particularly painful piece of scrambling. He regretted that he had not changed his light, thin-soled shoes for this expedition. And it was at this moment that he heard the noise behind and above him and turned to see a great boulder smashing its way down the cliff-face towards him, bounding, bashing, dragging pebbles, earth and stones big and little along with it. Straight at him it came, and for one agonized second he thought it had got him for, as he leapt to his feet in terror, he slipped and fell face-downwards among the seaweed and the jagged edges. It missed him by a yard. It crashed on a rock a yard to his left hand and, by the mercy of God, bounded away from him. A fragment flew off and struck him on the shoulder. Pebbles, earth, stones clattered about him and upon him: his head, his back, his legs, his arms.

Plumper swore and sweated; he leapt to his feet; his nerve was gone. The policeman was terrified. He cried out and started stumbling and clambering back the way he had come. He looked up the cliff but could see nothing. He slipped again and again. There was a lump on the back of his head; his shoulder ached; his knees were bleeding.

Another rock, huger it seemed than the last, fell ten yards in front of him and bounced off at right-angles towards him; but it fell short. Again he looked up the cliff. Nothing. Not a sign. It was getting dark.

There was an overhang before him—an overhang and safety. And a deep pool and a green slimy ridge between him and it. He jumped down into the water, landed awkwardly, slipped. Another crash behind him; a slithering of slate and stone above him. He thought of the Larcombe Head landslip. He tried to find a footing on limpets to get him over the slippery ridge. Big stones whizzed over his head and fell into the sea. He looked up again.

A man was outlined against the cliff-top; outlined but not silhouetted. The dark trees rose behind him, blurring his shape; but it was a man. A man stooping and throwing...

More stones clattered and splashed around him. He tore his nails, but he got to the top of the ridge. He slithered down a twelve-foot drop, landed, spread-eagled. He crawled under the overhang; lay on his face and, in safety, regained his spirit. Soon his panting gave way to cursing. He lit a cigarette and smoked hard and angrily. He got to his feet, limped over to one end of the overhang and cautiously surveyed the cliff-top. He could see nothing. And then, as he retreated to his cover, a solitary stone rattled on the rocks and splashed into the sea.

He decided to wait until it was quite dark—and the unpleasantness and discomfort of his waiting was intensified by his unnecessary anxiety about the tide. To be cut off by the sea was no more comforting a prospect than death by stoning.

The journey back to Pilchard Cellars was complicated for him by the darkness, the smarting and aching of his hurts, the necessity for silence, by his fear and by the irritating possibility that his attacker might well have left his post long ago. It took him a long time to reach the Cellars, even though no more stones or boulders fell.

At the Clove and Hoof you had to go through the Bar to reach the stairs. When Plumper arrived, the former was almost empty; only Rosa, Hannabus and Sam Bowle were there.

Dishevelled, wet, torn, bleeding, sore, he passed through without a word or a look. They stared hard at him, but did not speak—not even to say good evening, for the expression on his face was enough to deter the glibbest of gossips, let alone three astonished rustics.

He had a meagre bath of tepid water, daubed iodine on his cuts, changed his clothes, came down to the Bar again and started drinking whiskey. By this time, Scoutey and one or two others had come in.

Rosa smiled a timid smile at him and said, "I hope you don't mind cold supper. But, you see, we didn't know when you'd be coming in."

"Where's Yeo?" growled Plumper.

The girl looked uncomfortable. "He—he's still up in his bedroom, sir. He's locked the door, and whenever I go up to see if there's anything I can do or get for him, he just shouts at me and tells me to go away. I don't think he's in bed. He seems to have been rummaging about and shifting furniture. I can't think what's come over him. Did you want to see him special, sir?"

"No. And I don't think I'll bother with any supper. I'll have some sandwiches later."

And then Jeremiah Scoutey tried to be truculent. He bustled up to the detective. "What's all this about paint boxes?" he said. "What the hell's it got to do with the police what my daughter does with her own money? It's her money, isn't it? The maid can buy what she likes with it, can't she? And they call this a free country! Why don't the police do something about these murders instead of mucking about with kids' paint boxes? And I hear Jack Marsden was over at Charnock's too. I suppose we'll all be arrested for drinking beer soon!"

Plumper looked at him but said nothing, and the greengrocer, after waiting a few embarrassed moments for an answer and finding that no answer was forthcoming, blew his nose loudly on a red handkerchief and, as loudly, called for a pint of mixed.

Before Rosa had finished filling the stocky, light-blue cider mug, who should put his head round the door but the village constable.

"Could I speak to you a moment, sir?" he said.

Plumper tossed off his whiskey, jerked his head in the direction of the stairs and led the way up to his bedroom.

"I came up before, sir, but you were out."

"Yes," said Plumper, "I was out all right. I've been having quite a jolly time of it."

"Oh, sir?" said Jack, swinging his helmet by the strap like a little girl with her bonnet.

"Yes. But never mind that now. What is it? The paints?"

"Yes, sir." Jack handed over two paint boxes that had originally been identical. But whereas Annie Scoutey's was neat and clean, with the brushes still in their sockets, Master Charnock's was very much the worse for wear. There were indescribable messes of colour everywhere so that it was difficult to distinguish the various little squares of paint; several of these latter were missing—including the blue; there was one well-gnawed brush left, with perhaps four bristles to it. The constable explained. "Little Georgie's only seven, you see, sir. Now Annie, she's a bit of an artist. She bought these to paint the Cubs' and Brownies' notices with. They have Whist Drives and Jumble Sales and things; for the funds, you know. And she's done one or two things for Jeremiah as well. 'Shampoo and Haircut 9*d*.,' 'Shaving 4*d*.,' 'Singeing so-and-so,' the sort of thing he has up in his shop. And 'Eat More

Fruit!' That sort of thing, sir. When I went round, Scoutey kicked up a monstrous fuss, but Alan Charnock, he took it like a lamb." Jack smiled. "I really think I managed to impress him, sir."

"All right. Good. Leave these things with me and go and get some sleep. What time are you going up to Gedling's? About midnight?"

"Yes, sir." Jack turned to go but faced round again at the door. "Oh, sir, I don't know if it's worth reporting, sir, but that Costigan went off to Setterham by the afternoon bus. He was in his best clothes and he had a big suit-case with him. At least, so I heard."

Plumper jumped to his feet. "Worth reporting, man!" He rushed from the room.

The telephone was in the passage by the stairs, in full view and hearing of the Bar. Plumper cursed and dashed back upstairs. "Have you got your bicycle?" he snapped.

"Yes, sir." By this time, Jack was very flustered and fearful of having done something liable to spoil his pleasant relationship with the Scotland Yard man.

"Well, get back like all hell to your telephone. Get on to Blutton. Tell him from me that Costigan's gone. Tell him to get on to the Railway people to see what he can pick up there, and then to issue a general lookout. Tell him to get on to the Yard. Urgent. Go on. Fly! I'm going to see Gedling."

Almost instinctively, Plumper picked up a heavy walking-stick as he followed Marsden out of the room.

His hurried exit and the direction he took did not pass unnoticed in the Bar. There were grins. "Something's up," said Scoutey.

Sam the Lobster Man chuckled. "T'other one went that way in a hurry, didn't un? Didn't come back neither. Summat funny up there."

Hannabus plucked his beard. "Don't know what to make of that chap, I'm sure."

"He has such funny ways," said Rosa. And Scoutey summed up by saying that he was "a snotty scauffer."

The moon was hidden and the light from Peascod's cottage was the last in the village—but dark as it was, Plumper found the Vicarage road easy enough to follow. It was a different matter, however, once he had passed the drive gates. There was no light from Old Barton to guide him and the trees set up a black barrier on either side so that there were no tangible, no guiding limits anywhere except underfoot; he was unfamiliar with the place, and he was more than uneasy. Without having heard or seen anything out of the ordinary, he was sure he was being followed, not behind on the drive but to his right in the trees; not that there was any rustling or snapping of twigs; he just felt that someone was there, abreast with him, among the trees. He was uneasy; the memory of his adventure under the cliff was still very fresh. He pressed on as fast as he could without actually running.

When he came to the house, he found it dead—its outlines blurred, no light at any window, no noise, no sign of life. But almost before the echo of his bang on the door had died away, a powerful lamp hanging above his head was switched on, dazzling him with its unexpected brilliance. Nothing happened for some minutes; not a sound came from the house. Then an upstairs window was flung open and Gedling's voice shouted out, "Who is it? What d'you want? Clear away from here or I'll blow your head off!"

Plumper could see nothing, the light was too strong. He stepped back a little out of the glare and was able to make out the head and shoulders of the old man. He was still wearing his smoking-cap and there was a gun in his hand; he was muttering or, rather, gibbering to himself. "I'm from the police," cried Plumper.

Gedling laughed on a high-pitched, hysterical note. "Police! That's good, that is, very good! Damn lot of good the police are to anybody. Clear off! D'you hear? I don't want any more dead men round me. I've got a gun here and I can use it. D'you hear?"

"Why has Costigan gone away?"

"Costigan?" Gedling laughed again. "What's that to do with you? Be off! I've sacked him, that's what I've done. Can't stand him about the place." He laughed again, shrilly. "And now quick march, my lad, or I'll pepper you. And tell all your friends to keep their distance. This is private ground."

Plumper shrugged his shoulders and walked away. There was not much he could do.

All the same, he didn't like the look of Lionel Gedling; in the morning, with Blutton, he'd get hold of the old man properly. It wasn't healthy for him, in his present state, to be shut up in a house like that with one shotgun, one sporting rifle and one automatic pistol for sole company.

The window slammed shut and the light went out. As he turned away, Plumper had once again the impression that he was not alone. He hurried on, swinging his stick, watchful, uneasy.

The only occasion on which Jack Marsden had undertaken night duty (other than his tri-weekly bicycling from Larcombe to Corfield to Poridge and back again to Larcombe) for the past ten years was during the night and early morning of the Great Eclipse; then it had been his business to keep an eye on the concourse assembled on Crale Cliffs. That had been a convivial, a novel duty—almost a pleasure.

But this prowling among the bushes bordering the drive to Old Barton was not a pleasure. To him it was a nightmare. Unless you are a poet or a Sioux Indian, a wood—even an ordinary wood—is not the place to keep midnight vigil. In ominous woods, woods the scene of recent bloody murders, imbecile pranks and other monstrosities, you may be sure that there are no black pumas crouched to spring or boa constrictors coiled to strike, but of other things than that you cannot be so sure. And Jack was pestered with a lively imagination. The thought that England is a state drab and over-sane did not comfort him. His helmet, his buttons and his boots lent him no safe dignity in the middle of this murmuring wood during the small hours when the moon was dodging behind flying clouds. Reflection on the heroic deeds of members of the Constabulary—both County and Metropolitan—who had laid down their lives uncomplaining in defence of Law and Order, stood him in small stead.

He worked round cautiously to the front of the house and, to his considerable comfort, he discovered that there was a light shining from a ground-floor window. The surge of the tide echoed up gloomily through the Gap and the stream gurgled coldly. Jack lit a pipe; but the stem was clogged and foul and the tobacco was bitter to the tongue; the pipe went out. In the near distance, a dog barked. He leaned against a tree and tried to force his thoughts on to agreeable subjects—Tap Dancing, Jane McQueen, Strong Tea, his Cheap Excursion visit to London.

An hour passed. An hour and a half.

He was back among the bushes off the drive, close to the house. The moon was clear and round now and it was very cold. But quite suddenly Jack forgot the moon, his cold feet and his cold nose; he caught his breath and his heart leapt. There *was* something. Not near—not near yet—but coming nearer. Open-mouthed, wide-eyed, he clenched his truncheon with a sweating grip and strained to listen, head thrust forward. There it was again. A swishing, a crackling, a crunching. Regular. Coming closer. In front of him on the other side of the drive. But not *down* the drive. Too soft for that.

The village constable was rigid; he had been dreading this, and he didn't know what to do. There was no mistaking it; someone was coming through the wood. But at least it was in front and not behind; at least there was the drive between. If he kept still, he would not be seen. He felt a little surer of himself. Surer, but still rigid. It was very near now, louder. NOW!

Jack's rigidity collapsed. His heart pounded harder still by reaction and he very nearly took a step forward; but he didn't.

It was the Captain. It was John-Thomas Ridd who stumped into the moonlight from the wood opposite, who looked about him nervously, who tried to walk as quietly as he could the remaining few yards to the door of Old Barton, who entered the door which opened even before he had knocked, even before his foot was on the doorstep, and which closed again immediately.

Jack whistled softly, and as he whistled a slight sound behind him caused him to half-turn his head. Then a loaded stick hit him on that vulnerable spot on the back of the skull. A fiercer blow would have killed him, but this beautifully timed and measured blow merely knocked him out.

When precipitate footsteps clattered outside the Clove and Hoof, when a furious tantara was banged on the door, and when a wild falsetto voice cried out his name, Plumper was not asleep. He had recently awakened from a nightmare. His head lay uneasy on his hot, crumpled pillow and he was thinking. There had just occurred to him a disturbing possibility which, if justified, would spell more and more complication to his already tangled problem. This possibility was, in effect, that there was a maniac at large in Larcombe *as well* as a sender of threatening anonymous letters. Supposing that the Vicar had been threatened or blackmailed (as it would appear that Gedling was, after a fashion, being threatened or blackmailed). Instead of going to the police, he hires a private detective from some obscure agency not on Scotland Yard's books. This latter duly arrives and is last seen following him up to the Vicarage with the possible intention of mounting night guard, as Marsden was doing for Lionel Gedling. At this point, the homicidal maniac—a being quite unconnected with the blackmailer—marks his first *entrée en scène* by knifing the detective for no other reason than that which had prompted him to try to kill Plumper himself by rolling boulders down the cliff. The Vicar, finding his henchman dead, loses his nerve completely and determines, in drunken panic, on flight. He flees—but the blackmailer has anticipated this and is waiting for him on Crale Cliff; and in the heat of the argument or fight that follows, the Vicar gets a bullet in his chest.

That little possibility would leave—Problem One: Find the Larcombe maniac. And Problem Two: Find the Larcombe blackmailer. "Very fanciful," sighed Plumper. "Oh, very fanciful."

The whole inn seemed to tremble before the onslaught of the knocker.

Lights appeared at neighbouring bedroom windows; windows were thrown open; heads thrust out. Mrs. Busby, the butcher's wife, after shrieking "It's disgraceful, disgraceful! What's it all about? What's the matter *now?*" withdrew very suddenly as she realized that her hair was in curl-papers and her nightdress in comparative disarray, and sent her lethargic, unwilling spouse to the window in her place. Peascod whooped with joy on hearing the noise and a second later was scrambling into his trousers.

In the blackness of her little bedroom, Rosa shivered and goggled and was mute.

Old Hannabus went one better; he toddled down to his front door in his nightshirt and bare feet, a candle in his hand.

Plumper, as excited as any of them, leaned out of his window and shouted, "What is it, man?"

Jack, helmetless and dithering, squeaked, "Oh, sir, I've been stunned. Come quick."

Peascod and Hannabus were already commiserating with and questioning the constable, who was voluble, by the time Plumper got the front door of the inn open. Without a word, he hustled the constable inside, slammed the door, lit the gas in the bar, pushed him into a chair and was pouring out a very stiff brandy when Rosa stuck her head round the door. "Is he hurt bad?" she whispered.

"Get back to bed!" he roared.

Marsden's face was white, but the brandy brought colour to it with a rush; he had gulped it as he would have gulped beer. When his spluttering and coughing was over, he managed to answer the questions put to him. He had watched as Mr. Plumper had told him to watch without showing himself and without making any noise. He had seen the Cap'n come out of the wood and go to the front door of Old Barton. He had been hit over the head the very second the Cap'n had been let into the house. He had come to—he didn't know how long after—to find his legs tied up with his belt and his hands tied up behind his back with his handkerchief. He had vomited. He had shouted out loud and gone on shouting. He had stopped shouting because a window at the house had been thrown open and several shots fired in his direction. He had thought it safest not to shout any more and had vomited again because his head was like a very bad toothache only a lot worse. After a bit, he had felt better and had started trying to get his hands and feet loose. There had been no more shooting. And after what seemed like hours and hours, he had wriggled his hands free. The rest had been easy and he had run here as fast as ever he could.

Jack put his hands to his head and groaned.

Plumper leaned against the Bar, stroking his moustache, irresolute. He couldn't make up his mind whether or not to ring up Setterham to bring out Blutton and some reinforcements for any possible emergencies. But what emergencies? The shooting was perfectly explainable, in fact, almost inevitable: Gedling was in an abnormally nervous state and, after his disturbing experiences, suspicious of every sound and movement. The Captain's visit was admittedly odd and possibly significant, but not necessarily criminal. The really important thing was the attack on Marsden.

Was this attack, Plumper wondered, the work of the joker who had been pestering Gedling? Was it nothing more than a bad joke? At any rate, this new personage, the joker, had definitely established himself. And he wasn't Gedling and he wasn't Ridd—that much was clear. The man to look for was the man who did pointless and seeming crazy things; a man who might well enjoy sawing a dead head from a dead body to drop it into a pool where two lovers were.

Plumper looked at his watch. It was ten minutes past four. He decided to postpone his call to Setterham. "How d'you feel?" he said.

Jack smiled weakly and said he felt all right.

"Good. Come on then, we'd better go back and have a look round up there."

Plumper's chief difficulty and his chief desire was to get in touch with Gedling. It was still very dark and he had a feeling that the crazy old man was still prowling about from window to window, more than ready, anxious even, to take a pot shot at anything and everything. To march up to the front door at this time of day and in the present circumstances was to invite injury.

Accordingly, they made their way as quietly as possible along the grass verge of the drive until they were within thirty yards of the house. Then Plumper took the rash and unlawful but highly effective course of picking up a stone and throwing it hard. There was a crash of splintering glass, and then almost immediately the big outside light was switched on, a second-floor window was thrown up and a revolver banged away aimlessly into the darkness, bullets droning and spattering into the trees. The two policemen lay flat on their faces, and when the fusillade had died down, Plumper cupped his hands round his mouth and shouted as loud as he could, "Stop that shooting, Mr. Gedling! It's the police. There's nothing to be afraid of, but I *must* speak to you—it's most important."

A wild cackle came from an upstairs window. "Oh, it's the police, is it? And who d'you think's going to believe that, eh? You just step out into the light where I can see you—then we'll see what's what."

"What are we going to do, sir?" whispered Jack.

"We've got to chance it. Come on and keep your eyes open." With that Plumper walked forward into the semicircle of light and Jack followed him.

The laughter echoed out again. "Well, well! Now isn't that nice. Isn't that lovely, my pretties. I can see you now all right—oh yes, I can see you, my pretties, and I can put bullets in both of you if you come a step nearer. Both of you." Gedling cackled and began to sing:

> "Oh there was a little man and he had a little gun,
> And his bullets were made of lead, lead, lead.
> He went to the brook for to shoot a little dook,
> And he shot him right through the head, head, head…"

Jack shivered; he gripped Plumper's arm. "Oh lordie, sir, he's dotty all right. He doesn't know what he's doing, sir. He'll be potting us in a minute."

"Don't move. I'll talk him round." Plumper's nerves were jangling; he was far from having himself under strict control and he was in no mood to savour the grand eeriness of the old man's foolish song croaked out against a background of thin cloud streaking across the moon. He squared his shoulders and said in as commanding a voice as he could muster, "Now, Mr. Gedling, just tell me one thing and I'll go away. Is Captain Ridd in there with you?"

The question seemed to infuriate the old man. "Ridd! Ridd!" he screamed. "It's a damn lie. He's never been here in his life. He's a scoundrel. You're all scoundrels. It's a damn lie. I wouldn't touch him with a barge-pole. It's a lie. You're lying. But *I*'ll settle you!"

"The bushes!" yelled Plumper.

The revolver was banging away again, and this time at a mark. The two charged away from the light and into the bushes; then they fell flat and crawled farther into the wood.

Plumper wasted no more time. "Get along through the wood," he growled, "level with the drive. Then run as fast as you can to the Cloven. Ring up Setterham. Tell 'em to rouse up Blutton and as many men as they can get in one car. And tell 'em to come like hell. Then get along to Ridd's bungalow and knock him up. If you can't get an answer, break in and find out if he's there or not. If he is, make him come up here. If he's not, come back at once."

"Just break in, shall I, sir, if there's no answer?"

"Just break in," said Plumper.

Jack squirmed cautiously forward until he was within the cover of a clump of rhododendrons; then he cantered off and disappeared among the trees, his long legs swinging as awkwardly as stilts.

Plumper watched him go and then turned his serious attentions to the gunman in Old Barton. The light was still on over the door, but the night sky was turning to grey and robbing it of its brilliance. He cautiously worked his way round until he could just distinguish the outline of the old man perched at an open window immediately above the front door. From time to time he would disappear for perhaps five or ten minutes, and during his absence a few shots would ring out from the back of the house. As soon as he returned, there would be a further burst of haphazard shooting intended, apparently, to warn whomsoever the warning might concern, that the watcher was still at his post. In the twilight silence, Plumper could hear him muttering to himself; it was difficult to tell whether it was lunatic or drunken muttering. At all events, he took frequent pulls at a bottle.

The ground on which the detective crouched was damp and the dawn wind was cold, but he was, by this time, in a much healthier and easier frame of mind than he had been a short time before. He was even looking forward with excitement, if not with pleasure, to the outcome of this peculiar adventure.

After a little more than half an hour, at the time when Plumper was listening carefully for signs of the returning constable, footsteps sounded faintly at the far end of the drive. He cursed the man for a fool—for he was coming straight down, unconcernedly crunching the gravel instead of using the grass verge or working through the wood. Plumper couldn't see him, but it seemed that Gedling could, for he was now craning forward out of the window.

The former forgot himself in his anger. "The wood—you damn fool!" he roared. "Get to the wood!"

A bullet smacked into a tree, uncomfortably close to his head. More followed. Plumper jumped to his feet and rushed deeper into the wood bearing to his right, heading up the drive, shouting, "Marsden, Marsden—where are you, you damn fool?"

At last a figure emerged from the gloom of the bushes; but it was not Marsden. "Oh—good morning. What's going on?" said Christian Peascod.

Plumper snorted. "Good morning to you, and may I ask what the hell you're doing here?"

"I must confess that mere curiosity is largely responsible for my presence." There was less of ingenuous amity in his voice than there had been in his earlier conversations with the detective; he bore malice over Blutton's surly treatment of him over the question of the bloodstained handkerchief—treatment for which he felt Plumper was principally to blame. "I am awakened from my sleep," he went on, "by an agitated constable crying to high heaven that he has been stunned. I hear shot after shot coming from this direction. Is it to be wondered that I who have dedicated my unremitting services to the unravelling of this mystery—in spite of obstruction by over-bearing and recriminatory policemen—is it to be wondered, I say, that I should wish to be present when—"

"Shut up and go back to bed," began Plumper, and then suddenly softened his voice. "No. Just a minute. You can stay. Come with me and watch your step. Gedling's gaga and he's got a gun."

He led the way back to his original position, and Peascod followed, chuckling with pleasure and rubbing his hands. "Be careful, you—you pilgarlick!" growled Plumper: whereupon his companion moved forward with exaggerated slowness and care. But despite their precaution, Gedling heard them and greeted them with raking fire.

They crouched behind a tree. "I've never," whispered Peascod, "favoured whiskey as a *very* early morning drink, but I understand it comes in uncommonly useful in an emergency such as this. Have some." He held out a pocket-flask. Plumper shook his head angrily. Peascod took a commendable draught. "Tell me," he went on as soon as he was able, "is our friend here aiming specifically at you or has he merely been taken with ballistomania?"

"I really couldn't tell you. And if you want to stay here, you'll have to keep your mouth shut."

"But why—?"

"D'you think I'm having you here with me just for the pleasure of your company?"

Peascod grinned uneasily. "Well, Mr. Plumper, perhaps I wouldn't go quite so far as that. But, of course, I'm always useful in an emergency, and any helpful suggestions I can make, I—"

"Shut up," said Plumper. "And stay like that. The only reason I'm having you here is that I can keep my eye on at least one person in Larcombe. Do I make myself clear?"

"Crystal clear," said Peascod mournfully, and took another pull at his flask. With an ill grace and to the best of his ability, he obeyed the detective's order. From time to time, he turned his eyes to survey his companion's face, but the latter's eyes were always there to meet his—and this embarrassed Peascod.

At last there was a movement among the undergrowth to their left and the noise of it, slight as it was, provoked more stray shooting from Gedling. Marsden, dodging from tree to tree, appeared alone. With elaborate caution, he wormed his way forward. "Ridd's not there, sir."

"He's not?"

"No, sir. Bed hasn't been slept in."

Plumper swore and muttered something to himself. "Did you get on to Setterham all right?"

"Yes, sir. They said they'd get Inspector Blutton out right away. It's just gone half-past five now—I expect they'll be here in about quarter of an hour."

"Good," said Plumper. He studied the constable carefully: Marsden's long face was pale and thin at the best of times, but now it was looking very drawn and weary. "Give him some whiskey, Peascod."

Peascod, only too anxious to be of service, handed over his flask. "But certainly, my dear fellow. Certainly. Only too delighted, I assure you."

Marsden drank and colour flooded his cheeks.

"That better?"

Marsden blinked and made affirmative gurgles.

"Good," said Plumper. "I need you for just another half-hour and then you'll be able to go off and get some sleep. Now listen. I want you to go round to the other side of the house and keep watch there. You've got your whistle, haven't you? Now if there's anything worth whistling about, whistle as hard as you can, and don't let anyone get close enough to crown you this time. And be careful of Gedling too."

Marsden crept off the way he had come, and his departure was the signal for a fresh spatter of bullets.

Peascod looked appealingly at his companion. "Hadn't I better go with him? He's looking rather exhausted and it's not a very pleasant job you've given him."

"You'll stay just where you are." Plumper snapped the words.

But silence is irksome to eager youth, especially in the chill and cheerless hour of dawn. He tried again, "Old Lionel here isn't very sparing with his ammunition, is he?"

"He's got enough—don't you worry."

"If he's kept this up all night he must be getting pretty sleepy by now."

"I said shut up," said Plumper.

It was getting light quickly now. And they were, from time to time, able to see Gedling's face peering out from one or other of the open windows. Sometimes he would crane his neck to look down the drive, sometimes he would stare fixedly at one particular spot in the bushes for minutes on end, and sometimes he would fire a random shot into the air as if taking pleasure in the mere sound made by his new toys. And always he gabbled away unintelligibly to himself. Then suddenly the lamp over the door went out.

It was shortly after this that they heard a car groan its way up the hill.

"Come on," said Plumper, and started off through the trees.

Peascod expostulated. "But surely someone ought to stay here to keep an eye on the old man?"

"You'll do as I say. Come on. Quick."

It so happened that Gedling was on one of his visits to the other side of the house, so there were no bullets this time. As a consequence they were able to make quicker progress by way of the open drive. They met the car just inside the gates. Blutton, Jipps and four other constables were in it. After a quick greeting to the Inspector, Plumper turned to Peascod and advised him, in a very official voice, to go back to bed and get some sleep. "There's nothing to keep you now," he said.

Peascod seemed to have acquired the habit of obeying him without question, for he made no expostulation, merely shrugging his shoulders, grinning, saying, "Good morning, all," and marching off with his hands in his pockets. As soon as he was out of earshot, Plumper detailed off one of the constables to follow him discreetly to see that he went back into his house—and that he didn't leave it without escort. By the look on his face, Inspector Blutton approved heartily of this order.

Plumper concluded a brief statement of the facts by saying, "I thought last night he was heading for something like this. But the Lord alone knows where Ridd is or what he was doing here at all. Anyhow, that can wait."

Blutton whistled. "Gedling's really off his rocker then?"

"He must be—and it's not going to be easy getting hold of him. If he keeps this game up indefinitely, and I believe he'll try to, the best we can do is to get into the house, corner him in one room and wait till he comes to his senses."

"Sounds a nice job," remarked P.C. Jipps, who was given to speaking out of his turn and who was quite unabashed by Blutton's glare.

Plumper continued: "Bring any spanners and crowbars you've

got in the tool box. We'll need them—the ground-floor windows are all tight shuttered." He gave one of his rare smiles. "This is about as pretty a picnic as I've ever struck. Somebody tried to assassinate *me* last night!"

Blutton interpreted this as a piece of Plumper fantasy and paid no heed beyond saying, "Really?"

"Yes, really," said Plumper, still smiling.

"Really. Well now, do you think if *I* went and talked to this old chap he'd take a bit more notice? He probably remembers me after having sent me that note to go and see him."

"No harm in trying. But I warn you he's more likely to put a bullet in you than to take polite notice of you."

But the Inspector had been in the Force for twenty years and he placed great faith in the sobering effect of an official bearing. He had seen gangs of roughs take to their heels at the sound of a solitary police-whistle. He had seen armed and cornered malefactors surrender to a single policeman without calling on him to do so much as draw his truncheon. So he strode off down the drive with his head high, his shoulders back, his arms swinging and a set expression of Nowwhatsallthis? on his face, while two constables went off to relieve Marsden and while Plumper took the remaining one and Jipps round to his observation post behind the bushes. There was no question of Blutton being nervous; he was almost happy—for it seemed to him that things were really working themselves out at last and that all "mystery" was now at an end. The Chief had been right, Bughouse was the word he'd always used in reference to the man they were after.

This direct manœuvre of the Inspector's certainly seemed to have succeeded, for Gedling held his hand and did nothing to hinder his approach. He came to a halt immediately under the window over the portico—the one that Plumper had broken with the stone he threw. The old man sat very still, eyeing him like a malicious monkey, a whiskey bottle in one hand, an automatic in the other.

"I'm surprised at you, Mr. Gedling," shouted Blutton, "the way you've been carrying on! Come down and open this door at once. I want to talk to you."

For answer, Mr. Gedling put out his tongue and laughed. "Go away. Go away. You're a fool. You're all fools. Go away at once. The others as well. I can see them over there in the bushes."

"Are you coming down nice and quiet or shall I have to come and fetch you?"

Gedling suddenly changed front; his voice became a whine. "Surely you wouldn't harm a poor old man, not a poor old man like me?"

"I want to know at once where Captain Ridd is?" This question was a great mistake on Blutton's part, as Plumper could have told him if it had occurred to him to do so. Once again, reference to Ridd seemed to enrage Lionel Gedling. He yelled out a string of oaths and, in his fury, hurled the whiskey bottle down at him before he opened fire, which was very lucky for Blutton. Even so, it was almost a miracle that the cumbersome Inspector managed to get inside the porch without being hit, espccially as he delayed his desperate charge to cover until the bottle had smashed itself at his feet.

Gedling screamed furiously and disappeared. The three behind the bushes took their chance and dashed across to the porch to join Blutton who, in his element now, assumed complete command.

Under his orders and with his assistance, the agile Jipps climbed on to the other constable's shoulders, smashed the fanlight with a spanner, carefully removed the jagged edges of the glass, wrapped his hands in a couple of handkerchiefs, hoisted himself up and slowly wriggled through the window-frame. He dropped on the other side with a great clatter and a few seconds later the big door of Old Barton was open.

There was no sign of Gedling. The house was still and dark and it smelled of neglected emptiness. They stood in the hall and studied the lie of the land. A broad, carpetless staircase with a landing half-way up, was immediately in front of them: on their left were three closed doors: on their right, two.

Leaving the constable to guard the front door, Blutton, Plumper and Jipps proceeded with great and justifiable caution to search the ground floor—only to find that of the five rooms giving off from the hall, all but one were entirely without furnishings and offered no hiding-place of any kind. The last one was the big, encumbered room at the back of the house where Gedling had received Blutton and Plumper only twenty-four hours previously. It was shuttered now and though gloomy and more chaotic than ever, it had not the musty, twilit dampness of the other rooms; nor did it hide Lionel Gedling or John-Thomas Ridd. There was, however, evidence indicating that the former had recently entertained a visitor—evidence independent of Jack Marsden's statement; two tumblers that had recently held whiskey; the Captain's walking-stick; the dottle of a pipe in a house where, to all appearances, only cigarettes were smoked.

There were two bedrooms on the ground floor, but these were empty of everything but a few sticks of furniture, some very soiled linen and much dust.

When they came to search the first floor, Blutton stood in the middle of the hall with his feet wide apart and thought heavily; he rubbed his chin and looked up the broad staircase. The others halted with him and for a second or two the house was abominably still.

"It's funny," said Blutton softly.

"You're quite right," said Plumper.

"Eh?" said Blutton in his ordinary voice.

"I said you're quite right."

"Oh, I'm sorry. I must have been talking to myself. Ummm. Well, anyhow, what I was thinking was that it's funny that this Gedling should have been jabbering and banging about all night and that now he's gone all quiet like this. It's as quiet as the—"

"The grave. Yes, it is," said Plumper.

"And I've got a feeling that he's watching us now—now at this very minute. It sounds foolish—but I've definitely got that feeling. Or maybe it's just this house giving me the creeps."

Plumper was impatient. "Maybe, Inspector. But come on now, what exactly is it you're driving at?"

"Well, it's those stairs as a matter of fact. We've got to go very careful. I've got this feeling that he's waiting for us at the top of those stairs—and if he *is* and he gets us in a bunch half-way up, well, I mean… And it's not as if we could rush them. They're too long." The Inspector was seldom at a loss for words or hesitant in his speech, but he was on this occasion.

"What d'you suggest then?" said Plumper.

"Well—er—there's a big table in the sitting-room there and I was wondering if it wouldn't be a good thing to carry up in front of us, or something."

"Just as you like, but let's get it over quick."

They took the huge, round, mahogany table and with unsteady steps (it was a remarkably heavy table) advanced on the staircase under cover of their testudo.

They made an almost comic sight as they trod with the ponderous regularity of stage-policemen, their boots creaking and echoing on the bare, hollow boards, their heads poking out warily, their faces grave. Comic especially as their precautions were quite unnecessary for there was no sign of Gedling at the stairhead.

Nor was there any sign of him, or of Ridd either, in any of the empty, dusty rooms on the first floor. And the attics were as bare and deserted as the rest of the house.

Jipps it was who eventually ran him to earth in one of the cellars and who, in doing so, got a bullet in the fleshy part of his thigh. A regular siege followed.

The crazed old man, determined to sell his freedom dearly, had entrenched himself in an angle of the cellar behind some tubs set on a heap of coal. He had, however, committed a grave tactical blunder. The angle in the wall made him secure from rear and flank attacks, and his tubs, coal and armaments provided him with a good frontal guarantee. But he was vulnerable from the air, having unwisely taken up his position immediately underneath a coal-chute. Nevertheless, it took his besiegers some time to discover this defensive flaw.

The only approach to the cellar was down some stone steps from the kitchen, and it was a dangerous approach, as Jipps had very soon come to realize. Blutton, venturing to poke his head into view to shout a brief but pointed exhortation against folly and a statement concerning the Inevitability of Justice, had to skip back very nimbly as a charge of shot splattered itself against the wall. Then Gedling made things worse by shooting out the light.

It looked very much as if it was going to be a long job, a question of starving him out—until Plumper precipitated matters by finding the iron cover to the coal-chute and, subsequently, a length of old and leaky hose in a garden shed. "I think," he said to Blutton, "that a little drop of water wouldn't do him any harm."

The Inspector viewed him with much less distaste than usual. "A capital idea, Sergeant!" And he even rubbed his hands as if in boyish anticipation of a bit of fun. Thereupon the cellar door was bolted from the outside and Gedling warned that if he didn't surrender he'd be flooded out. But he merely screamed and jibbered and blazed away at the open coal-hole.

Blutton gave a signal and a constable turned the water on.

The moment the hosepipe came into action, the screaming jabber from the cellar increased in volubility and ferocity, but the firing stopped.

"Are you going to be sensible?" roared Blutton.

There was no intelligible answer.

For a quarter of an hour the water poured in. Plumper was looking rather uneasy. "D'you think he's had enough?"

"I don't know," said Blutton. "He's certainly a bit quieter." He went as near as he dared to the coal-hole and asked the old man once again whether he was going to be sensible. Again there was no answer.

And then Blutton lost his temper and did a thing which he was to regret all the days of his life. In a loud voice, he shouted, "All right then, drown, you old lunatic!"

There followed a single sudden report that echoed and boomed in the cellar, and then a silence that was unbroken.

"Oh lord!" said Blutton and turned to Plumper, but Plumper was racing for the front door.

They found Gedling with the front of his head blown away. The last report had come from the shotgun. The old man had evidently sat on an upturned tub, leaned forward, rested his chin on the muzzle and pressed the first trigger with the knob of a poker round which he had wrapped his handkerchief to prevent it slipping; he had thought very carefully about his death.

But they didn't find the Captain in that cellar—or in any other. After much splashing and fumbling and unpleasantness in the dark, they got the body up into one of the empty rooms and laid it out as best they could. Blutton felt very uncomfortable and did much fussing over minor details such as examining with zeal all the pots, pans, tins, jars and jugs in the scullery and larder, asking Jipps every ten minutes how his leg was getting on and going through the pockets of every piece of clothing in the dead man's wardrobe. He also said on five separate occasions, "Well, that's that. That's that job over and done with."

Plumper, for his part, went about with a very long face and refused to say a word to anybody. Rain began to fall heavily. The morning was dismal.

The young constable patrolling the big lawn at the back of the house was lamenting the dispositions of Providence which caused a man to be hauled from his bed in the coldest, deadest hours of night and put to walk, on an empty stomach, aimlessly up and down a stretch of grass in the pouring rain while his more fortunate fellows indulged in the intriguing pastime of sensational, bloody detection. To be so near to possible opportunities for promotion and yet to be in such damp, such monotonous remoteness! And then it was that he caught a glimpse of the man in the mackintosh and the soft felt hat pulled down over his eyes. It was only a glimpse—but it was more than enough for the young constable.

With the brisk, ungraceful efficiency of all policemen, he moved forward in the direction of Starehole Gap and he soon had his man under observation. This latter was behaving oddly. At one moment, he was poking about in the bushes with a walking-stick, at another, going down on hands and knees to examine the muddy ground at close quarters, and at yet another, standing stock still with head bent as if lost in profound meditation. The young constable waited patiently: always give your man rope enough was one of his mottoes.

And patience was rewarded—for his man obligingly made himself a trap and walked straight into it. He climbed a tree.

The constable strode forward and called up to him, "Oi, you!"

His man looked down from his perch with an astonished jerk of his head, said "Oh," lost his grip with one hand, panicked and began to slither; he tried to get a grip of the slimy trunk but failed, and in a couple of seconds he was sprawling in the muddy leaf-mould at the constable's feet. The latter, chortling, pounced; he grasped him by the coat collar and jerked him to his feet; then seized one of his arms and twisted it behind his back, and bundled his captive off towards the house, grunting "Ha! you would, would you?"

His captive writhed and struggled, expostulating indignantly. "Take your hands off me, you brute. Let me go, you—you nasute manticore!"

But his writhing and expostulation availed him nothing. The constable hauled him through the front door and held him with unnecessary vigour while the Inspector and the Sergeant were fetched to examine the prize.

"Peascod!" shouted Blutton.

"My dear fellows," cried the captive artist, "you can't let them badger me about like this. Really and truly you can't. I'm working on this case. I'm giving it enormous thought. In fact, I haven't done anything else for days. I've already made some valuable suggestions, haven't I, Plumper? Be honest."

Plumper was angry; Blutton truculently suspicious.

"How on earth can I go on making these suggestions if you stop me looking for clues and tracks and so on. Behaving suspiciously! Folderol, sirs, so much mumbo-jumbo!"

"Take him into that room over there and keep him there."

"I think we ought to take him in on suspicion," grumbled the Inspector. "He's no alibis for any of these jobs, and there's that metronome and that handkerchief into the bargain. He was up here early this morning and now he's back again. He seems so fond of this place, I'm wondering if it wasn't him knocked Marsden on the head last night."

Plumper's anger had gone. "If you take my advice, you won't arrest him. For one thing, if he's really been up to any tricks he's been so damn clever and cautious about it before that he's not likely to go blundering into us like this for no reason at all."

"Maybe he wants us to arrest him. I've known that happen before now."

"Maybe. Anyhow I'm going to take him off for one more talk. When you've finished up here, pick me up at his cottage and we'll go straight on to Ridd's bungalow."

The detective picked up his bowler hat and went into the hall: he found Peascod trying to rub green slime and mud off his clothes under the triumphantly glowering eye of the young constable.

"Come on," said Plumper.

Despite his bumps and bruises, Peascod leapt to his feet.

"Can you manage him by yourself, sir?" said the young constable anxiously.

"Who? Him? Oh yes, I can manage him all right. Come on."

Then, as they walked away from the house together, he said, "I want you to enlighten me on a little matter that has been puzzling me for the last ten minutes."

"Are we going anywhere in particular?" interrupted Peascod.

"That depends on you, my friend."

"Why—?"

"As I was saying, I want your help. You see, when I last saw you earlier in the morning, you were going back to your 'Nook' and at a discreet distance behind you went a police officer whose duty it was to see that you went to 'The Nook' and that you didn't leave it without an escort. Now what I want to know is this. How did you manage to get away from your cottage without the constable seeing you, and how did you manage to slip past the man on duty at the drive gates who had a perfectly good view of the road as far as the Vicarage?"

Peascod spoke in a superior, airy way. "Exactly! I thought as much. How did I do it? When I answer you that question Mr.—I mean Detective-Sergeant Plumper, I answer a question that ought to have occurred to you several days ago. A question of paramount importance. A question upon which this whole case hangs. *I* could have answered it days ago. Why then, you ask, did I not? I will tell you. We Peascods are traditionally good-natured. We are always ready to give assistance to our fellow-men, to stretch out a coadjutant hand to all and sundry. But our good nature draws the line at insolence, suspicion, intimidation, discourtesy. Why should I help the police? They are churlish, they are unmannerly boors."

Plumper was patient and polite. "I'm sorry. But you see, in this pleasant village of yours three men have already died violent deaths and two have disappeared within a week. A policeman's nerves are apt to get a trifle frayed when he is making absolutely no progress in the solution of such an unpleasant business. His superiors are bitter and unsympathetic over his impotence, his colleagues grow more thick-skulled every day. Can you wonder that when a young man like yourself cavorts all over the place—and especially highly compromising places, in a seemingly strange way, can you wonder that the policeman should feel disinclined to chatter and hobnob with him whenever he appears?"

Peascod clapped him on the back. "Ah, bravely said, my dear fellow. Now that's the way I like to hear you talk. Urbanity, polysyllables, gentle conceit—that's what I like. Splendid! I forgive you everything."

"That's more than generous of you. And now what about the answer to my question?"

"Ah, my secret route. Well, I'll give you a practical demonstration this very instant. Come, sir—this way, if you please."

So saying, Peascod branched off to the left just as they were coming in sight of the drive gates and set off through the wood in a north-easterly direction. The ground was rising, there were no paths and the trees were thick. Plumper began to lose his bearings, but Peascod carried on confidently. After a good five minutes he altered his course and went right-handed, almost due east. The ground flattened out and then began to slope away from them; the trees began to thin a little, and in a very few minutes they came out of the wood to find themselves on the very brink of an escarpment, looking straight down on the back and the roof of the Clove and Hoof with Peascod's and Hannabus's cottages to their right and those of the majority of Larcombe's inhabitants farther along to their left, and looking on the road which ran along the ledge splitting the cliff into two perpendicular parts; and on the road, in front of "The Nook," stood Peascod's guardian constable gazing idly out to sea.

"So that's how it's done," said Plumper softly. "Well, well, well! That's very interesting indeed. But it looks impossible from the road."

"Ah, that's because, when you're on the road, this upper half of the cliff seems to stand parallel with the walls of the houses. It isn't really—as you can see for yourself when you get up here."

Peascod began to slither down the sharp slope and Plumper followed him rather more cautiously. The rain had made the going soft but it was not very difficult and in a minute or two they were at the back door of "The Nook." Nor had their passage been noted by the policeman on the road.

"Have six cold sausages smothered in scrambled eggs," said Peascod, "and two bottles of Guinness's Dublin Stout, a breakfast that is second only to cutlets and claret!"

Plumper was very thankful. "I'll have anything, I'm starving."

When they had broken their fast, Peascod pulled up two chairs to the fire and made other preparations for a cosy interlude of post-prandial chat, saying, "And now as a reward for my invaluable assistance and hospitality, tell me about everything."

But Plumper refused to make himself comfortable and it was only after considerable hesitation that he permitted himself to say, "You will be sorry to hear that Mr. Lionel Gedling has committed suicide."

Surprised and shocked as he was at this piece of information, Peascod was by no means satisfied with it. "Well, go on," he cried.

The other silently stroked his moustache.

His host was impatient. "Oh, a truce to misprision! You might at least tell me who felled our Marsden. And it's no use looking at me as though my knowing *that* were further evidence against me. The man himself was broadcasting the news in a strident falsetto at four o'clock this morning."

Plumper rose from the chair upon whose very edge he had been sitting.

"For an excellent breakfast, I thank you. If there have been no more sudden deaths in the meantime and if you yourself are still alive and in Larcombe, you must dine with me to-night, if I haven't been recalled for inefficiency."

"You're not going?" pleaded Christian.

"Oh yes, I am. I have a little business to attend to. But before I go, would you mind telling me where you were at dusk yesterday."

Peascod made an impolite grimace. "I was with my grand-mother. She was holding an egg-sucking soirée and she sent you her kindest regards."

"Perhaps you'll tell me to-night," said Plumper, who then left the house and sought out Inspector Blutton.

He found him up at Ridd's bungalow and he found that he had reduced Jane McQueen to tears. Blutton was exasperated by the girl's apparent daftness and as a consequence had frightened her few wits out of her. She knew nothing. Nothing, that is, except that she had made the Captain's bed and that he had not lain in it. She was sure, however, that something terrible had happened because the Captain had been carrying on so.

"What d'you mean, carrying on?" rasped Blutton.

"Well, sir," she sobbed, "he hadn't been down to the Cloven for days."

"What else?"

"Oh, nothing else, specially."

Plumper interposed. "Where d'you live and what d'you do?"

"Oh, sir, I lodges with my uncle in the Orchard, my Uncle Jerry, you know."

"Scoutey?"

"Oh yes, sir. We're orphans you see, me and Rosa. I do a bit of washing and I do the daily for the Cap'n whenever he's at home." And then, as if definitely to establish her respectability, "Jack's courting me, too."

"What time did you leave here last night?"

"About seven, sir. After I'd got him his supper."

"And you came back at eight this morning?"

"Oh yes, sir."

"You know where he keeps his shirts and clothes and razor and toothbrush and so on, don't you?"

"Oh yes, sir."

"Well, find out double quick if anything's missing, the slightest thing."

"Fine goings on, Inspector!"

Blutton shrugged. "Ah, but I think we're getting near the end now."

"You're feeling warm, are you?"

"Eh?"

"You think," smiled Plumper, "that you know where you're up to?"

"I think I do."

"I only wish I did," said Plumper.

Blutton frowned and was about to make some further observation when Jane returned to assure them that everything in the house, to the superficial eye at any rate, was in its appointed place. If John-Thomas had decamped, he had taken nothing with him except the clothes he stood in, not even his passport or a clean handkerchief—as they discovered when they had searched the bungalow as carefully as they had searched Old Barton.

The only objects which engaged their special attention were a licence for a revolver and an empty revolver-case, and an undated letter written on a scrap of lined paper torn hurriedly from some notebook. They recognized immediately both the paper and the handwriting of this letter, which ran as follows: "For God's sake come up to-night. Come at 1.30 and come by the old way. It's safest. It's for you as much as for me. For God's sake don't fail me and burn this as soon as you've read it." It was signed "L.G."

"That settles it," said Blutton hurriedly as if fearing interruption and thumping the table as if to warn it off. "I thought as much. Gedling! Mad as a hatter. Took a dislike to everybody in Larcombe and just set about wiping 'em out. Some sort of what d'you call it phobia. First the Vicar, then this stray detective chap who was showing so much interest in the Vicar, then he tried to do you in, if what you were saying's true."

"Oh, it's true enough," said Plumper, smiling.

"And now Ridd. Shoots himself when he thinks we're on his track." He ended on an embarrassed note. "It's not watertight, I know. But it's the first theory we've had that's at all workable. And if you're looking for the man who's been playing these cock-eyed tricks that have been putting us off the track, you don't need to look much further than your artist friend."

Plumper merely nodded non-committally: what he was thinking about was the potential significance of the phrase "by the old way" in the letter they had just discovered—but what he said was, "I'm going to take a boat out to have another look at the rock at the mouth of the creek."

Half an hour later, he was taking another look, but he looked in vain for any one-legged corpse or for the trace of any corpse in that place.

The Police were busy all over the country and their efforts were directed mainly towards the threefold object of finding Gedling's late servant Costigan, of whom nothing had been seen or heard since he stepped off the Larcombe bus at Setterham, of finding John-Thomas Ridd, and of identifying the butchered "detective."

Plain-clothes men lurked in railway stations and public houses; a strict watch was kept at likely ports; cars were stopped in Devonshire lanes and their drivers questioned; in London, a hundred people were interviewed; the B.B.C. broadcast urgent police messages; the Press published descriptions of the missing men; bloodhounds were brought to Old Barton in an attempt to follow up the Captain's trail through the woods—but the rain neutralized their efforts; a specially-trained squad of police searchers explored every nook and cranny, every bush and pool, every shed and ditch in the Larcombe area for anything and everything that might have a bearing on the mysterious tragedies. Nor were Inspector Blutton and Det.-Sergt. Plumper idle.

The day after Gedling's suicide, the shy, red-headed boatman Alan Charnock came into Hannabus's shop to buy a caulking-iron. Peascod was there, theorizing on Crime and munching barley sugar. Hannabus himself was dogmatizing on the same subject and making rabbit-traps.

"The very man!" cried Peascod.

"What's up?" said Alan.

"I'm eliminating, and I haven't eliminated you yet."

"You can eliminate till doomsday and it won't do you any good," mumbled Hannabus with strings dangling from his mouth. "I tell you old Mr. Gedling's been doing all this 'ere. He's crazy, and everybody knows it. Now he's dead we'll have a bit of peace—you see."

Charnock said, "I don't know about that, Seb, but I do know all this 'ere's messed up the Cloven proper what with John-Thomas gone and all these nosey parkers about."

"Ah," said Hannabus.

"And there's summat funny with Bert Yeo too."

"Is he ill or something, then? I haven't seen him for a day or two."

"I've just been talking to Jane McQueen," said Charnock, "and their Rosa told her that when he came down yester morning—and he hasn't been down for days, you know—he was all grey like. She says he looks like he has consumption or something. Well, anyhow, when she told him about Gedling being dead and Cap'n having run off, he fainted right over, just like a girl, fell down all of a heap. A man of his age too!"

"D'you know what I think?" said Hannabus. "I think old Bert knows something. I don't say he's had anything to do with it, mark you—far from it. But he's seen or heard something and he daren't speak. It's got on his mind."

Peascod was derisive. "But he could only have heard or seen something in connection with somebody in Larcombe—and you're not going to tell me there's somebody in this village that he's afraid to inform on! Think, man. There are no sinister villains knocking about this place, with the possible exception of myself. You're all honest, God-fearing men. Take Mr. Charnock here. Busy from morn till night with his beloved boat, wedded to the

Sea. What time's he got for villainy? And you yourself, you might as well suspect Father Christmas of infanticide!"

Hannabus grinned and shook his head. "That Plumper's got his eye on me, all the same. 'Where was I at such a time?' 'What was I doing on the second day of May, 1906?' 'Why do I keep paints?'"

It was at this moment that Alan Charnock began to go red in the face. He looked from one to the other as if weighing up his chances in a boxing match. "Talking about paints," he rubbed his hands together uncomfortably, "you know about Marsden coming and taking Georgie's paint box I give him for his birthday? Well—I don't know what it's all about, but this came yesterday morning." He took from his pocket a letter, a letter whose contents were brief and to the point. "You keep your mouth shut." And these five words were not written by pen or pencil, they were painted in blue water colour.

Peascod yelped his wonder, seized the paper and examined it as if he were looking for a flaw in a diamond.

"What have *I* got to keep my mouth shut about?" said Charnock.

Hannabus shook his head. "All this fishiness beats me. Has it something to do with this business, d'you think?"

"Merciful Heaven! The man asks, has it anything to do with this business?" Peascod was almost prancing with excitement. "This has come straight from the murderer, don't you realize that? Hot from his bloody hand." He turned to Charnock. "Don't stand there dithering, man. Don't you realize you hold the key to everything? All unwitting, you've stumbled on the villain's secret! Quick, quick, what is it you've seen, heard, felt, smelled, dreamed?"

Charnock was alarmed. "I'll have nothing to do with it. It's nothing to do with me. It's fishy. Someone's up to something."

Peascod forced him to sit on a battered sea-chest. "Now for God's sake think. Think hard. Think as you've never thought before!"

"About what?"

"First of all, Sunday night. What were you doing at midnight on Sunday night?"

"What d'you think? I was asleep."

His interlocutor groaned and made elaborate gestures of despair.

"People who sleep at the witching hour are damned! Oh, why were you asleep? Think what you were missing."

"Don't be so daft." Charnock half rose from the chest. "Give me that letter. I must be getting along."

Peascod pushed him down again. "Wait, wait, wait. I've got it. Tuesday afternoon, the time of the decapitation. Where were you then?"

"I was out fishing like I always am."

"Of course you were. That's right, up and down the creek. I've seen you many a time. Yes. Out past the rock, slowly back level with the Cloven, out again fast to the island, slowly back to the Cloven, a hundred times. I know. I know. Fishing! That's what we want. You were out there, you could see everything on both sides of the creek, you could even see round to the Gap if you got out as far as the rock. Now, if you love me, tell me what you saw. There's only one possible reason for this letter. You saw the murderer on his way to or from Starehole—and the murderer knows you saw him. And I'll bet my boots he thinks you know you know you saw him, which it seems that you don't—more's the pity!" Peascod was more or less incoherent.

Charnock snatched the letter away from him and stuffed it in his pocket. "You're as bad as a bloody detective, you are. I saw nothing at all, I tell you—I was too busy with my lines. And anyhow, if I had seen anything, d'you think as I shouldn't have spoken up? But I'm going to say nothing about this 'ere and I hope you'll say nothing neither. I don't believe in meddling."

"That's right," said Hannabus. "And anyhow, it's all finished now Gedling's dead, and that's all there is to it."

"My poor, poor poppets!" cried Peascod wildly and dashed from the shop.

The fisherman rasped his stubbly chin with the back of his hand. "I'm a fool to go showing him that letter. There's something funny about him. I don't like him. I never have. He'll only go making trouble."

Hannabus tapped his forehead significantly. "He's all right though. He's only a boy."

But Charnock was very uneasy. "Honest, Seb, I don't like this letter. If he's right and it *has* something to do with this business, it sort of mixes me up with it, don't it?"

The old shopkeeper pooh-poohed the idea. "If you know nothing, you've nothing to be afraid of. If it was me, I'd say nothing more about it. And I'll bet you a bob the fellow who sent you this is the same one who's been playing these other practical jokes, and I've got a pretty good idea who that is."

"Ay, I think we've all got a pretty good idea," said Charnock, who was by now so agitated that he left the shop without having fulfilled the purpose of his visit, which was to purchase one No. 5 caulking-iron.

FOURTH DEATH?

Gedling's death had brought the Press to Larcombe. The papers were full of the "Larcombe Mystery."

The favourite headline was "DEATH Stalks Through DEVON," and "Hell Let Loose in Quaint Village," "Work of Secret Society?" "Who Next?" "Murderer Strikes under Nose of Police," "Lunatic at Large!" were popular too.

The Own Special Correspondent of one of the newspapers which claims to have as many readers as there are miles to the moon, stated, in Great Primer, on the front page, that

"Larcombe to-day lies under a Death Pall! A sinister cloud hangs over this Valley of the Shadow that but a few short weeks ago was the playground of merry kiddies laughing and sporting by the sunlit sea! Panic reigns where jollity held sway! This quaint picture-village has become a ghastly charnel-house! Terror-stricken inhabitants gather in sombre knots at every street corner! What have these men and women to say to one another? Are they discussing the weather? the day's catch? the Leader in yesterday's issue of this paper? NO! They are asking one another with bated breath, 'Who next? Where will the Killer strike NOW?' White-faced mothers keep their kiddies indoors! Every girl in Larcombe is a typical unspoilt Devon Beauty as sweet as cider apples and with a complexion like Devon Cream—but none venture out with their sweethearts after dark! Even the bronzed sturdy fisherfolk who have spent their lives laughing in the face of howling gales and mountainous seas and braving the perils of the 'deep' are uneasy, watchful, S U S P I C I O U S! As Mr. Jeroboam Scouter, prominent Larcombe worthy, put it to me only an hour ago over a foaming tankard of mellow cider in the picturesque ancient inn, 'Where is it all going to end? We are at the mercy of Unseen Forces! The police are powerless to avert what must rank as a hundredpercent tragedy in the annals of British Crime!' We are back in the days of Jack the Ripper!!!"

There were many photographs of Old Barton.

"The Mystery House under whose roof a grim Drama of Life and Death has just played itself out. Many tales are told in Larcombe of this weird place! Of the unearthly cries heard by night! Lights flickering in and out! Sinister shadows! From the windows of this house the mysterious and crazy recluse armed to the teeth held the police at bay throughout the ghostly hours of early morning before dying by his own hand after a desperate fight in a waterlogged cellar in which P.C. Jipps and P.C. Morden showed great gallantry, both receiving severe wounds!"

Another London journal which is justly proud of the bulk of paper it uses per issue, contented itself with the report that

"The untimely death of Lionel Gedling, Esq., of Old Barton, somewhat complicates the issues in the Larcombe case. We are given to understand that the police were hoping to obtain from the deceased certain information relative to the recent tragic occurrences in South Devonshire. Mr. Gedling was educated at a small Public School in the West of England."

As a whole, Larcombe infinitely preferred to be interviewed by the Press than by the Police. The former were flattering and cheerful and generous; there was no menace in their voice; they smiled continually and encouraged exaggeration. There were some, however, who would have nothing to do with the reporters.

Bert Yeo, for example, although two of them were staying under his own roof, was surly and silent. He kept very much to his own room and left the conduct of the house more and more to Rosa, who had never been happier in her life. She wanted to get Dr. Girdwood to come and have a look at her master but Bert cursed her hard for such a suggestion.

"It's me nerves, I tell you," he had shouted. "I'm as sound as a bell inside. I'm just upset. Leave me alone and mind your own blamed business!"

Peascod would not talk either. When Dundas of the *Echo* had first sidled up to him in the street and wheezed very respectfully, "Good morning, sir. You're a stranger hereabouts, I suppose?" he had scowled and said loudly, "It is no use, my man. I will not be drawn. I know perfectly well what your intentions are. You wish to pick my brains and use such information as you can get for publication in the Yellow Press. I will talk to you only when this affair is settled."

That little speech had not made life any pleasanter for Peascod, for Dundas of the *Echo* passed the word round among the boys that he was a "good thing," and the boys had done the rest. Christian was pestered to the point of fury. Wherever he went, a reporter was on his heels. If he went down to Crale Cliff, if he tried to dodge the police and get round to the Gap, Dundas or one of his mates was there, watching, smirking; if he went to have a look for clues on the *Saucy Sue* or round John-Thomas's bungalow or in the small boats moored by the quay, some elderly youth with a cigarette at the corner of his mouth would saunter up to him and say, "Looks as if it's blowing up for a storm, doesn't it?" or "I wonder if you could tell me the time?" or "Could you oblige me with a match?" And in the end, he was forced to barricade himself in "The Nook" and to confine himself to pure Theory at long range.

Blutton just dismissed them with a wave of his hand. He had learned his lesson before they had been in Larcombe an hour. He had never before dealt with Fleet Street in the flesh and he had graciously and importantly issued a statement: "We know a little bit more than we knew before," he had said, "and I think it won't be long before this business clears itself up." The afternoon editions had blazed him forth in streamers "Inspector Confident of Immediate Arrest," "Working on Secret Information," "Has the affair well in hand and confidently assures me that the criminal will be brought to book with the utmost despatch." Blutton had raged—but the reporters were used to rage: their only reaction was to give him a very bad press the next day. Blutton raged again. The next day there was no mention of him whatsoever in any penny paper.

Plumper knew Dundas of old and merely smirked back at him when questioned and referred him to Inspector Blutton.

But the man from the *Echo* did not confine himself to the routine details of crime reporting: he had his eye on a possible Human Feature for the most sickening of all Sunday newspapers and managed to work up some wonderful local colour from those of the villagers who would talk. With his Feature in mind, he tracked down one day the Oldest Inhabitant. Dick Bowle, the ancient, bald, bowler-hatted, bedridden tobacconist, had a fairly strong claim to this title, and even if there were one or two men his seniors in Larcombe, he at least was by far the most featureable of them all. A column on Dick practically wrote itself... "How many of my readers can number in the circle of their acquaintances an old gentleman who wears his bowler hat in bed? Here the old tobacconist lies, smoking his pipe and meditating serenely on his quiet past, undisturbed by the sensational and bloody happenings going on around him."

From old Dick he learned, among other things, that Lionel Gedling had not always been a recluse. Old Dick could remember a time, ten, twelve years ago in the days before his baldness had come upon him with the suddenness of a rocket from a bottle, when Mr. Gedling had been a regular patron of the Clove and Hoof. Not once but many times had he been helped home up the hill at midnight, singing songs at the top of his voice and now and then falling flat on his face despite the steadying hands, themselves none too steady. But for some reason he had drifted away. No. Dick didn't know why. Perhaps some in the Cloven had taken shameful advantage of his generosity. Perhaps he had wearied of buying popularity by the pint.

Had Mr. Gedling had a love-affair—a disastrous love-affair?

The stricken tobacconist summoned his strength to laugh. "A love-affair? Well, the barmaid in they days, not the one before

Rosa, she was a Presbyterian or something she was, but the one before that, she was a regular bit of all right. So there was no telling, was there? And Mr. Gedling once had a housekeeper, a widow; she left in a hurry, folks said. Oh yes, Mr. Gedling was a real good sort at one time. Friendly with everybody."

Dundas wanted to know if he'd been friendly with Ridd.

"Yes, most certainly he was. Of course, the Cap'n was friends with everybody."

Dundas stayed on at the cottage in the Orchard to probe further into the seamy side of Mr. Gedling's past. And by the time he was done with probing, he was resolved to do yet another Feature for his Sunday paper, this one to be entitled "The Women in Their Lives!" "they" being the Larcombe corpses.

There being no time like the present, he hurried back to the inn and swallowed three bottles of stout preparatory to taking the bus into Setterham in quest of Woman No. 1—Mrs. Helena Fitzroy, housekeeper to the late Vicar.

Meanwhile, Sergeant Plumper was returning Peascod's hospitality at "The Nook," by entertaining him to dinner in the back room of the Clove and Hoof. The dinner consisted of a sort of soup; hard, tepid pork, turnips and coarsely chopped cabbage; and tinned apricots with Devonshire cream.

Peascod had come in with shining eyes, an excited brain and a mouthful of news—but the meal sobered him and made him postpone his bombshell until they had retired to the Parlour. Plumper, weary after a futile day's work and realizing that his guest was in extravagant mood, tried to quell him by forcing upon him a port which was nothing if not a blend of syrup of figs and vinegar. But turnips or no turnips, port or no port, the news had to come out at last.

The young man crossed his legs, smoothed back his hair, raised his eyes to the ceiling and said in what he considered to be a very off-hand manner, "Oh, by the way, I've stolen a march on you."

"How astonishing!" the detective replied.

Peascod uncrossed his legs, shifted his gaze to his host's face and abandoned his off-hand manner. "I knew you'd say that! You make me angry, you do really. If you were doing very clever work on this case, making brilliant deductions, discovering things that had escaped everybody else's notice and so on, there'd be some excuse for your confounded superciliousness. You say nothing and pretend to know everything. Actually, I believe you know less than I do." Plumper mimicked him. "Ah yes, but do you not see? That is precisely the impression I wish to convey. My policy is to lull the criminal into a false sense of security. At the same time, my air of confident inaction gives him to pause. But apart from all that, out with it—what's this great march you've stolen?"

Peascod struggled with his sulkiness. "I've been to see the postman," he grumbled.

"Yes, I know you have. He told me so himself just an hour and a half ago."

Peascod made great eyes.

His host went on: "I told him to let me know the moment you asked any questions—just as I've told most other people of like importance. You've learned, I suppose, that there's been an epidemic of painted letters?"

"Yes, I have," said Peascod with enthusiasm and quite forgetting his resentment. "The Vicar, Gedling, Ridd, Charnock, Scoutey, Hannabus and Yeo have all had them. Charnock showed me his this afternoon." He paused. "But look here, why did you tell the postman to tell about me? Surely I'm not still under suspicion?"

"Under suspicion? Good heavens, no. Inspector Blutton and I consider it a privilege to be allowed to work with you. Naturally we like to be kept informed of our colleague's activities. If you'd like to know what you've been doing to-day—hour by hour—I can tell you in a minute. I have it all here in my little book. But I've no doubt you know perfectly well yourself without me having to jog your memory. And by the way, if you're thinking of taking the air late to-night or very early to-morrow morning, you might jot down the things you do and the places you visit, then we'll be able to compare notes when we meet again, as I've no doubt we shall."

Peascod laughed in a perfectly friendly way and said, "I think, sir, I like you even less than your abominable port. But do tell me before I go—as go, you imply, I must—do tell me what you think about these painted letters. To my mind they are of the most tremendous importance. Really staggering. I can understand the Vicar getting one and possibly Mr. Gedling—and as Ridd seems to have disappeared, I suppose there's no reason why he shouldn't get one either. But Charnock! Scoutey, Hannabus, Yeo! Why in heaven's name should they get them? Charnock's simply said, 'Keep your mouth shut,' or something like that. But he swears black and blue that he's not the slightest thing to keep his mouth shut about. Beyond suggesting that these crimes have all been committed by one man what do these letters mean?"

Plumper looked at him long and solemnly and said, "They may mean anything."

Peascod stared back at him and then said uneasily, "You don't—er—by any chance suspect me of having sent them, do you?"

"What an idea!" said Plumper, still solemn. "What an idea!"

Peascod sighed a sigh of half-hearted relief. "Well, that's something, anyway. And I take it you're not inclined to have a little chat over these letters?"

"You've taken it," said Plumper. "But there's no need for you to go yet. I'll order another bottle of this port wine, if you like."

"I do not like," said Peascod, and so saying went, disconsolate, out into the night.

It was precisely at this moment that John Costigan, the ex-factotum of the late Mr. Gedling of Old Barton, was opening a tin of sardines in a very half-hearted, inefficient way. He did not feel particularly hungry, but as he had not eaten for many hours, he considered that a little fish might well serve to maintain his strength and re-enliven his spirits. If he had not bought this same tin of sardines the night before, intending it for his breakfast in the morning, he would not now have been opening it for his supper twenty-four hours later.

When John Costigan had stepped out of the Exeter Express, he had walked out of Paddington Station feeling safe and exhilarated as one who has come through a battle unscathed. He had looked at the policeman on point duty at the junction of Praed Street and London Street; and the policeman had taken not the slightest interest in him. He had taken a bedroom in one of the dilapidated houses in Star Street, locked his suitcase safely in a cupboard and taken the key away with him to the Load of Hay, where he had drunk bitter beer and an occasional white port till time had been called. Then he had consumed two cold veal-and-ham pies and a cup of tea at Jack's Bar in the Edgware Road and, at the same establishment, purchased the tin of sardines for his breakfast.

But on the Friday morning he did not break his fast. He had risen and gone out to buy bread and a newspaper. He had bought the newspaper first and had glanced through it on his way to the bread shop. He had not been reading for more than a couple of minutes before he suddenly crumpled up the newspaper, stuffed it in his jacket pocket and shuffled back to Star Street as inconspicuously and as swiftly as possible. What he had read was this:

> "In connection with the Larcombe Mystery, we are asked to state that the Police are anxious to trace the whereabouts of John Costigan, the manservant of the late Mr. Lionel Gedling of Old Barton, Larcombe, who left his place of employment yesterday afternoon and is understood to have taken a bus into Setterham. It is believed that Costigan may have left Setterham by train. He is a man of about forty years of age, clean shaven…"

He had sneaked up to his bedroom and stealthily locked the door. He had sat on a rickety chair, shivered, re-read the paragraph in the paper, read it again a hundred times—or rather, stared blankly at the print for nearly an hour, occasionally peeped through the yellow lace curtains into the street below, reclined on his tousled bed, smoked cigarettes and shivered.

Luckily for him, his landlady was the mother of six and likely to be of seven: a very harassed mother whose waking hours were exclusively devoted to the feeding, thrashing, washing, dressing, scolding, healing, undressing, bedding and unbedding of her brats. She had no time to spare for newspapers except on the occasions of Royal Weddings when she liked to look at the pictures. So if her lodger had behaved himself, not fussed her and kept regular hours, he could have had the room for as long as he wanted, as far as she was concerned, and gladly. It would never have occurred to her to wonder if he was a Wanted Person.

Costigan did not know this; throughout the long day, he imagined her studying his description in the Press, conferring with her neighbours and eventually putting on her hat to go to the Police Station or sending her eldest boy to call the man on point duty round the corner.

But it began to grow dark and none of his more immediate fears had materialized. He did not dare to hope, but some of the maddening tension went from him. He stopped thinking and opened his tin of sardines. He ate them all and wiped his fingers on his socks. He went to the window and saw a boy pushing a wheeled soap-box down the street; in the soap-box were the evening papers. Forgetting caution, he hurried downstairs and bought three. Back in his room, he read of the death of Lionel Gedling and of the redoubled efforts the police were making to get in touch with him. He read on and he felt sick. He reached for his cigarettes—but the packet was empty. It was dark now, but he dared not go out for more.

The papers were full of it, of him! But there was no photograph.

They wanted Ridd too, Ridd and Costigan. The entire Police Force of the British Isles were on the lookout for John Costigan and for John-Thomas Ridd. He put out the light in futile precaution. He lay on the bed sweating and shivering. He tried to make a plan. He tried to think of somewhere to go, somewhere safe. He had only been to London twice before and he thought of it as a place limitless as the Sahara. There were countless criminals in London and the police only managed to find a few of them. The East End! He had heard it said that there was an Underworld in the East End where a man could lose himself. A man was safe from the police in the East End! He had read of "Mysterious Limehouse," "Sinister Dockland." He would go to the East End.

He waited till the clock struck three, then he took off his boots, carried them in one hand and his suitcase in the other; fumbled slowly, quietly, with infinite care, his way down the stairs; let himself out into the street; padded along to the nearest shadowed shop doorway; put on his boots, pulled down his hat, turned up his coat collar and after a few seconds' puzzled hesitation, stepped out down Star Street, due west.

He was apprehended before he had gone two hundred yards.

There is a church whose front is in Norfolk Square and whose back is in Star Street. It is a sad, silent church. Only the Deaf and Dumb worship there. Leaning against the railings that guard the dark portico, was a police constable and, having several minutes to wait for his point with the Superintendent, he was stealing a few puffs at his pipe. When he heard footsteps behind him hurrying along the pavement by the side of the church, he stuffed his pipe away very quickly and spat the inevitable clove out of his mouth. But he did not move. A small man looking now to right and now to left, with coat collar turned up, hat well down, suitcase in hand, came scuttling into Norfolk Square as hard as he could go without actually running. The policeman moved, and as he moved, he shouted, "Hey you."

The policeman didn't anticipate trouble and he didn't get it—for John Costigan was trembling like one palsied.

Dundas of the *Echo* was drunk, communicative, inspired and lucid. Alcohol and his business had kept him very late in Setterham and he had had to hire a car to drive him back. He had banged on the door of the Clove and Hoof and it was Plumper who had come down to let him in, because the fastidious Rosa was loth to leave her bed and show herself in pins and face-grease to any man, and because Bert Yeo had lost interest in everything else in this world beyond his own urgent problems.

"I've got something for you," said Dundas.

"Good," said Plumper. "Come up to my room and have a drink."

"Lead me to both," said Dundas.

Plumper coaxed and poked the dying fire into life, wrapped his dressing-gown tight about him and curled up in the arm-chair. For want of a bar, Dundas leaned against the mantelpiece and puffed appreciatively at an unlighted cigarette. "Ever met Mrs. Helena Fitzroy?" said Dundas.

The detective replied that the pleasure had not been his, but that his colleague Blutton had taken a fairly adequate statement from her.

"Pity you haven't met the old girl. You'd have liked her. I've just spent a jolly evening with her. She talked for about three hours solid. Gin started her off and gin it was that stopped her. It cost me an awful lot, but I think I've got a line on your Vicar. Possibly a line on Gedling too."

Plumper licked his lips ostentatiously and leaned forward in his chair. "I'm all agog," he said.

"Oh no, policeman. Oh no! Let's get this thing straight. I've got something *you* want and you've got, or at least you will have, something *I* want. Will you swop?"

"That depends," said Plumper.

"Well, listen. Don't for a minute think I'm grousing about the stuff you fellows are giving us. I'm not. You've given us muck enough and to spare. But this is what I want. I want you to give me the inside stuff *now*—without waiting for the grand daynoomong. I won't use it and I won't whisper a word till the minute you give me the tip-off that I can get in first with it. You know me. And that's all I ask. You see, I need to know really what's been going on so as to get properly lined up with what old Helena's been spouting. Honest I do. It don't make much sense as it stands, but it might mean a whole heap to you."

"If it would do you any good and if there *was* any inside to this story, I'd tell you. There just isn't any inside as far as we're concerned. And that's fact. Apart from details, you know everything, and these details don't help. They do just the opposite as far as I'm concerned. They seem, most of 'em, to be just slipped in accidental like, to put us off."

"Honest?"

Plumper nodded.

"All right. Let it go. I'll be content if you'll just tell me what *you*'re thinking about it all. Tell me, for example, if there's any blackmail in it."

"What makes you ask that?"

"Just a hunch."

Plumper was thoughtful. "Yes. I think there is. There have been letters, a plague of 'em."

"Good. That's what I like to hear. Now just let me have Amos's own sidelight on the problem."

Plumper smiled. "Well, so long as you remember that this is not much more than theory—and I'm quite sure Blutton thinks very differently. Someone, almost certainly in Larcombe, has got something on the two solidest people in the village, the Vicar and Gedling; and they start blackmail. But it wasn't straight blackmail. At least, not in Gedling's case. The Vicar got one of these funny letters, but we don't know what was in it. Gedling got a letter too, but it was merely a hint that pressure *might* be brought to bear. It was very sly and it had been led up to in a very sly way. Even before he got the letter, fantastic jokes had been played on him, fish in his bed, his milk tampered with, airgun shots at his window, and so on. The planting of the body may have been part of the same game. Maybe not. Anyhow, I'm quite sure in my own mind that blackmail was at the bottom of it. Not blackmail for money, as far as one can see. But just, how shall I put it? just sheer terrorist blackmail. For some reason of his own, the blackmailer wanted to hound these two out of the place. God knows why. I can't find any sign of either of them having done the dirty on anybody, or anything like that. Anyhow, blackmail it is. It must be for something really serious because the Vicar tries to bolt and Gedling turns his house into a little garrison. The Vicar realizes he's ruined. Gedling realizes he's up against somebody who wants his blood, not just his money. Again I say it's something pretty serious, something vital. The Vicar comes a cropper on the cliff. Gedling blows his own head off. And that, in essentials, is how things stand at present. Now Blutton thinks that Gedling was a lunatic and polished off the Vicar and our unknown 'detective' friend in real lunatic fashion and from real lunatic motive. He thinks that Gedling defended himself and shot himself because *he* thought that we knew he was the murderer. Blutton also thinks, quite illogically…"

Dundas interrupted him. "Pardon me." He tiptoed over to the door, but before he had got his hand to the knob there was a succession of squeaks on the boards of the corridor outside, squeaks that might have been made by man or rat; but when he opened the door, there was no sign of any living thing and there were no more squeaks. The two searched the corridor and stairs, and listened carefully, but they heard and saw nothing.

"Nice little girl, Rosa," said Dundas.

"Nice big man, Yeo," said Plumper.

The latter continued in a lower voice, "Where was I up to? Ah, yes. Blutton's got a little idea that Peascod, that's the artist fellow, is responsible for all the theatrical incidentals, the fake footprints, the comedy at Old Barton, the letters. Perhaps he's right. That hokum certainly needs some explaining. Oh, and there was a burglary at the Vicarage and a bloody handkerchief left behind—Peascod's. And the matter of a metronome in Gedling's bedroom—Peascod's. So you see, Blutton's case is that a crazy Gedling did all the killing and that a dotty, mischievous Peascod put in, on his own, mind you, and quite distinct from Gedling, all the little fancy bits."

"And I take it you don't agree with that?"

"No, I don't. But I'm afraid I've no definite theory of my own to offer. All I've been able to do so far is to reconstruct what happened—and even that in very rough outline."

"How does the stray detective fit into your outline?"

"He doesn't, unless he was part of the blackmailer's intimidation scheme."

"Hired to intimidate the Vicar?"

"Yes."

"And why was he killed and cut up? Dead men tell no tales?"

Plumper poked the dead fire for want of something better to do with his hands. "Probably. Probably also to provide more intimidation—on Gedling this time."

"Sounds like your blackmailer's crazy."

"He is."

"Crazy as Gedling?"

Plumper stood up, stretched himself and yawned. "Crazier."

But Dundas showed no desire to go to bed. "What about the absent Costigan?"

"I don't think he's very important. He might be able to tell us more about Gedling—but that's about all."

"And Ridd?"

Plumper frowned. "I don't know what to think about Ridd. But I have a very uneasy idea that he was next on the blackmailer's list. Somebody tried to plant the Crale Cliff job on him, you know."

Dundas made appreciative clucking noises and then fell silent as if lost in thought.

Plumper broke the silence by saying, "Now you tell me something. What's this line you've got for me? Where does Mrs. Fitzroy come in?"

Dundas went over to the door, opened it and made sure that there were neither rats nor men in the corridor. "Well," he said, when he had returned to the mantelpiece, "if you curse me for having got information on false pretences, I shan't blame you. It's nothing stupendous, but my newshound's nose tells me it's *something*."

Plumper smiled. "All right. Let's have it."

"It all began with me trying to dig up some dirt about Gedling for a nice human story I'm going to do for the *Sunday Emetic*. 'Women in his Life,' and so on. Old Bowle tells me that Gedling was once a bit of a lad, the Maecenas of the Bar, the chucker-under-the-chin of maidens, brides and even matrons. There was once a bit of scandal going round about him and his housekeeper, the widow-who-left-in-a-hurry, and she's one of the birds I thought you might be interested in. Quite apart from this blackmail theory you've talked about, I thought you might be interested. But now the thing has reared its Ugly Head, it seems to me she might have something to say quite enlightening from your point of view. Remember, if Gedling *was* being blackmailed, it's a hundred to one it was during his loose-fish, rake-hell days that he put the foot wrong which he's just paid for."

"Who was she?"

"Ah, now there you have me. If, when I asked old Bowle that question, he'd been a man with a fine head of hair, he'd have scratched his poll and grunted; as it was, he rubbed his finger along the side of his nose and said after five minutes' deep thought, 'Urr, sur, I can't rightly say. I know un come fer Lunnon and un's name beed 'Ammond or Evans or Corlett or summat, but I be an old man you know, and it were a long time ago.'"

"That helps a lot."

"I know, I know, but wait a minute. I thought the same as you. I said to myself, 'Dundas, you've come to a dead end—it's fresh ground you'll have to be after breaking.' So I ups and I sees what I can do about the Vicar. They tell me that his late house-keeper is now resident in Setterham. I hop on the bus. I run her to earth. I find her dressed in black lace and whalebone and so on, you know, a bit stiff like. N.b.g. for the *Emetic*, if you see what I mean. Nothing daunted, I gave myself out as a representative of the Ecclesiastical Commission for the Biographies of Country Clerics. 'Madame,' I say, 'we must know everything about the life of the martyred Vicar. And you alone can help us.' She was a bit stand-offish at first, but by the time I'd got her—by easy stages—to the Private Bar of the Hen and Chicks she opened up a bit. Prompted by me and pink gin, she admitted that the old boy had been an indisputable soaker. Unhappily, during the five years or so she'd been with him, he hadn't given her much opportunity of reading many of his letters—and what she had got hold of were not worth the paper they were written on. However, I probed her about her predecessor. That was sheer inspiration on my part. From what I heard, this predecessor, a Mrs. Faith Lapworth, was a gem and a half. Her parting words to Mrs. Fitzroy when she came to take over had been: 'Watch your step, dearie, and if ever he tries anything, just you let me know—*I*'ll settle him!' And she lent substance to this warning by giving Mrs. Fitz her address." Dundas searched his waistcoat pockets and handed over a slip of paper on which was scrawled "Mrs. Faith Lapworth, 12 Ariel St., Fulham."

Plumper was impatient. "So what?"

"That's all," said Dundas. "Aren't you satisfied?"

The former said nothing; he seemed to be weighing up the pros and cons of something or other.

Dundas pursued his point. "If you want to know why the Vicar and Gedling were being blackmailed, there's a first-class chance of learning the answer from these two girls, Mrs. 'Ammond or Evans or summat, and Mrs. Faith Lapworth. And they're both in London."

"You mean they were several years ago. And besides, d'you think the violent deaths of three men have been brought about by the ancient indiscretions of a couple of clacking housekeepers?"

In his excitement, Dundas lit a cigarette. "Look here, Amos, I feel so certain now that I'm on something good that I'll go up to the Metropolis to-morrow at my own expense and run these two dames to earth. On one condition. If anything new turns up here, you'll ring me up at the office and let me have what you think fit of it before you give it to the other boys."

Plumper sneered. "Very kind of you, I'm sure."

"Not at all, not at all, anything to oblige an old pal. But look, you'd better take me on before the mood wears off. I've got a hunch, and though it's me that says it as shouldn't, my hunches are usually good. Are you on? Make up your mind—I'm sleepy."

"It seems a pretty one-sided bargain to me—but I'll see you. It can't do any harm, anyhow."

Dundas yawned. "O.K. But there's one more little thing I'd like to know before I go. Our friends Costigan and Ridd. Would you mind telling me why you've taken such a rooted objection to regarding them with even a shadow of suspicion?"

Plumper sighed an embarrassed sigh. "Well, let's take Ridd first. Blutton has an idea at the back of his mind that he could have got from Symouth to Larcombe on Sunday night by car and got back to his bunk early enough on Monday morning for nobody to have been any the wiser. There was only one boy on board and he says he didn't wake till seven. By car, he could have done it. But if he came by car there must have been someone to drive. A complication which I don't like. There are enough people in it already, and the Symouth police haven't been able to trace any car at that time of the morning. No, I don't like it. There's more to it than my own personal feelings. There's the question of Ridd's patent-leather shoe which is the only one that fits the cliff-prints. The old boy was wearing his sea-boots on this voyage, and according to the crew there was no sign that he had any other footgear with him. Blutton saw this patent-leather shoe with his own eyes and he says it hadn't got a speck of dirt on it. Jane McQueen testifies that she brushed it herself and that it hadn't moved a fraction of an inch from where she'd left it. I know that, strictly speaking, the crew's and Jane's evidence doesn't let the Captain out. He may have fixed his own men, and Jane may have some reason for not wanting to give him away. Only the other day, through my telescope, I saw him trying to make love to her. It's just remotely possible there may have been a conspiracy, but I don't like it. In any case, where is Ridd now? A man as conspicuous as he is, and without even so much as a toothbrush, can't just disappear in the night. He only had a few hours' start and there have been search-parties out for him ever since. Between you and me, if you ever see John-Thomas Ridd again, you'll see him on a slab in the mortuary."

The reporter rubbed his hands together cheerfully. "And Gedling was the last person to see him alive! Is this getting good? I was going to suggest that Ridd's potential pal with the car might have whisked him off somewhere. But the other's much more in my line. You're sure you couldn't manage any secret panels in Old Barton where Gedling could have slipped the corpse?"

"I don't believe Gedling did kill him and I shouldn't be a bit surprised if his body's lying at the bottom of Larcombe Creek."

"The blackmailer and his boat?"

"Exactly. There were at least four people near Old Barton that night. Gedling, Ridd, Marsden and the fellow who knocked Marsden out."

Dundas kicked the fender in an ecstasy of excitement. "Don't tell me, don't tell me. Let me tell you! The blackmailer, having bungled the first part of his campaign against John-Thomas, keeps a close watch on the old boy. He follows him up to Gedling's house and sees him safely inside. Unfortunately, your village Robert is there too. With his eye on the immediate future, the blackmailer biffs him one and ties him up. Lurks in the bushes till Ridd comes out, ambushes him in the wood, carts him down to the Gap, rows him out to sea, ties a mill-stone round his neck and dumps him overboard. Then off home to bed. Am I right?"

"As near as makes only a little matter."

"The interesting thing about this case is that you seem to know the exact moves of the murderer at the important times, and yet you can't put your finger on him. You clever policemen are as accurate and as circumstantial as a Bradshaw. It's a pity you're not as foreseeing."

Plumper looked at his watch. "Don't you worry. You'll have your Sensational Court Scenes before you're much older. But it's a quarter to four, I'm going to bed."

"Just a minute—you haven't said anything about Costigan yet."

The Clove and Hoof was an old house; its walls were thick and its doors solid. The telephone bell only sounded faintly up in Plumper's room—but he was on his feet at the first note.

He groaned. "I'll bet that's more slaughter!"

Together they clattered downstairs. Dundas was chirruping with excitement. "It's probably only the brewer ringing up about the empties."

The detective snatched the receiver. "Yes, yes, speaking." He smiled. "Good. Excellent. I'll come up myself. Yes. Right away. Very good." He hung up and turned to the reporter. "Give me the address of Mrs. Lapworth." He grinned. "I'll save you the trouble of talking to her. I'm going up to Town myself."

The other was rather piqued. "Hey, what's all this?"

"They've caught Costigan."

"Well, well," said the reporter, "now isn't that nice." He wrote down Mrs. Lapworth's address on the back of an envelope—and while he was doing so Plumper rang up Setterham; he asked for a car to be sent out straight away.

"When will you be back?" asked Dundas.

"Who can say? To-morrow night possibly."

"Well, go easy with my Faith, be kind to her, be gentle, be generous. Remember that corkscrews open bottles better than brickbats."

The next morning, before he had been in Larcombe quarter of an hour, Inspector Blutton received a deputation. One pert and three sheepish men stopped him as he was passing Hannabus's shop. Hannabus himself acted as spokesman for the little group. "Oh, good morning, sir," he said. "Could we have a word with you? Would you mind stepping inside for a minute?"

Blutton cast a suspicious eye over the other three—Jeremiah Scoutey, Alan Charnock and Christian Peascod, and then, as they stepped aside to let him pass, he walked into the shop without a word. Once inside he stared at Peascod in open disapproval—but the young man was unabashed. "It really is a lovely day, isn't it, Inspector?"

Blutton scowled. "I've seen worse. And now what's all this about?"

The three sheepish men remained sheepishly silent.

Peascod cleared his throat and took his chance. "Perhaps—er—I had better explain, as I am directly responsible for this pleasant little gathering. What you are about to hear, Inspector, will probably stagger you. I say, probably, of course, because some of us know more than we pretend to, don't we now? Ha ha ha!"

Blutton did not return the well-intentioned wink. "For goodness' sake get on with it. I've not got all day to waste."

Scoutey broke in, mumbling, "It's about the letters."

"The painted ones," said Hannabus.

"The highly-mysterious ones," said Peascod.

"It's summat funny," said Charnock.

Blutton ran his eye over them like a schoolmaster over his class.

"So that's what it is, is it? I was wondering how long you were going to try to keep it dark. Let's see 'em."

"I would like to point out——," cried Peascod.

"*I*'ll do the pointing out here. You didn't get one of these letters, did you?"

"No."

"Well, you'll oblige me by stepping outside and waiting somewhere handy till I need you—as I very likely shall."

Peascod shook his head sadly as he turned to go.

"Ingratitude, ingratitude! Was ever man served thus? One day, Inspector…" He did not finish this last remark, but slammed the door behind him instead.

"If it weren't for him," said Scoutey, "we'd none of us be here."

"Never mind him," growled Blutton. "Let's hear what you've got to say for yourselves."

"Well, speaking for meself, I got this letter Thursday morning and I haven't had a wink of sleep since. It's all right for young nibs like Peascod to go getting themselves mixed up with the police, nibs like him seem to think it's funny—but us chaps don't like it. The less you have to do with the police the better. That's…"

"That's it," said Hannabus. "People talk."

Charnock nodded, without ceasing to bite his nails.

The barber-greengrocer continued: "You may be all innocent, but your customers ask for nothing better than to gossip about you, and the fishier they can make it the more they like it. Marsden coming and taking Annie's paints away was bad enough, and now this painted letter. I thought it best to say nothing about it."

"I warn you, once and for all—all of you," growled Blutton, "that you're letting yourselves in for a pretty serious charge if you withhold anything that looks like evidence."

Charnock objected that he didn't know it was anything to do with evidence.

"And anyhow," said Hannabus, "I thought it was all settled when old Mr. Gedling shot himself. He was the murderer, wasn't he?" said Hannabus.

Blutton gave the taxidermist a long, hard stare. "That's neither here nor there. And now let's see these letters."

They handed them over and Blutton laid them side by side on a table from which Hannabus had hurriedly removed much dust and some torn strands of a purse-seine. All three had been posted in Larcombe at the same time and all three bore the same message. "You keep your mouth shut." Blutton examined them cursorily and put them away in his pocket. He then proceeded to do his best to bully the three men into making some kind of a statement, though his heart was not in his task; he had his own theories about the letter-writer, his purpose and his motives. He looked out of the window as if half-expecting Peascod to be eavesdropping at the keyhole. But Peascod was not in sight.

The Inspector glowered and folded his arms. "You heard what I said about withholding evidence, didn't you? Well, now, what about it? Somebody"—he tapped his pocket where the letters lay—"seems to think that all three of you know something. If it wasn't important, you wouldn't have got these letters." He paused and then almost shouted: "I want to know what it is you're keeping back. You've already shown that you're willing to withhold material evidence—I'm going to give you one more chance and one more only! What is it you've seen, heard or *done*—singly or all three together—since this business started?"

Charnock had gone very red in the face. Hannabus hung his head and scratched the back of his ear. Scoutey tried to cover his embarrassment with a facial show of unconcern. But none of them spoke.

Blutton held himself in check and tried in vain to get something out of them in turn. He was convinced that they were all telling the truth and it gave him a certain amount of satisfaction to find his theories being borne out.

"The only thing," declared Hannabus, "which I heard which would do you any good, is what I've told you already. I heard what sounded like wheels running down the hill very quiet in the middle of Sunday night when I got up for some alum. Beyond that I know nothing. I only wish I did."

Jeremiah said: "It's no use going on asking me. I know nothing. I'd tell you fast enough if I did. I'm no murderer, you know, and anyway, I'm short-sighted and a bit deaf in my left ear."

Charnock merely shook his head repeatedly and dumbly.

"Well," burst out the Inspector at last, "have you any idea who could have sent these letters?"

"That there Peascod!" Scoutey was truculent. "He's as mad as a hatter, as everybody knows, and it's just the sort of thing he would do. High-flying pranks, thinks he's funny. And he's a painter, isn't he?"

Blutton half smiled and turned to the door. "All right. We'll leave it at that. But in the meantime, if any of you can think of anything—I warn you, it's in your own interests to come and tell me straight away."

Charnock spoke. "Peascod says Bert Yeo got a letter too."

"I know, I know. Don't you worry about that." The Inspector left the shop and, for once in a way, did not slam the door behind him. The three Larcombe men were uneasily silent for a space. Scoutey looked at Hannabus who peered back at him through his dark spectacles without speaking. Alan Charnock looked at neither; he looked at the floor. A bluebottle buzzed suddenly loud in the little cobwebbed window. Sebastian Hannabus pulled out a very dirty red handkerchief and blew his nose upon it. The barber-greengrocer pulled his old trilby hard down on his head and turned to go. "I'm just about sick of all this," he said.

"So'm we all," said Hannabus. "But it's no use talking that way. There's nothing we can do about it. And if you ask me, it'll all blow over pretty soon."

Scoutey snorted indignantly, averred that there was more in it than met the eye, and went his ways.

Alan Charnock made as if to follow him out, turned back again, opened his mouth to speak, changed his mind about speaking, grinned at the floor and said, "Oh well, so long, Seb." And went out.

Old Sebastian shrugged and shuffled back to the bench whereon lay a half-stuffed screech owl. It looked as if Peascod's little plan to help the police had been unsuccessful.

The first thing Detective-Sergeant Plumper did on arriving in London was not to follow his inclination and go hot-foot to Chelsea to embrace his bride, but to go to the police station in Paddington where the suspect Costigan was held. And he did not waste much time before putting the latter through his paces.

The wretched man was sitting on a high stool in the middle of a bare, antiseptic room. There was a policeman taking notes at a table. There was another policeman with his back to the door. The dirty morning light came through a barred window. Plumper was pacing backwards and forwards in front of him. There had been a dead silence in the room for at least three minutes.

Plumper stopped, with his legs apart and his hands deep in his trouser pockets. "And you mean to say you left Larcombe for the one and only reason that Mr. Gedling had sacked you?"

"How many more times must I tell you that?" whined the prisoner.

Plumper glared at him. "And the knick-knacks in your bag?"

Costigan stepped down from his stool; but he was pushed back. "Look here, sir, this isn't America, you know. I've admitted I pinched those candle-sticks and the cutlery, and that's all there is to it. He sacked me for no reason at all, and I was sore. He's a crazy old man, I said to myself, and he'll never miss 'em—and it'll serve him right for sacking me like that. So I just pops 'em in me bag. Honest, sir, that's the truth. I've had nothing to do with these murders and I didn't know he was dead till I saw it in the papers last night."

Plumper took a step towards him and he thought he was going to strike him; but Plumper's hands never left his pockets. "You're prepared to swear that Gedling never had any visitors during the five years you've been with him?"

"Not a soul." Costigan was emphatic. "Nobody ever came near him, and I don't blame them. He was bats."

"Think hard, think very hard. What about when you first went there? Did the Vicar, for example, never pay a call?"

"Now that's funny, sir. I should never have remembered it if you hadn't mentioned it. The Vicar, of course he did. Now as far as I can remember, he came once or twice when I first went there." Costigan pondered. "He'd come in late at night, perhaps once or twice a week, stay for an hour or two and drink whiskey. Even when I first went there, Mr. Gedling used to like me to be with him all the time, but when the Vicar came in he used to clear me out. Yes, it all comes back to me now. But it didn't last long. He came half a dozen times or perhaps a dozen after I first went there—and that's all. He just stopped coming. There wasn't no row as far as I could make out, or anything like that. He just stopped coming."

Plumper began to pace the floor again. "Did Mr. Gedling get many letters?"

Costigan was regaining confidence; his eyes were less frightened.

"Very few, sir. Very few indeed. Income Tax, a few circulars and bills, but hardly anything what you might call personal."

"You read them all, I suppose?"

"Lord no, sir, I never got a chance." He tried to grin. "He used to burn 'em all as soon as he'd read 'em."

"Did he say anything to you about that painted letter he got a week or so ago?"

"Not 'alf, he didn't. Talked about nothing else. What with all the funny business that had been going on and that letter, he was just about going even battier than he really was. And he used to say to me: 'Costigan,' he'd say, 'I'll get the so-and-so, I know who it is. I've been expecting this for years. I'll blow his brains out for him if he shows himself, the so-and-so.' Yes, sir, I asked him many a time who it was who was doing all this—but he always shut up like an oyster then and told me to mind my own business. But he was scared all right. Look at the guns he bought."

"Did he keep a boat?"

Costigan shook his head. "No, sir. Never as far as I know."

"There's never been a boat kept up the Gap, then?"

"No, sir, I shouldn't say as how there has. Though, mind you, I never went down there much myself."

To Costigan's infinite relief, Plumper turned his back on him and made for the door. "All right," he said. "Take him away."

Looking at it in one light, Chelsea is on the way to Fulham. Plumper looked at it in that light and paid a surprise flying visit to his bride. He stayed for nearly an hour and enjoyed one of her omelettes, two cups of her Turkish coffee and an infinity of her kisses. Then he fled guiltily from the flat and sought out Mrs. Faith Lapworth.

Ariel Street turned out to be a gloomy, grimy thoroughfare flanked by ill-kept houses, the majority of which bore cards in their front windows or in their fanlights announcing Apartments, Board Residence, Bed and Breakfast or Flat to Let. The fan-light of No. 12 sported two such cards—Board Residence and Bed and Breakfast.

The front door was open and Plumper walked up the steps to look into a narrow lobby papered with greasy, faded wallpaper. There was a smell of food cooking; not a savoury smell; there was mouldiness in the air. Plumper knocked hard. He waited two minutes before knocking again. There was no sign of life within the house.

A child passed by, rollicking along the pavement on one roller-skate.

"Does Mrs. Lapworth live here?" shouted Plumper.

The child shrieked, "'Course she does," and at the same instant slithered sideways and came a cropper in the gutter. Plumper grinned and threw a copper to the tearful child, who pounced on it, knuckled his eyes and disappeared, whooping. Plumper took a step inside the lobby. "Is there anybody at home?" he shouted.

From the bowels of the house there came the sound of an opening door and a muffled noise as of water flowing away down a pipe; and then a strange sound as of someone drawing a heavy roll of carpet along an uneven floor. Plumper stepped back to the front door and waited. It appeared that someone was coming up from below stairs; yet a minute, two minutes passed before anything stirred at the other end of the lobby, at the head of the basement stairs. Then two people came to light. A ludicrously fat old woman and a much older man. The latter, who was bent almost double, wore a dressing-gown and he was clinging to his companion as if to life itself. Between them, with great puffing and blowing, they managed to shuffle down the lobby at a snail's pace.

"Good morning," said Plumper.

"Full up!" wheezed the fat old woman jovially. She opened a door to the left, urged the ancient through it, followed him and without taking any further notice of her visitor, slammed the door. Plumper imagined that she might return—but she did not. He went up to the door and knocked, shouting, "I'd like to speak to you a minute, Mrs. Lapworth."

The door opened immediately and Mrs. Lapworth poked her head out. Plumper's intrusion had made her a little less jovial, though the wheeze remained. She held her hand to her heart and smelled of gin. But as he stood there, hat in hand in her lobby, looking respectable and respectful, she forgot her momentary pique and waddled out to him. "Now what d'you want? I've told you I'm full up," she gasped.

"I'm from the police," said Plumper.

"Mrs. Pailing at 29 might do something for you, though I can't recommend her, you understand. I don't know anything about her, if you see my meaning."

He shouted hard. "I'm from the police."

"Oh, that's different, isn't it? So you don't want a bed?"

"No. I want to talk to you."

Mrs. Lapworth was still puffing and blowing. "Do you really? Nothing to do with the drains, is it? And it can't be the wireless licence because the wireless I use doesn't belong to me."

Plumper shook his head and shouted: "Is there anywhere we can go and talk?"

The balloon-like woman rubbed her heart as though it itched. "Well, it's awkward. You see I can't go upstairs because of me heart. I got it bad the time me eldest daughter had her mental trouble. Husband left her. I have a nice sitting-room up there, but I haven't been in it for donkey's years. We could go into old Tom's room—but it's not very nice. He won't have the window open and he's very, very old, you know. Bedridden, been there for twenty years. He was in it when I took over this place. Lasted out three landladies. Mind you, there's nothing wrong with him—it's only old age. I've just been giving him his bath. We can go down to my kitchen, but I don't mind telling you it's in a bit of a muck."

"You are Mrs. Faith Lapworth, aren't you?" yelled Plumper, just to make sure.

"'Course I am," she panted. "Who else d'you think I'd be?"

She had said that the kitchen was a bit of a muck. It was an enormous muck. She removed a stew-pan from a chair, wiped the seat with a piece of newspaper and urged Plumper to make himself comfortable. She herself leaned against the sink, tapping the open palm of one hand with a wrung-out dish-mop. For a landlady, she was (thought the experienced Plumper) absurdly unselfconscious.

Working under great difficulties, he managed to outline the purpose behind his visit.

"Larcombe?" said she when, through the fog of her tipsy deafness, she had perceived what he was driving at. "God bless you, 'course I remember it. And the Vicar, Mr. Pratt, that's right. Terrible, wasn't it? Fancy murdering him! I read all about it in the papers."

Plumper allowed her to ramble off into her Devonshire reminiscences. Then, gradually, he brought her round to talk about the Vicar's mode of life during the years she was with him. "Oh yes, even in them days he was what you might call fond of his bottle." As she talked her eye, despite its bleariness, grew roguish. "Yes, in lots of ways he wasn't like what you'd imagine a Vicar to be. He was a bit of a lad, him and Mr. What's-his-name, Mr. Ged—Mr. Gedling from the big house. Mind you, it was Mr. Gedling took most to drink. He was the ringleader as you might say. Coo, the times they had. What's that, sir? Mr. Gedling's housekeeper at that time? Well—the least said about her the better." Here Mrs. Lapworth rapped the hot-water tap sharply with her dish-mop. "She was No Lady, and the least said soonest mended. Mind you, it's always the man's fault, always, there's no getting away from that whatever walk of life you're in. Fun's fun and fun's fun—but Mr. Gedling he went too far, and though he is dead, it doesn't excuse him." She went on to say that in the old days, the Rev. Pratt had been a regular visitor to Old Barton in the evenings.

There had been parties there that John-Thomas Ridd (the great one-legged monster—as she called him) had also attended. And if Plumper wanted to know about the carryings-on at these parties, Miss Walsh, Gedling's housekeeper that was, was the one to talk to. No, Mrs. Lapworth didn't know where *she* was. She'd need a bit of finding, that one. If you asked her, she was in her grave by this time—or in an Institution. She was that sort.

Plumper described the dead "detective" to her as best he could and asked if she had ever seen anyone like him at the Vicarage. She said that she couldn't remember anyone like him, but that of course it was such a long time ago. Nor did she know anything definitely damaging to the Vicar's reputation except his heavy drinking and his associations with Gedling and the dubious Miss Walsh. She had plenty of ancient and petty Larcombe gossip, chiefly connected with the youths and maidens of her day, and Plumper learned nothing that seemed to have any bearing on the case in hand.

It had been a difficult job starting the fat, deaf old lady off on the subject, but once started, she was very loth to stop. It was years and years since she had had an opportunity of talking about her old life in Larcombe—and she was determined not to miss it. She even set about brewing vast quantities of tea in an enamel teapot to sustain her asthmatic garrulity, and whenever Plumper chipped in to say that he must be going now, she would turn stone deaf and feign not to have the faintest idea what he was talking about. In the end, he was forced to walk out of her reasty basement while her back was turned and she was babbling away happily about a certain Perse Swinhoe of Corfield whose wife stole her famous and closely-guarded recipe for Hog'd Pudden, and used it for her own considerable profit.

Plumper fled to Scotland Yard where, in his tiny office, he dealt with reports which had come to hand in connection with the identity of the Stranger. The Larcombe Mystery had become a national sensation and letters were coming in from all parts of the country.

No less than sixteen women claimed and complained that a man answering his description was their long-lost, lawful wedded husband who had deserted them one—five—ten—fifteen years ago, leaving them and their offspring dependent on reluctant relatives, harsh officers of Relief and their own efforts. These hardly-treated women enclosed photographs of their husbands. Some of these were fairly like, some fairly unlike, but none very like. Photographs of his alleged children too were sent to strengthen the claim, since they were averred to be the "spit," the "living image" of their father. Children in swaddling clothes, children rigged for Confirmation.

Three young women wrote to say that such a man had knocked them off their bicycles in dark country lanes and robbed them of their handbags, virtue, etc. A ship's steward, recently dismissed the service of an American Line, begged to report that on his last voyage he had served a gentleman closely resembling the Stranger in every way except that he was bald. A recluse from Newcastle said that, while he had never known anyone at all like the murdered man, he wished to offer a theory. The Russian Communists were very astute in the choosing of their spies for this country. They picked men whose appearance would never create suspicion. Who less suspicious than a large, fat man with big feet, dressed in a dirty raincoat and looking more like a plain-clothes policeman than anything else in the world? The recluse recommended that Plumper should enquire as to which retired or cashiered policemen had been known to hold extreme political opinions. A clairvoyant dowser volunteered to reveal the identity of the man on receipt of a cheque for five guineas. There was a great pile of letters and they provided Plumper with much entertainment and no profit whatsoever.

Scotland Yard was taking an unusually long time to trace the man, even allowing for the fact that they had no clothing to help them, no peculiar features on the body, no photograph, but Plumper was not unduly worried by the delay. He did not regard the identity of the "detective" as essential to the solution of the mystery. He knew that, sooner or later, they would discover who he was: he must have had some belongings, some luggage, some lodging, sometime, somewhere; he must, at least, have had some acquaintances. There was one man who would, of a certainty, know who he was—and that man was the blackmailer of Plumper's fancy. Plumper was unreasonably confident that he would have his blackmailer in a very short space of time.

He returned to Setterham by train. It was a long journey, but throughout its tedious five hours his mind was obsessed with thoughts of one person. Jeremiah Scoutey.

His recent preoccupation with the problem of the Stranger had led him to regard the barber-greengrocer with more than customary ill-favour. The fact that the Stranger had lodged, or rather, intended to lodge with Scoutey seemed significant. A stranger to Larcombe, with no prejudices against licensed premises, would, as a matter of course, put up at the Clove and Hoof. It was not expensive. There were also three regular boarding houses, all empty at this time of year, which would have been the next obvious choice; but to go straight to Scoutey's shop and ask for the one spare bedroom in the house was not what a stranger to Larcombe, without consulting any of its inhabitants and, in particular, Scoutey himself, would have done. As a further deterrent to a strange visitor, Scoutey's shop stood in the Orchard back from the cliff road and some distance from the Clove and Hoof where the bus from Setterham put down its passengers. According to reliable evidence, the Stranger had alighted from the bus and proceeded immediately down the hill to the Orchard and Scoutey's. He had not asked to be directed. He had visited no other house. He had spoken to no one.

This obviously argued a knowledge on his part of Jeremiah Scoutey and of the spare bedroom which occasionally housed surplus visitors in the summer. Yet Scoutey denied all knowledge of the Stranger and denied it with conviction.

There were three conclusions to be drawn. One, that Scoutey was a liar. Two, that some casual summer visitor who had had occasion to use Scoutey's bedroom, had recommended it to the Stranger. Three, that someone in Larcombe itself had previously told him of it.

The second was a possibility remote and unpromising, the third less remote and more promising. And in that case, the "detective" would have been acting on the instructions of his accomplice, the blackmailer. The first was interesting and was giving Plumper much thought. Scoutey had more than one qualification for suspicion. His alibi for the small hours of Monday morning was that he had been fast asleep in bed; and that was an alibi that rested on his word and his word only. He had a boat. He knew every inch of the district and the ways of its people, for he had lived there all his life. He was friendly with John-Thomas Ridd. Jane McQueen, who was servant to Ridd and had cleaned his shoes, was own niece to him and lodged at his house. His daughter had recently acquired a box of water-colours. He had been in the bar of the Clove and Hoof and had thus had opportunity of learning that Old Barton was to be deserted on Tuesday afternoon. On Tuesday afternoon he had been at his allotment, very near to Old Barton—and no one had seen him for several hours. His house abutted on the cliff which gave access to the woods above, through which lay a route (a hidden route as Peascod had proved) to the grounds of the big house. Add to all this the fact that the Stranger, on arrival, had gone straight to his undistinguished dwelling. The more Plumper reflected on Jeremiah Scoutey the vaguer grew his eye, which had hitherto been engaged in a dispirited survey of the flamboyant, hugely-fragrant Jewess sitting opposite him. By the time the train ran into Newton Abbot he was hardly conscious that she was there at all.

The tragedies had brought a great change to life in Larcombe. The people of Larcombe were not gullible yokels; and after the first novelty of being interviewed by newspaper men and others had worn off, they had taken up an attitude which was almost scornful, cynical. There was little profit to be made out of the sightseers, so they grew surly and affected to be weary of the whole mysterious, tragic business. There had been too much fuss. And this was bad for the police, this hard core of hostility.

The deaths of the Vicar and Gedling were not, in themselves, of very great importance—for Gedling had become more of a stranger to the place than even a visitor like Peascod, and Pratt had been loved by none. The people talked of these deaths, but they regarded them as subjects faintly disreputable, not to be spoken of in the hearing of children. There was a strong local feeling that Gedling's suicide had settled the matter, and without meaning to be sensible, even the most prominent gossips considered that the whole thing were better left alone. "There's summat nasty somewhere which is nobody's business. It doesn't do nobody any good to go stirring up muck." At the Clove and Hoof, Larcombe men talked about boats or the weather or their illnesses or the Harbour Dues or Football Pools, or they held their counsel. But the Clove and Hoof was no longer what it was. Journalists, sneaky pryers, rabid sightseers, silly strangers held the floor in the room of the peerless John-Thomas and the jovial Yeo. Even such stalwarts as Hannabus and Scoutey were missing, or if they did come in it was only for a quick and silent draught.

But however aloof the people stood over the deaths of Gedling and Pratt, the disappearance of Ridd affected them deeply and there was incessant speculation. The speculators were divided into two camps—those who believed that Gedling had "done John-Thomas in" as he had done in all the others, and those who were of the opinion that the Captain was lying low for reasons which he, in his unrivalled wisdom, considered good and expedient; when the time was ripe and not before, these wise ones said, John-Thomas would come back, and he wouldn't come back to no purpose, they said: he'd show the police a thing or two and no mistake: there'd be more than one would rub their eyes at the things John-Thomas would have to say, they said. There was also a small minority which held that the police had arrested him and were saying nothing to nobody—which superstition had its roots in the antipathy and suspicion with which Blutton and Plumper were regarded.

Everybody knew that Bert Yeo had taken to his bed and he too had everybody's sympathy. He was closer to the Captain than most and he'd be worrying about him. He was a sensitive man despite his fat, they said, and he'd be taking these dreadful murders to heart; he was upset, poor man. It was only right that he should keep himself to himself like he was.

That the police seemed more interested in Charnock, Scoutey and Hannabus than in anybody else was treated as a subject for derisive comment on these same police. Look at young Alan Charnock for instance, as shy and quiet a chap as you could meet; Alan Charnock wouldn't say boo to a goose—let alone harm a fly. And Jeremiah! He was a cussed old fool of course, who would always have his say and argufy over nothing at all till he was purple in the face—but as for him running about killing people, that was just the daft sort of idea that the police would think of. The same with old Hannabus, old Seb with his funny beard and his stuffed birds and the acid-drops he always had in his pocket for the children!

Peascod was just a fool and would be getting himself into trouble if he didn't look out. There was no saying what a potty young fellow like him might do. He meddled too much, he was always peeping and prying. And it wasn't as if he belonged to Larcombe, anyhow.

But however surly and hostile the people were becoming to the police and the Press, Dundas of the *Echo* usually managed to find out whatever he wanted to know. He went to the one man in Larcombe whose principal joy it was to talk with anybody and everybody, and with strangers for choice; the man who could not have enough of talk; Dick Bowle, the bedridden tobacconist. Dundas used to call on him nearly every day and the old man used to look forward to his visits, not only for the conversation but also for the Egyptian cigarettes his visitor brought him. In two days, Dick Bowle had conceived a passion for Egyptian cigarettes. And this was a strange thing, for from the day of his thirteenth year, when he had first worn his father's cut-down trousers, he had smoked a pipe; and as he grew in strength and age so did his tobacco—until now, bald, bowler-hatted and stricken, he sucked away without interruption at a short clay stuffed with a certain very rare black plug which is chewed by the most virile of Scandinavian stokers and smoked only by heroes. It was remarkable, therefore, in the first place that he should ever have accepted a cigarette from Dundas, but that the fumes of the emasculate Egyptian weed should have ravished his charred palate was well-nigh incredible. But it was so—and Dundas was not slow to follow up his advantage.

At about the time when Plumper's train was snorting through Bulleigh Hill tunnel, he was offering the old man his third cigarette in twenty minutes and questioning him about the more sensational features of Larcombe's history during the past half-century.

"Well, you see, mister," mumbled Dick, "as I said before, there's a lot of things as would seem startling to me as likely wouldn't to you. Like when Peter Belcher... this was when *I* was a lad... Peter Belcher from Poridge fought my cousin Lomax in the middle of the Orchard with his bare fists, with all the women looking on and shouting for close on two hours. He beat Lomax down and then started on the constable who tried to stop 'em and walloped him too. Now would you call that startling?"

"Ah, those were the days," sighed Dundas dutifully. "But what about deaths? Haven't you had any murders before or anything like that?"

Bowle puffed away with fantastic speed at his cigarette. "Now, let me see. My cousin Jem Bowle got a kick on the head from a horse what you could nearly see through. That was a killing all right. And Argeant's two children, he has a farm just up beyond Marsden's cottage, got smothered in a hayrick. That's only three summers ago. Yes. I've just remembered about young Scriven too. It was just after the War, it was in winter, in the November month I think 'twas and we were having a bit of a blow from the sou'west—nothing to speak of really. And young Scriven went out one night and never come back. Some say he was blown over the cliff, some say he put out to sea. It was never cleared up proper, but I don't see how he could have put out to sea because there was no boat missing. It's funny, you know, this being a fishing village and us losing so few men to sea. I can only remember one beside Scriven, my cousin Harry Staples. That was a squall on a nice fine day in Spring. Course *he* was a damn fool. He could no more handle a boat than Beecham's Pills can lace boots. We lose a boat or two in winter but we never lose any men, touch wood. We're lucky down here."

"I suppose the Vicar was never mixed up in anything unusual?"

"Oh, wasn't he just! You ask 'em at Corfield if he wasn't. Though I suppose there's not very many remembers it up there. They have a little church up there what he goes to, or what he went to, I should say, every other Sunday, or something like that. Well, he was never popular, you know. Once he missed 'em out at Corfield and didn't turn up. There was an awful shindy at that, and next time he went up not a soul turned up for the service except daft Fred who goes round with him to pump the organ. Old Prattie was wild. I think he'd had a drop, too. He stalked down through Corfield looking like the devil, with everybody staring at him through their windows. If nothing else had happened, I suppose 'twould have blown over, but unlucky like, one little lad who I suppose had heard his mother and father talking about it, put his tongue out at him as he went past—and what did Pratt do but give him a slash with his stick. Well, there was a terrible row. They say they all came out into the street, and they very nearly set about him, the women most of all. I wish I'd been there. It must have been grand."

"Have another cigarette," said Dundas with childish joy in his eye. "And tell me some more."

"Thank you, mister, but I don't know as there's much more as I can recollect."

"Oh, go on," pleaded Dundas.

"Well," said old Dick, "did I ever tell you about the heiress we had down here once? The heiress who wore trousers and was fair mazed about shrimps?"

"No," said Dundas, "you didn't."

"Well," said the invalid, "it was like this."

It was just before closing time when Peascod came into the Clove and Hoof to find the Bar empty except for Rosa, who was washing dirty glasses and mugs. He came in like a conspirator, furtively peering to left and to right and behind him and yet, when he leaned confidentially over the bar, there was something plaintive about his face and voice. "Rosa, darling Rosa," he whispered.

"Miss McQueen to you! What can I serve you with? You'll have to hurry, there's only another two minutes."

"Oh, why is everyone so unkind to me? What have I done? What would I not do to have you smile on me again, to have you give me your ear and your sympathy—I will not say your love!"

Rosa was peevish. "Oh, what is it you want?"

"Rosa, I must talk to you. I have so much to say. There is so much I want to hear you say. Could not we walk together this afternoon?"

"Not likely. Not after what happened last time we went walking. Besides, I've something better to do with my time."

Peascod sighed. "Oh well, in that case—" He did not finish the sentence but leaned both elbows on the bar, propped up his chin with the palms of his hands and stared in gloomy silence at the array of bottles facing him.

Rosa began to clean down the bar with a wet cloth. "Pardon *me*," she cried, "your elbow's in my way."

He lifted up his head and uttered one word in a voice so pathetic, so urgent, so desperate that Rosa so far forgot herself as to be deeply touched. "Rosa!" he said.

She gulped with quick emotion, nervously dried her hands on her apron and said in a very small voice, "What'll you have, Mr. Peascod?"

"Your heart," he whispered.

Rosa blushed: something extraordinary had happened to her: she was experiencing the most delightful palpitations, and even if she'd tried, she could not have reprimanded him for his impertinence. "What about a Peach-Blossom Dream with me?" she said.

"Yes, oh yes."

She turned and reached down from the shelf a bottle with a pink and green label. "Ready made," she said.

"How wonderful!" he said.

She filled two glasses with the cloudy pink liquid and raised one daintily to her lips, her little finger at rigid right-angles. "Good health," she said solemnly.

He gulped his drink down without tasting it and without taking his eyes off her eyes. "Another Peach-Blossom Dream," he murmured.

They drank another Peach-Blossom Dream and then passed quite naturally and effortlessly to the bottle labelled in green Mermaid's Delight, and then to the yellow June in January. Peascod rejected the Side Car and the Bronx Special because of their ugly names, and Rosa would have none of the White Lady because, as she said, it reminded her of the emulsion she had been forced to drink as a child. At the conclusion of a second Mermaid's Delight, Peascod took her hand in his and said, "Miss McQueen, I regret to have to inform you that you are tiddly."

She giggled and withdrew her hand. "I'm surprised at you, Mr. Peascod! It's not me who's tiddly. It's you."

"No," he said, "you're wrong. I can say with perfect confidence and reasonable accuracy that far from being tiddly, I am merely spree."

"It doesn't matter what you call it—but the fact remains that you are."

"On the contrary, my blooming Hebe. It matters very much what you call it. There's as much difference between a man who's squiffy and a man who's oiled as there is between a Port-Salut and a Double Gloucester. You've only to consult Roget to see what I mean."

"Who's Roget?" said Rosa.

"Roget! You don't know who Roget is? Peter Mark Roget, member of the Literary and Philosophical Societies of Manchester, Liverpool, Bristol, Quebec, New York, Harlem, Turin and Stockholm, author of the Bridgewater Treatise on Animal and Vegetable Physiology, and the *sine quo non* of every British author!"

"No," said Rosa. "Was he a great drinker?"

"I couldn't tell you that—but he must have known something about it because he grades the state of intoxication not only into that of being drunk, tipsy and inebrious, but also into that of being temulant, fou, elevated, cut, boosy, flush, flustered, disguised (you didn't know that one, I'll warrant!), groggy, potvaliant, glorious, overtaken, whittled, corned, raddled, sewed up, lushy, nappy and obfuscated. He also makes nice comparative distinctions—such as being as drunk as a piper, as drunk as a wheelbarrow, and as drunk as David's sow. So you see, you have to be careful."

"There's no call at all for me to be careful," said Rosa, popping a preserved cherry into her mouth. "I'm as sober as a judge." And before he had a chance to contradict her, she burst into a fit of giggles, pointing all the time at the clock over the door. "To think of all the policemen wandering about Larcombe," she tittered, "and us here an hour and a quarter after time without even so much as locking the door!"

He joined in her giggles. "What on earth started us off toping at this time of day?"

Rosa suddenly remembered what it was that had started them off—and as suddenly stopped giggling. She gathered the glasses up and spoke brusquely. "You'll have to go—and see that nobody sees you."

"Your brow is like ivory," said Peascod, "and your teeth are pearls of price. And your eyes! Argent-lidded, amorous with lashes like to rays of darkness!"

"The things you say," she smirked, relapsing into near-giggles. "What *would* Mr. Yeo say if he found us!"

"Let's not stay here," he urged. "Let's go out for a walk. We need air. Air! Come, my queen, let's stalk the headlands hand in hand together."

"Well," she hesitated, "you know what happened last time we walked out?"

"Of course I know. It was splendid. Nothing like that ever happened to you before. You loved it. You wouldn't have missed it for the world. Come on. Something just as magnificent may happen this time."

He had his way with her and in twenty minutes they were walking up hill towards Larcombe Head—she striving hard to be prim and stiffly seemly in spite of Peach-Blossom Dreams, Mermaid's Delights and Junes in January, he all but prancing. "This is splendid," he cried. "You should let me walk you out every day."

She became very coy. "If I let you do that, people would start thinking you were serious."

"But," he protested, "I'm nothing if not serious."

"That remains to be seen, Mr. Peascod. Never trust a man further than you can see him—that's my motto. But anyhow, I don't see why you shouldn't take me to the pictures now and again. There wouldn't be any harm in that."

"You like the cinema, then?"

"Oh, I *adore* it." She sighed. "I'd *adore* to be a film star."

"What a funny idea! I think film stars are silly."

"Pooh! What nonsense, Mr. Peascod! Who ever heard of a film star being silly! And silly or not silly—living in Hollywood must be simply divine. The life they *lead* out there! Coo."

"It is my considered opinion," said Christian Peascod gravely, "that Hollywood as a community is more absurdly moral than Geneva ever was and that film stars are as self-consciously virtuous as Calvinistic Methodists."

"I never heard such rubbish in all my life," cried Rosa, up in arms. "They have the most marvellous goings-on. You've only to read the papers. Look at their divorces."

"Exactly! Their divorces. It's nothing for them to be divorced half a dozen times and more. But I contend that they're so moral, these film stars, that they steadfastly set their faces against any love-making that isn't blessed and regulated by the law. If a married man-star falls in love with a married she-star or vice versa, they don't cuddle under the rose tree or conduct an *affaire* in holes and corners like ordinary decent men and women. Far from it. They immediately buy a divorce and regularize everything until they fall in love with someone else—at which time, the process is repeated. And they're even as carefully moral with their grounds for divorce. It's never adultery! Oh dear me, no. The mere mention of such a word would shock all Hollywood to the core. It's always 'Mental Cruelty,' 'Incompatibility of Temperament,' 'Political Differences,' 'Peculiar Habits,' or some such milk-and-water folderol—"

Rosa, who had long since given up listening to him, suddenly gripped his arm and whispered: "Look!"

They had reached the Vicarage and were just about to branch off on to the cliff-path leading round to Larcombe Head, when Rosa stopped dead.

"What's the matter?" said Peascod, who had much preferred to go on talking about Hollywood.

"Look at Yeo," she said.

Peascod looked and, to his surprise, saw the innkeeper coming with great strides down the road towards them, having presumably just emerged from the Old Barton drive. Peascod's surprise turned to bewilderment when the man came near enough for him to be able to see his face clearly in the afternoon light. The pink, heavy-jowled, boisterous face of Yeo was white and hard; his breathing was audible at twenty yards; he was moving his eighteen stone of fat and bone at a rate so unprecedented that it would have been ludicrous but for the obvious fury that was driving him on.

Rosa gripped Peascod's arm and her grip grew tighter and tighter as her master drew near. "I thought he was in bed," she gasped.

On came Yeo. His arms were swinging, his eyebrows were beetling over hot eyes, he was looking straight in front of him, and yet he seemed not to be looking where he was going. The happy publican made a fierce sight upon that empty road.

As he came abreast of the fascinated couple, Peascod shook Rosa's hand off his arm and took a step forward. "Good afternoon, Mr. Yeo," he said in a forcedly even voice.

Mr. Yeo's eyes did not swerve a quarter of an inch from the line they were holding, his pace did not slacken, his face did not soften. He had not heard or seen Christian Peascod. He lumbered on and away down the hill.

Rosa clung to Peascod's arm again. "Oh!" she said.

Peascod was so excited that the hand he laid on her hand was trembling. "D'you remember what I said when I first came into the Cloven this afternoon?" he whispered. "I said I wanted to ask you some questions, didn't I?"

"Yes."

"Well, I don't want, I don't need to ask them now," he said.

Rosa McQueen was very frightened. "Whatever's happened?"

"That's just what we're going to find out," he quoted. "Come on!"

"Oh no—I must get back and see what's the matter with Mr. Yeo. He's ill, you know."

"That can wait," said Peascod firmly. "Something's going on at Old Barton, and we're going to find out what it is. You must come with me because I shall need you as a sort of alibi if the police find us up there. Come on now, we'll get up on to the Head and then work round through the Gap. They've probably got someone on watch in the drive." He started off at a brisk pace and a reluctant Rosa followed him. When they came to the place where the recent landslip had brought the path to an abrupt end, they were forced to scramble up the steep bank on their right, through heather and gorse and over mossy boulders.

Rosa was soon out of breath. "We oughtn't to be doing this," she gasped. "I ought to be seeing to Mr. Yeo."

They had reached the highest point of the Head and the west wind was blowing there with considerable force. Christian, who was ahead of her, turned, and in turning, his hair was blown into a yellow whirling mop. "Don't be silly!" he howled. "I tell you, we've got to get to the bottom of this. We may be on the brink, on the very threshold of—" He broke off as a voice behind him called out his name. He spun round to find Sebastian Hannabus—his beard streaming in the wind, his dark spectacles bobbing up and down on the bridge of his nose as he hurried over the craggy headland towards them. Peascod went forward to meet him, but the old man waved him back.

"No, no," he cried. "You mustn't go any farther."

"Why on earth not?" said Peascod.

"Oh, Mr. Peascod—I'm glad I was in time to warn you!"

Sebastian was now standing beside him and Rosa had come up too: her blue eyes were wide and frightened, her mouth ajar. "There hasn't been another murder, has there?"

"No, no," said the old man. "No, it's nothing like that. But you must go back, you mustn't go any farther. The police are over there and you'll catch it hot—you especially, Mr. Peascod, if they find you."

"But Bert Yeo——!" exclaimed Peascod.

"I know. I know. I saw him. And that makes it worse. If they catch you after the bit of trouble they've just had with Bert."

"What's he done?"

"I don't know. I was just up there after rabbits when I see them come up to him and yank him off. There's half a dozen of 'em up there."

Hannabus took Rosa by the arm and began to walk her off the way she had come. Peascod followed, protesting. But there were two voices against his one: Rosa was only too anxious to get back to the Clove and Hoof and Hannabus was loud in his insistence on the risk and folly of going a step nearer to Old Barton. "Besides," he said, "I've something particular interesting I want to show you. It's something I've found and it's something that'll make you open your eyes proper, I can tell you." He wouldn't say what this discovery of his was and Peascod's disappointment was somewhat tempered by the thought that it might prove to be an enlightening clue.

Rosa left them at the shop door and hurried off to find out what was wrong with her master and whether she could be of any service to him.

"Come in," said Hannabus to Peascod.

The young man was, by this time, thoroughly excited again and he needed no second bidding. "Now!" he cried. "Now let's see what it is you've got hold of."

The taxidermist shuffled over into the dark, mouldy recess at the far end of the shop, opened a drawer and shuffled back again with a small cardboard box in his hand. "Just you look at that, my boy!" he said with melodramatic emphasis on the "that."

Peascod looked: the little box was lined with cotton wool and in the cotton wool there nestled a light green egg with faint grey markings on it. "But—!" he burst out.

"That egg, Mr. Peascod, is rarer nor gold. It's a September Chuggie—that's what it is! And there hasn't been one of them found on the British Coasts not since before the War—think of that, Mr. Peascod, getting on for twenty-five year!"

"But I thought—But this hasn't anything to do with the murders!"

Old Sebastian chuckled deep down in his throat. "Ah, but eggs is interestinger than murders," he said with a sagacious shake of his head.

Peascod's exasperation dissolved in a great gust of laughter; coughing and choking with it, he flopped down on his accustomed lobster-pot and gasped. "Give me a piece of barley sugar, Mr. Hannabus. For charity's sake a piece of barley sugar!"

Down by the quay, Inspector Blutton was waiting. At the best of times he hated to have to wait, for it left him with unscheduled time on his hands and it implied the gross vice of unpunctuality in the person he was expecting; but to have to wait for Plumper was unbearable, especially unbearable as it meant that because of Plumper he would be at least twenty minutes late for his high tea. The police car had gone back to Setterham to meet the Detective-Sergeant's train—and Inspector Blutton was dependent on the police car to get him back home to tea.

So there he waited by the quay, his fingers drumming the top of the breast-high concrete wall, his eye on the dirty reddish water that gushed from the pipe below him out on to the sand. He had been staring gloomily at this water for several minutes. Then he suddenly swung round and away from the quay wall. "Pah!" he muttered to himself. "A sewer." Blutton hated Larcombe and all its works.

Five minutes later P.C. Jipps brought the police car to a standstill by his side. "Had a breakdown, Jipps?" said Blutton.

"No," said Plumper, sticking his head out of the window.

Blutton snorted hard and then spoke a few words in perfunctory enquiry as to the success of the former's visit to London.

"I got nothing," said Plumper. "You have any luck?"

"We found Yeo on the cliffs by the Gap this afternoon."

Plumper raised his eyebrows. "Dead?"

"Oh no. Very much alive. Said he was just getting a breath of air! He was shaking like a leaf when Rogerson challenged him. The man's ill. I thought I'd just tell you."

"Thank you, Inspector. I think I'll have a chat with Yeo. I've been meaning to for some time."

"Right," snapped Blutton. "And now I'll be getting along. Shall we drive you up to the public or..."

"Oh no. Don't bother," grinned Plumper. "It's only a few yards, after all."

"Right." Blutton got into the front seat, banged the door and said to Jipps: "Get on!" Jipps put his foot on the self-starter.

"Farewell," said Plumper.

"Eight-thirty in the morning," said Blutton.

When Plumper got back to the Clove and Hoof, he found Dundas of the *Echo* gulping whiskey in the empty Bar. "Well?" cried the reporter.

Plumper smiled faintly and shrugged. "Well?"

"Don't tell me! I can see it in your face. You haven't got a sausage out of Mrs. Lapworth?"

"Oh, I won't say I got nothing. At least she bore you out over your *Cherchez la Femme* idea. I've put the Yard on to Gedling's old housekeeper, the Miss Walsh—though I doubt if anything will come of it. Mrs. Lapworth seems to think she'll have come to a bad end by this time. Anyhow, I'm sure there's more behind this blackmail than doubtful relationships between employer and employed. Well, I'll see you later."

Plumper went straight upstairs to Yeo's room and knocked on the door. There was no reply for a second or two. Then he heard Bert cross the room and call out: "Who is it?"

"Plumper."

"What d'you want?"

"You."

There was silence again. Yeo growled something to himself and then…

"Just a minute." There was a slight noise as of a drawer or cupboard being shut, or the lid of a box. Yeo unlocked the door. He stood as if to prevent the detective from entering, but the latter pushed past him unceremoniously. The innkeeper looked very ill and distraught. He had neither shaved nor washed for three days, and he was collarless. His great rolls of fat seemed to have retreated, leaving his flesh pouched and baggy. He was no longer fat in the merry, tight way; especially when he sat down, you got the impression that one day soon his belly would sag down as far as his knees. It was difficult to hear what he said because he kept his mouth loosely open so that flakes of froth accumulated on his lower protruding lip. His left eye had a slight cast. He was breathing noisily and supporting himself with his hands tightly clenched on the back of a chair. He was too weak to be convincingly truculent as he growled, "Well?"

"I just came to see how you were."

"What's my health to do with you?"

"Oh, your health is very important to me." Plumper was sneering.

"It's nothing to do with you if I'm ill. Come on——what is it you want?" Yeo was rather hoarse. He let go of the chair and moved over unsteadily to the bed, flung himself on it, glaring and panting. The other said nothing for a while but busied himself in pressing down the cuticle of his finger-nails with his thumb-nail.

"You're getting rather worked up, aren't you?"

"You tell me what you've come to say and then you get out."

"Suppose you tell me something," smiled Plumper. "Suppose you tell me first of all what form your illness takes. Have you pains in the head or over the heart or in the small of the back, and if you *are* ill, why don't you see a doctor? I'm sure Doctor Girdwood…"

"What business is it of yours?" The colour was rushing back in Yeo's grey face and he was shouting.

"Oh, everything in Larcombe is my business just at the moment. But we'll leave the question of your health for the time being and turn to the question of that remarkable man, John-Thomas Ridd."

"I knew it was that. I knew'd it!" The man was yelling.

"What did you know?"

"Just because he was a friend of mine, just because I had a bit of a row with him, you think *I* did it. I know, I know."

"Did what?"

"Did for Ridd, of course… what d'you think?"

"Oh, he's been done in, has he? He's dead, is he?"

"Of course he's dead. Everybody knows he's dead. He'd have shown up before this if he wasn't. That devil's done for him as he's done for all the others and as he'll do for all of us before he's finished! You'll see."

"What devil?"

Yeo banged his pillow with his fist, childishly but hysterically. "The one out there waiting, waiting, just waiting to have a go at somebody else under your very noses. But I tell you—if you let him get me!"

"Why on earth should he want to get you?"

Yeo got off the bed and stumbled across to a little table where his glass of whiskey stood. "He's trying to get everybody else, isn't he? Why shouldn't he want to get me too?"

"Have you got such a thing as a gun?" said Plumper smoothly.

"What if I have?"

"I'd just like to have a look at it. Hand it over, will you?"

"I will not."

"Hand over your gun, please."

"What right have you got? You've got no right…"

Plumper stared at him in silence. Yeo descended from the hysterical to the surly. "It's in that drawer over there." And then from the surly to the petulant. "You police have got to stop him. It's up to you. It oughtn't to be allowed."

Plumper pocketed the gun, a revolver of an old pattern. Then he said: "So you walk in fear and trembling, Mr. Yeo? I can understand you being upset because your old friend the Captain is missing, or, as you prefer it, dead. I can understand that perfectly well. But I put it to you quite frankly—you're overdoing it. It's making you ill. And as for getting the wind up over the murderer picking on somebody else, as far as I can see you're the only man in Larcombe who's making any fuss at all."

"More fools them."

"Perhaps you've some special reason for being afraid?"

"What d'you mean by that?"

"Just what I say."

"Well, understand this, mister—I know nothing about nobody nor nothing connected with this business. Understand that, d'you hear? All I know is that there's somebody going about that means mischief, more mischief. And I'm not taking any chances." With something very near a sob, he went over to the window, drew the curtain back and peered out and muttered to himself, "John-Thomas, old John-Thomas."

"Talking about walking in fear and trembling," said the detective, "I'd like to know exactly why you chose to take your constitutional up by the Gap this afternoon."

Bert swung round from the window. "I've told that damned copper once already when he came chasing me off. What harm is there in going up there for a breath of fresh air when you're feeling low like I am? It's nice and quiet up there. I didn't think there'd be anyone about."

"But, my dear Mr. Yeo, if you're as frightened as you make out—surely up round Old Barton is the last place you'd choose for a little stroll? It may seem fussy of me, but I really would like to know just why you put your head, as it were, into what is the lion's mouth as far as this mysterious affair is concerned."

Bert went back to the window. He was having difficulty in speaking. "Oh—I—oh—I dunno. I never thought of it that way."

"I see. And by the way—and again you must excuse me if I seem fussy—how did you get up there on to the Head?"

The other still faced the window. "Why—I—damn it, there's only one way. What way d'you think I'd go?"

"So you went up past the Vicarage and cut across the drive and up over by the Gap. That way?"

"Yes. How did I know I was doing wrong?"

"You're sure you went that way?"

"I've told you already, haven't I!"

Plumper took a long shot. "I'm sorry to have to disagree with you, but the constable on duty at the drive gates says that you were never on the road up past the Vicarage."

"He's making a mistake."

"Oh, come on, Yeo, we're wasting one another's time. Let's get it over. You climbed up the cliff at the back here, didn't you, and went round through the woods?"

"What if I did?"

"Oh, nothing, but why didn't you say so at first?" Plumper went on before he could reply. "And there's another little matter I'd like to talk to you about. Why have you said nothing about that letter you got? You know, the one with the blue paint?"

"Blue paint? I don't know what you're talking about."

"Don't be silly. Let me see it."

"You can search the whole place. I don't know anything about it."

"You've burned it, have you?" Yeo said nothing. "And you won't tell me what it said? Ah, well, I must be going now. You'll think over what we've been talking about, won't you? It would be a good thing if you did, you know—because I shall be coming up again in the morning just to see how you are. Inspector Blutton may call too. He's just as much interested in your health as I am."

Yeo turned from the window; his face was splodged with tears. "You get the murderer, mister—and don't bother your head so much about me."

Plumper was at the door. He put on a heavily sinister voice. "Oh, I don't think you'll have much to worry about from him."

FIFTH DEATH

By the time Blutton had digested his high tea of boiled cod and cold marmalade pudding and taken off his big black boots, he was enjoying a sweeter humour than he had experienced for several days. In the beginning, Plumper's prestige had somewhat intimidated him and this intimidation, coupled with a real dislike of the man, had worked on the Inspector's bile. The dislike was natural enough. Plumper was a younger man. Plumper cultivated an aloof, disconcerting, at times churlish manner. Plumper had no gift for co-operation. Plumper was not self-consciously, rigidly a policeman. Plumper was not a teetotaller or a Nonconformist. But Blutton was so accustomed to being on an unsympathetic footing with his colleagues—for twenty-one years he had looked for nothing but unthinking, mechanical obedience from his inferiors and cold politeness from his superiors—that his dislike for Plumper was, in itself, no bar to a good relationship. But the intimidation was a different matter. It had hampered him, put him out of his stride. However, the feeling that he owed the Scotland Yard man an almost obligatory respect—not respect for rank but for reputation, achievement—had now disappeared and the Inspector could now and again find time to smile in his little heart if not on his big face. Plumper was not up to standard. He was making no progress, or rather, progress in the wrong direction. He was bigotedly running a fanciful theory for the simple and regrettable reason that he, Blutton, had got his teeth into something else, something solid!

Blutton was sitting on a hard arm-chair with his legs neatly crossed, in front of a fire of small coals in the living-room of the house which he shared with his sister. This sister was eating oranges.

"You're very quiet to-night, Percy," she said, letting a pip fall from her mouth into a saucer which she always had by her when eating her evening orange. "Is it that man again?"

Blutton stretched his arms almost luxuriously. "No. I've stopped worrying about Plumper. No. I was just getting things straight in my mind. There's only one little piece that doesn't fit. If only I could explain about the Tuesday afternoon, the rest would go like clockwork."

"Are you going to bring it up to the Coroner when the Inquest comes on again? or what? I'd like to see *his* face when you do!"

"Don't be silly, Girlie. I shall put it to the Chief to-morrow in a proper report. He knows most of it already, but he'd better have it official. He'll call in Plumper and Plumper will have to like it or lump it. Mind you, I know for certain what he'll say. He'll tug at that ridiculous moustache of his and look down his nose. 'Very—er—nice—er,' he'll say, 'so long—er—as we—er—shut our eyes—er—to—er—the happenings of—er—Tuesday afternoon.' And then he'll come out with his stuff about boats and blackmail!"

"Yours is so much nicer. It'll save all the fuss of a trial. But why are you having so much trouble with Tuesday afternoon?"

He snorted. "However crazy Peascod is—and it's as clear as a bell to me that he's been writing these letters and playing these other funny tricks—he's not crazy enough to go cutting that fellow's head off. Besides, the girl from the public house was with him at the time."

Girlie Blutton had a bright idea. She spat out the last pip. "Percy, d'you know what I think? I think this Peascod could have done it easy. What if what the public-house girl said she thought she saw wasn't just a head, but a head with a body on it! Only the body was under the water and she couldn't see it—not liking to look too close. Then while this girl's gone off to fetch you, Peascod fishes it out, cuts the head off—and there you are!"

Blutton gave a fairly good imitation of a short, sharp guffaw. "You ought to join the Force, you really ought, Girlie," he said. "Well, I'm going to bed. I'm tired and I've got a lot more work to do in the morning."

"You work too hard, Perce. You should let somebody else do a bit sometimes."

"Hard work never did anybody any harm," said Blutton half-way up the stairs. "Good night, Girlie." His bedroom door slammed.

Girlie Blutton gazed fondly at the ceiling as her brother clomped about in the room above: she loved and admired her brother more than anything else in the world.

Back in the Orchard at Larcombe, Alan Charnock was sleeping badly and it was not the snoring of his wife that was keeping him awake. She had snored ever since she had had her false teeth fitted and he was as accustomed to it as he was to the rumble of the breaking sea. He was thinking about Hannabus and Scoutey. He was wondering why they had both kept silent when he had told them about the strange letter he had received. It was funny that they should have said nothing at the time, for they had each received one too. You'd have thought that at least they'd have mentioned it. It wasn't friendly not to have mentioned it. He'd trusted them—why couldn't they have trusted him? Charnock the boatman sighed and became conscious of his strident spouse. He drew up his knee and jabbed her hard in the back. Mrs. Charnock did not wake, but sputtered as a recalcitrant motor-car sputters and stopped snoring.

Christian Peascod was sleeping badly. He had awakened from a nightmare in which Plumper, Rosa and himself had been the chief characters. Peascod seemed to have been serving them as gondolier in Venice or some such place and Plumper had been busy carving a hole in the bottom of the boat, with Rosa raptly kissing his feet as he worked. Peascod had said, "Oh, but you can't do that to my gondola," and for reply, Plumper had stuck Rosa head-first into the hole so that her legs waved stupidly in the air, and then had come at him with the huge, jagged knife now dripping with blood. The knife was at his throat as he woke up.

His waking thoughts prolonged the Idea of Plumper the Villain. He'd hoped for better things from Plumper. Who would have thought, on that exhilarating afternoon when they rowed across the mouth of the creek to the rock and then on to the Gap, working on Peascod's own illuminating theory, who would have thought then that this man would want to damp all his ardour for the chase, to cramp his detective abilities and even—monstrous thought!—to look at him askance and with suspicion? Was this a just reward for hours of concentrated thought, for hours spent in painstaking, often laborious search for blood on boats and garments and rocks and blades of grass, for unstinted confidences, for a good dinner? Peascod smote his coverlet with the palm of his hand and said aloud, "But I'll show him, I'll show him yet, the Monster."

Rosa McQueen was sleeping badly. She wasn't thinking about anyone or about anything specifically or consecutively. She couldn't think why she had wakened up. She had been tired when she came to bed. She hadn't had any cheese or any apples for supper. She hadn't even been dreaming. She just suddenly found herself awake and sweating slightly. For her age, she had an unreasonable fear of the dark. If the telephone bell had rung or if someone had banged at the front door, she would have let them go on ringing and banging and pretended to be fast asleep. She turned her head to the wall and pulled the bedclothes up over her shoulders. But she was sweating. She was afraid and she longed for sleep. She strained to listen for the slightest sound and her concentration soon closed her eyes. She dozed, and in her doze she thought again of that wet afternoon when she'd found herself in the caravan with that dirty old gypsy at Setterham Fair. "Dearie," the crone had mumbled, "you have Hidden Power. You're claryvant, that's what you are. Wouldn't you like to know how to be able to tell the Past, the Present and the Future? Wouldn't you like to hold Destiny in both hands? I'm not telling you this to get any profit out of you. I'm telling you it for your own good. You're one in a million. For ten shillings I can give you a globe of crystal what was used by Cleopatter herself! Now what about it? The chance will never come again." Rosa hadn't bought the crystal because she hadn't the ten shillings, or even the five which was the rock-bottom price. But she'd remembered the words. Claryvant! Hidden Power! Wouldn't it be lovely if it were true? She went deeper into her doze. Only to waken again suddenly, unreasonably, violently. This time she sat bolt upright. Her undefined fear had vanished. She sniffed. She sniffed again. So that's what it was. It was gas.

She scrambled out of bed and lit her candle. There wasn't a gas-bracket in her room because she slept in the smaller half of a long, partitioned room. It was in Yeo's half that the usual fittings were. She cautiously opened the door and stuck her nose out, sniffing hard. There could be no doubt about it. It was gas and it was much stronger out in the corridor. There was a bracket down at the other end, at the head of the stairs. It must be that.

She hesitated a moment or two, then resolutely bit her lip and creaked off down the passage. But she didn't get far. She didn't get past Yeo's door. It was gaspingly strong there.

"Mr. Yeo!" she screeched, "Mr. Yeo!" and banged hard on the door, blowing out her candle as she did so, for she had read stories of explosions.

There was no response from Mr. Yeo, but there was from Mr. Dundas. He must have been awakened by the first knock and out of bed by the second, for by the time her scared soprano was shrilling through the house, his door was open and he was charging down the corridor towards her, hitching up his disreputable pyjamas as he came. The wan moon filtering through the skylight gave him just light enough to see by. The amount of gas in the air told him more than he could have professionally hoped for. "Go and wake Mr. Plumper," he gasped, and a second later he was charging his shoulder against the panels of the bedroom door.

Plumper was sleeping like a boot and his immediate reaction to Rosa's cries was not nearly as swift and definite as Dundas's had been. He was fuddled and he even wasted time putting on slippers and a dressing-gown; but by the time he was helping to smash in the door, he was much more self-possessed and knowledgeable than the reporter. He was shouting orders to Rosa as well as battering at the panels. Gas was thick in Yeo's room and it came swirling out at them when eventually they broke the door down. With a handkerchief to his face, Plumper blundered across and got the window open. Yeo was lying on the hearth-rug. He lugged him out by the heels and they carried him into Dundas's room. The jolly landlord was dead.

A good half-hour later Dr. Girdwood from Corfield confirmed the obvious fact that death had resulted from coal-gas poisoning. "No complications as far as I can see," he said. "But we'll make sure at the post-mortem. What's been the matter with him?"

Plumper shrugged. "I only wish I knew."

Girdwood snapped the catch of his black bag and began to draw on his gloves. "What's that row?" he said.

"That'll be Dundas," said Plumper.

It was Dundas. He was at the telephone downstairs yelling at a sleepy operator to get him through to the Central Exchange of London without an instant's delay, and at his side were three fellow reporters, yelling at him to hurry up and give them next use of the instrument.

When the body had been taken away to Setterham and he had dealt with the buzzing gang of newspapermen, Plumper descended on the dead man's room like a carrion crow. He searched principally for letters. But there was no farewell note such as suicides habitually leave, and to all appearances, Yeo's correspondence had been very inconsiderable. There was an old desk in one corner of the room—for this had been his office as well as his bedroom— and this desk was full of communications from brewers, distillers, tobacco factors and the like, but of very little else. There were three or four letters from someone who signed herself "Peg" and appeared to be a married sister living in the north of England; several faded, brown photographs showing Yeo as a younger man in sea-boots, high-necked fisherman's jersey and peaked cap, one showing him arm-in-arm with Ridd, another, portentously holding up for display a freak fish which seemed to be a cross between a skate and a conger; a recent bulletin from the Hon. Secretary of the South Devon Affiliated Darts and Skittles Guild; a jumble of circulars and club cards, and that was all.

Judging from his books, his financial position was good, very good, remarkably good for the landlord of such an establishment as the Clove and Hoof. A most scrupulous examination of the contents of drawers, cupboards, chests, trunks and boxes revealed nothing which would indicate any reason why the man should have taken his own life or anything (and it was for this that Plumper was chiefly hoping) to link him with the chain of deaths in Larcombe. That he had taken his own life was fairly obvious, for the feed-pipe of a small gas-fire had been wrenched loose and bent round so that it lay on the hearth-rug where they had found him.

Plumper went back to the desk and turned up the oldest of a pile of brewer's Delivery Books. He discovered that Yeo had taken over the inn on June 4th, 1921. But apart from this fact, he found little to hold his attention.

It was remarkable how little the several efficient searches, made in connection with this affair, had revealed. They had drawn a blank at the Vicarage, unless the bloody handkerchief were to be taken into account. Even in respect of the burglary, no finger-prints had come to light other than those of the Vicar and his housekeeper, Mrs. Fitzroy. It had been the same at Old Barton and the "Moorings" and in the *Saucy Sue*. There had been nothing extraordinary, nothing that they did not expect to find, nothing that was in the remotest way helpful except to confirm their estimates as to the characters and habits of Gedling and Ridd. Plumper had instituted a thorough search of the neighbouring coastline for any stray or suspicious boats or for any articles of clothing, etc., washed up by the tide, with no success. Every boat in Larcombe had been examined for traces of blood, and no traces had been found. Nor had John-Thomas Ridd or John-Thomas Ridd's body. Only the soft ground on Crale Cliff had yielded any evidence, and that was confusing and savouring of the preposterous. This lack of evidence made theorizing not only justified but inevitable. Any of a dozen theories held a certain amount of water—but not one of them was watertight. Plumper's only comfort was the melancholy thought that, at least, his Short List was narrowing itself down of its own accord.

When he had disposed of bath, breakfast and Blutton, Plumper stepped round to "The Nook" to see Peascod. The young man was frigid and over-courteous. "I'm afraid if you've come to ask me for my collaboration, you are foredoomed to disappointment," he said. "I made a solemn resolution not an hour ago to wash my hands of the whole affair. Crime is so sordid and the people who make crime their business seem to make a point of stultifying and sullying innocent zeal. Henceforward I shall concern myself solely with my old love—the Spirit."

"It is about a more recent love of yours that I have come to see you. You'll have heard of the death in tragic circumstances of your neighbour Yeo?"

"I have indeed heard," said Peascod with an air of boredom. "But I fail to see that it has to do with any recent love of mine."

"I believe you had a little conversation with Rosa McQueen yesterday afternoon? She says you behaved somewhat strangely and that you had wanted to know something about Yeo."

Peascod blushed prettily. "Rosa said that? Well, well, I wouldn't have thought it of her! Still—love is as much a part of my past as detection. The questions I meant to put to her constitute my last act as a detective and as a lover. But I must say that I don't remember behaving strangely and I can assure you that the questions I intended putting were of the most ordinary nature, questions which Inspector Blutton or yourself might well have put."

"They were?"

"Oh, I merely wanted to know whether Yeo had any sea-charts of the neighbourhood: whether Miss McQueen had seen anything of the painted letter which I knew he had received: whether he was taking any physic for his indisposition: whether he was in the habit of saying his prayers aloud at night, and so forth and so forth."

"And what made you want to ask such odd questions?"

"Odd? Perhaps they are. But one day, my good friend, you will learn that Truth herself is odd. Odd, perverted, as a double-hearted onion or as a flying swan."

"Am I to believe that you were considering Yeo in relation to the murders?"

Peascod looked at Plumper very seriously. "My friend, if you'd come an hour ago, I might have answered that question. I might have taken it up with you and debated it with you. I might have outlined to you a rather brilliant theory which occurred to me only yesterday. But it is too late now and if you'll excuse me—I have some colours to grind."

Plumper smiled and stroked his whiskers and purred coaxingly, "If I were to apologize for having treated you, during the last few days, in a rather summary fashion."

"I think you mean high-handed."

"As you will. But if I were to apologize here and now and admit that some of your work on this case has been brilliant to a degree, would you not honour me again with your confidence?"

"Ah, you crystal-clear flatterer! You Janus, you! You uncharitable pickbrain. I know your artful stratagems and I'm not to be caught napping four times. No. The past is a sealed book. All I will say is that it did occur to me that Yeo *might* have been a criminal. But not wild horses, let alone a hirsute Detective-Sergeant, could drag anything from me at the moment. Perhaps one day I shall write a little monograph on the subject and have it published in one of the discreeter monthlies. Yes, I think I shall certainly do that."

Plumper bowed. "Very well. As you wish. Silence covers a multitude of sins."

But the poet had the last word. When his visitor was out in the road, he put his head through the window and shouted loudly: "Ask yourself this. What is the focal point in this affair? Where lies the nodal brick? What is the geographical, spiritual, commercial, inevitable centre? What secret holds the appropriate Cloven Hoof? What is the relation of a hoof to a wooden leg?" Before Plumper could make a suitable retort or grimace, the window had been shut with a bang.

The Chief Constable had summoned a council for three o'clock that afternoon, and regretted having done so as soon as it was assembled. Plumper was playing the rôle of acid obstructionist. Blutton seemed to be on the verge of losing his temper. And the Chief Constable did not know what to say to either.

It seemed to him that his Inspector's arguments were as sound and as sensible as could be expected in dealing with such a fantastic case. He turned to Blutton. "Let's have it just once more. And make it as clear as you can."

Blutton sighed in controlled exasperation. "I maintain that there's no need to look further than Gedling. We know for a fact that the old chap was crazy, and as you yourself have worked out, Plumper, he'd certainly had associations in the past with both the Vicar and Ridd. What those associations were, apart from drinking and so on, we don't know and we probably never shall know. But their break seems to have been so definite and complete and—as far as I can make out—so sudden that it's quite on the cards that it was brought about by something, to them, serious. And don't forget that it was just at the time of their break that Gedling shut himself up and lived like a hermit. You'll admit a man doesn't do a thing like that for nothing. The Vicar and Ridd may have offended him—or done something much worse than just offend him. We don't know. But there's motive for you. The old man may have brooded over it for years until it became very definitely an obsession with him. And when eventually his brain did crack—well, you know what happened."

"But we don't even know that Ridd's dead," complained Plumper.

"We'll find him yet and it won't be a hundred miles from Old Barton either, you mark my words."

"It seems fairly all right to me," said the Chief Constable, chewing the end of a pencil.

"There are," growled Plumper, "twelve irreconcilable points that even a Blutton can't reconcile."

The Chief Constable frowned. "You don't seem to be able to do much better yourself. And if you were to look at this theory a little more sympathetically, *you* might be able to help with the reconciliation."

The other sighed. "For the thousandth time, sir, may I make

the point that this theory falls to the ground for the very simple and incontestable reason that Gedling and Costigan were in Setterham here on Tuesday afternoon? You say, without proof of any kind, without any argument, without logic, without even offering a motive, that Peascod has been writing these letters more or less for fun."

"We haven't been able to search his house for proof."

"You say he has been playing these pranks because he's just as crazy as Gedling—only in another way. He thinks all this is funny, as an undergraduate would think it funny. But that Tuesday afternoon prank is a prank he did not play."

"You mean the woman from the public house says he didn't. How do we know he didn't persuade her to think it was funny too?"

"Come, come," smirked Plumper. "Come, come. That girl's no Judith. Are you going to suggest that there's yet another humorist in Larcombe?"

"I'll admit," said Blutton, "that that's the one weakness. But I won't admit that it necessarily destroys my whole case."

"All right. And I suppose you're going to say that the decayed fish, the metronome, the milk and the air-gun shots were just a put-up job by Gedling with, incidentally, the shut-eye co-operation of the rogue Costigan. And I suppose you think that Peascod burgled the Vicarage with great thoroughness just for fun, and left his own handkerchief there to draw attention to himself without, I may add, leaving any finger-prints. And what about Crale Cliffs? I suppose Gedling hired the stranger to shoot the Vicar and then knifed him because dead men tell no tales. And then I suppose he took him and laid him naked at the edge of his own lawn for someone who by rights has no business to know that he was there at all, to chop his head off?"

Blutton fought down his anger. "You suppose a lot, don't you? As you put it, it doesn't sound too good. But you're dead against it. If only you'd look at it with a little less prejudice, you'd find it wasn't quite so absurd, and if you really put Costigan on the rack, he might just be able to fill in a few of the gaps."

The Chief Constable did some humming and hawing. "I must say I agree with him, Plumper. In all my long experience, I've never yet met a case where there was so little straightforward, honest-to-goodness evidence, so much that we don't know and don't seem likely ever to know. What else is there we can do but theorize? You can say what you like—but the combination, the accidental, quite accidental combination of—what shall I say?— of viciously crazy old Gedling and mischievously crazy young Peascod seems to be, in the light of what little we do know, as sound as any of the other damn theories that have been popping up like mushrooms all this week. Now you've been doing a goodish bit of criticizing—have you yourself anything less vulnerable to offer?"

"Oh, yes. Mind you, I don't say it's less vulnerable. Its only virtue is that it happens to appeal to me more. Its principal weakness is that it doesn't offer a motive. If I had the remotest idea why my man's done what I think he's done, I'd be asking you for a warrant this minute. As it is, I'm not sure whether it wouldn't be better to risk it and jump on him now. There *might* be something at his house. On the other hand, Yeo's death is a tricky question."

Blutton was trying to register rather aloof, condescending scorn, but his features were so coarse and inelastic that he only succeeded in looking faintly comic. It was as if he had got a smut on the end of his nose and was having difficulty in seeing it because of chronic myopia.

Plumper smiled quite openly. "Jeremiah Scoutey has no alibi for any of the vital times. For Tuesday afternoon he had quite unrivalled opportunity. For the small hours of Monday morning he had as good a chance as anybody else, and—there's no getting away from it—the Stranger went straight to his house the minute he arrived in Larcombe. Furthermore…" Plumper proceeded to outline all the theoretical, circumstantial evidence against his suspect that had occurred to him on his recent train journey from London.

His colleagues seemed as biasedly dubious as he had been of the Gedling-cum-Peascod theory. The Inspector blew his nose precisely. "But Scoutey's an oaf—as dull as they make 'em. If you're looking for someone out of those public-house chaps, I should have thought that Hannabus was much likelier. He's a foxy enough customer. I don't trust him an inch. He even looks the part with that beard and his spectacles!"

Blutton intended these remarks to be heavily sarcastic—but Plumper took him up seriously. "Don't worry. I've got him down too."

Blutton tried again. "Pity that old Bowle is bedridden. I suppose you'll have to leave him out."

"I think it would be a grave mistake to leave anybody out in this case," said Plumper solemnly.

The Chief Constable intervened. "What about Yeo? I take it neither of you are proposing to link his death up with the other affair."

Plumper and Blutton both began to speak at once. But both behaved in an elaborately polite fashion and there was much "After you"-ing and "My dear fellow"-ing before a reply was forthcoming. "It's most definitely not unconnected," murmured the former. Blutton added, "They seem to have been worrying him in an extraordinary way. He hadn't spoken to anybody for days and I understand he was under some sort of delusion about being the next victim."

The Chief Constable spat out splinters from his pencil and pondered.

"Well, what are we going to do? It seems, at the moment, that we've got to decide between Gedling and Scoutey. I'd like us to have made up our minds for the resumed Inquest on Wednesday. However—it's up to you."

Blutton was emphatic; he even slapped the table. "We must find Ridd first! If only the creek was sandy, we could trawl for him—but the rocks put it out of the question. In any case, I'm convinced he's somewhere round about Old Barton. We're going over it inch by inch. We'll find him—we're bound to. Meanwhile, if we were to give Costigan a real grilling…"

"All right," grinned Plumper. "Does this suit you? If you haven't found Ridd by Wednesday and you haven't got anything out of Costigan, d'you agree to us taking Scoutey in on suspicion?"

"Yes. If you'll help me to grill Peascod too."

The Chief Constable was more than relieved to leave it at that.

Jack Marsden was off duty and was employing his leisure to further his suit for the hand of Jane McQueen.

They were strolling together up the Larcombe valley, along the lane that led to Corfield and Poridge. Jack was tasting the pleasure that comes with the confession of suspicion recently allayed. "When Plumper told me that he'd seen you kissing about with John-Thomas, I didn't know what to say."

"'Twas a shameful lie," cried Jane. "He's tried to do it before, but that time out in the garden when I was hanging out the bit of washing was the very last—because I'd told him then and there that I'd told Uncle all about it and that if it didn't stop there'd be trouble."

"Oh, you'd told your uncle, had you?"

"Yes, I had, only a day or two before. Because, Jackie dear, it had been getting worse since he came home this last time."

"What did Jeremiah say?"

"Oh, he was vexed proper and he said he'd talk to John-Thomas at the Cloven. But I don't think he got a chance because the poor man never came down there again after Wednesday, did he? Oh dear, d'you think he's dead?"

Jack wagged his head solemnly. "Ah, my dear, it's a mystery, proper mystery."

"And now, poor Yeo. Our Rosa thinks it's a curse, but I don't know. There certainly never was such a thing as this has been. But, Jackie, if you'd done something about it, wouldn't you have got promotion?"

"Everything's being done that need be. That Plumper will get his man, you see if he doesn't. He's a very clever chap and he knows a lot more than he says. When it all comes out, you'll get a real shock. Oh, yes, a real shock!"

"Uncle Jerry says it was Costigan and that first detective fellow between 'em. Says they was a couple of London robbers and that Costigan will have to hang. He says they were planning to rob Old Barton and perhaps the Vicarage too, and in the dark, they all got mixed up in the shooting."

Jack snorted. "Old Jeremiah thinks he knows a lot, doesn't he? Got mixed up in shooting!" They walked on a little way in silence and then he said: "Are you glad I'm with you, Jane?"

"Ooh, Jackie." The girl's blank, undistinguished face almost shone as she lifted it up to him. And for some time, as they strolled through the dusk, they talked no more of death.

SIXTH DEATH

Back in Larcombe, Hannabus was addressing himself in a very agitated manner to Plumper. "I tell you, sir, I think I've discovered something very important. I don't think, I'm sure!"

"A cave?" said Plumper.

"A cave," repeated the old man. "I came on it quite unexpected when I was out after the bunnies. You'd better come along with me right away, sir." He was tugging at the policeman's sleeve in his excitement. The latter looked at his watch. "There'll be only one man up there by this time—and he'll be patrolling the drive. All right, we'll go straight away. Come on."

They hurried on up the hill, but when they came to Hannabus's shop, the old man stopped. "Just a minute, sir. I'd best get a torch. We might need it. I've got one inside." He was out again very quickly and, almost gasping with eagerness, led the way up past the Vicarage. Before they came to the drive gates, he turned sharp left and climbed up through the heather and brush in the direction of Larcombe Head. Plumper followed at a short distance. Conversation was difficult because the going was very uneven and it was getting dark. But after a time, the undergrowth gave way to bare rock and they were able to trudge on side by side.

"Did you find anything in this cave?"

"Well, sir, to tell you the truth, I didn't look. I was that excited at finding it at all—I just came rushing straight back to you."

"What puzzles me," grunted Plumper, "is that we haven't found it before. I've had men out for days and for miles along the coast looking for nothing else but caves and places where you could keep a boat, or anything else for that matter."

"Doesn't surprise me they didn't find it," chuckled Sebastian, "not this one! Whoever would think of looking for a cave at the *top* of a cliff? Might never have found it till doomsday if it hadn't been for the rabbits."

"You're sure about all this?"

"Sure? Well, you'll be able to see for yourself in a minute."

They had wound round over the Head and down almost to the Gap. Hannabus flashed his torch on a small mound of boulders not more than two or three yards from the edge of the cliff. "Here we are," he said. One of the boulders, not a very big one, had been rolled out of place leaving uncovered a small round hole.

Plumper dropped down on his knees and took the torch. The hole seemed to be about four or five feet deep, narrow and sloping slightly. He was disappointed. "Is this all there is? You don't call this a cave?"

Hannabus chuckled again. "Give me the light—and you watch me." Nimbly he lowered himself into the hole which was just wide enough to take him. In a minute or two, he had completely disappeared. His thin voice echoed up. "Come on. It seems to be quite all right."

With his heart beating a little faster, Plumper followed. He discovered that the hole shelved away sharply, broadening out slightly. And then suddenly his feet were hanging over into space. Twelve feet below him was Hannabus and the light at the bottom of a ladder.

"Easy—isn't it? Was I right?"

"Were you right, by God!" Plumper lowered himself over the ledge, got a footing on the top rung of the ladder and slithered down.

They were in a good-sized cave. He took the torch from Hannabus and flashed it round. There was a boat suspended from a sort of davit clamped to the rope. But the strange thing was that there did not seem to be any opening at the other end of the cave. Next to the boat there was a table, or rather a sort of work bench, and on it stood a big oil lamp. Near the foot of the ladder lay a large sack.

Plumper stood peering about him, breathing hard, his hand clenched tight round the torch. He shone it on the lamp. "Light that," he barked.

Hannabus shuffled across, struck a match, and in a few seconds the whole place was brightly lit. The old man turned from the lamp and in his hand was a neat, small automatic. He said nothing.

Plumper swore and flung the torch as hard as he could at the lamp. It missed and smashed itself against the wall of the cave.

Hannabus passed the back of his hand wearily over his forehead and speaking in a much softer, deeper voice than he had used before, said, "Please don't do anything like that. It won't do you any good because I shall shoot you if you move again without permission."

Plumper had recovered himself. "Would you like me to put up my hands?" he sneered.

"For a few minutes, yes. I think that would be a good idea. That's right. Well over your head. Believe me, I'm not at all anxious to do you any harm, but it is essential for my purpose that you do exactly as I tell you. If you will just sit here." He indicated a wooden chair by the side of the bench.

Plumper obeyed promptly.

Hannabus stepped behind him. "You may put your hands down now."

With extraordinary dexterity, the old man slipped a noose over the other's shoulders, pulled it hard—and before the unfortunate Plumper could offer any resistance, had wrapped the free end of the rope round his neck and was pulling that hard too. Plumper was too concerned with getting his breath to struggle. His chair was tipped backwards and Hannabus dived for his legs like an inside three-quarter stopping a cut-through. In another few seconds, he had buckled a leather belt round and round his ankles. And Plumper was effectively trussed. Hannabus, however, was not satisfied; he wound several more lengths of rope round him and the chair and then he released the rope's stranglehold on his neck. "Easier than I imagined," he panted. "You could have got me if you'd been quick enough when I went behind the chair. I had to use both hands on the rope."

The detective's face was regaining its normal colour and he was breathing more easily. "I don't see what you're going to gain by all this. People saw us going off together, you know."

Hannabus smiled rather wearily and shrugged. "Who said I wanted to gain anything? It will only be a question of an hour or two in any case. But just as a precaution, I think I'll go and see what I can do about fixing the stone up there. I don't want to be disturbed." He climbed up the ladder out of the cave and disappeared into the tunnel.

Plumper wriggled and squirmed, but he soon gave it up. He was expertly pinioned. He looked about him. The cave was perhaps thirty feet long and half as broad at the far end where the boat hung; it narrowed down considerably as it approached the ledge and the tunnel. The roof was very uneven and varied in height; it was a good twelve feet above Plumper's head where he sat, but where it met the wall on the opposite side of the cave it was no more than a couple of yards from the ground. The lamp gave a very bright light, but did little to dispel the chill, the dankness of the place. At the foot of the drop, by the ladder, lay a sack; it was partly in shadow, but it seemed to him that something very like a wooden leg was sticking out at one end.

Sebastian returned. He stood peering at his prisoner, apparently expecting him to say something. He half-smiled through his beard. "At least," he said, "pay me the compliment of telling me that you're very surprised."

Plumper grunted. "Oh, I'm surprised all right—at this place I mean. Not so much at you. The jury will be—at both."

"You have suspected me then?"

"Not as much as several other people. But as I reported to my colleagues only this afternoon, I've had my eye on you."

The other smiled again and again his smile was rather weary. It was certainly not a grin of triumph or malice. "So I'm even to be denied the satisfaction of having pulled the wool over your eyes completely? Oh, well, I hardly expected it. From the very beginning this has been a most unsatisfactory tragedy." He pulled out a box from under the bench, placed it in front of Plumper's chair and sat on it, wrapping his arms round his knees and hunching them up under his chin like a schoolgirl hugging herself before Lights Out.

"Nothing has gone according to schedule. I hoped you'd be full of bluster, straining at your ropes and saying things like, 'Why have you lured me here, you old devil?' 'Am I to be your next victim?' But no—you're giving me none of my cues! You don't ask any questions, so I suppose I shall have to use the very dull method of telling you the story right from the beginning."

Plumper glowered. "I'll ask questions all right, but I'll ask them in another place. And I don't mean hell."

Hannabus waved a deprecating hand. "Have it your own way. Meanwhile, whether you like it or not, I shall tell you the story. Now where shall I begin? Perhaps I'd better tell you about myself. Yes. You shall hear about me—all about me. Well, first of all, I want you to understand that I'm a perfectly ordinary elderly man. My tastes are very simple. For instance, I take far greater pleasure in doing little things like breathing good sea air or drinking fresh-tapped beer than in fingering diamonds or being whipped by a young lady in high-heeled boots, if you see what I mean. I don't spend all my day breathing and drinking deep— naturally. But I think it illustrates my point. By no manner of means am I a monster or a madman, at least I don't think I am." He scratched his head and grimaced good-humouredly. "Oh, dear, this isn't as easy as I thought it was going to be. I was never very good at talking. However, I dare say you'd like to know who I am and where I come from. That's easily told. I was born and bred in Larcombe—but I'm afraid you won't be able to look me up in the Church Register under 'Hannabus,' because my name isn't Hannabus at all. As a matter of fact, it's Scriven, William Scriven. You won't have heard that name, I expect. Not that it matters. Well, I was a clever child and thanks to the persistence and generosity of the then Vicar, Pratt's predecessor, I was allowed to go to the Grammar School at Setterham. But that isn't important, is it? No. I must keep to the important things. Anyhow, after that, I came back and helped at the village school, did odd secretarial jobs for the Vicar and made myself generally useful. But I was too ambitious to be happy—and there were no prospects in Larcombe, obviously. I was always hankering to go off to London, but it never got beyond hankering. Oh, I hope I'm not boring you with all this. It's quite important, as a matter of fact, quite relevant."

"Get on with it," said Plumper.

Hannabus ignored him and went on slowly, haltingly and very carefully. "I got a clerk's job at Setterham and stuck it for a few years, but it was no good. Back I came to Larcombe, and it was about this time that Mr. Lionel Gedling began to take an interest in me. In those days he used to spend half his time at the Cloven, that was before Yeo had it. And it was there I got to know him. Him and Ridd made it a really lively place; oh, really lively, and there always used to be a good crowd there. Sometimes of an evening he used to take two or three of us out of the Bar up to Old Barton, and we used to have some fun I can tell you. I went up there perhaps half a dozen times with the others, and then one night he got me up there by myself. I don't know how it came about—but he just managed it so that there was him and me together. I can remember it very well, even though it is thirty years or more ago. I was a good bit nervous, being by myself, for though he was free and easy with everybody, we still looked on him as a bit of a cut above us. But he plied me well with the whiskey and made me very much at home. Then he gradually brought the conversation round to me and my future. What was I going to do for a job? He flattered me by telling me how he'd noticed that I was certainly qualified for something better than fishing or shopkeeping or even teaching at the village school. 'I hear you want to go to London,' he said. 'Mr. Gedling,' I replied, 'I'd give anything to go to London. I've got ambition.'

"He left it at that and gave me some more to drink. He was looking at me in a peculiar sort of way, half smiling, half appraising. He was a handsome chap in those days—only six or seven years older than me and his nose hadn't started to go funny then. Well, anyhow, he came down to brass tacks at last. What he wanted to know was—would I like to work for him? 'D'you mean in London?' I said all excited. He nodded. 'Mostly.' I told him I'd be only too glad to do anything in the world so long as I could go to London. But he wouldn't say what he wanted me to do, not for a bit. All he'd say was that it was highly confidential work, and yet very simple and very well paid. When he'd said that, he put his glass down and came and stood over by my chair, looking at me in a very peculiar, fierce way. 'Well paid—and dangerous,' he said.

"I didn't care about that. 'I tell you, Mr. Gedling, I don't care what it is,' I said. But I'm wasting time. To be brief—he made me swear on the Bible that whether I took the job or not, I wouldn't tell a soul what he was going to tell me now. I swore all right. This is what he told me. My job was simply to consist in taking packages which Gedling would give me up to London and there delivering them at a certain time, at a certain place, to a certain person. All the London side of the business would be arranged for me well beforehand. Being highly confidential work, I should have to cover my movements by setting up as a commercial traveller working the Devon area for headquarters in London. And that was all. It seemed too soft to be true. I laughed. 'Where does the danger come in, and why all this secrecy?' He laughed too. 'So long as you do exactly as you're told and so long as you say *nothing* to anyone, anyone about the collection and delivery of these packages, there'll be no danger. None whatsoever.' I was young, full of enthusiasm. The chance was too good to be missed whatever it might turn out to be. I took on the job.

"Most of the time, I was on the commercial job which Gedling had got me—the job to act as cover to my movements. Selling tea it was, as a matter of fact. Then every month or so, I'd make the trip up to London and meet a man in some appointed pub, a different one every time, and hand over my suitcase. Nothing more, nothing less. It was the easiest thing in the world. And that's how I came to take an active part in the smuggling trade! Me—at my age, a drug-smuggler! It didn't take me very long to find out all about it. Gedling was the organizer and the brains of a flourishing concern. And his henchmen were, but you can guess? His henchmen were Herbert Yeo and John-Thomas Ridd. Gedling arranged everything and these two worked the boat, went to meet the foreigners five or six miles out and brought the stuff in. It was this very cave that made the business possible and it was this cave that made it fairly safe. Without it they wouldn't have lasted five minutes. And they were proud of it too, I can tell you."

The old man got off his box and walked over to the far end of the cave. "I'd better explain. This end looks over the Gap. And I suppose you'll have noticed that from down below—or from up on the Head for that matter—you can't see any trace of a cave. They were helped of course by the fact that there isn't any cliff, no cliff to speak of on the other side of the Gap. It was lucky it running to sand like that. Oh, very proud of their cave they were. And it took 'em some time to fix it up, for you see they had to block up the hole in the cliff face. They did it," Hannabus banged with his fist on what had seemed to Plumper, in the shadow as it was, to be a dead end to the cave, "by making these two doors.

They're a bit rickety now, but they weren't when they were first made, I can tell you. Heavy wood faced with slate and rock-slabs. It took 'em months to do it, but it was worth it. From down below it looked like there was a solid wall of rock—and even now there's hardly a crack shows. The rest was simple. There's a slight overhang and all they had to do was to run out this bar." There was a very long rusty iron rod, rather like a single railway metal, running along a levelled stretch of the roof through rings... "clamp inverted davits on to it and sling the boat on to them, open the doors, slide the bar out to its full length over the edge and pulley the boat down. Gedling was much more particular about his property in those days and he kept good fences round the whole place, so that no one had much chance to see what was going on. Old Barton itself was very useful too, with it standing up exactly in a straight line with the Gap. Naturally, they always worked at night and they were able to have the house lights to guide them. As soon as they got back, they hoisted the boat up again by the pulleys, swung back the doors, and there you were! Not a trace of anything. That was before the War. After a bit, of course, they let me in to the whole affair and I stood on an equal footing with the others. And I must say we made a fair amount of money. By the way, our dear Vicar, Mr. Pratt, had been in on it from the very beginning as a sleeping partner. When Gedling first planned all this, the only obstacle he could find was the lack of a bit of capital because he himself was as broke as the devil. Now Pratt had become a friend of his and Pratt, like a fool, had got mixed up with Gedling's housekeeper, who was a piece and no mistake. Pratt had a little money of his own, so Gedling had simply said: 'Ernest my boy, if you don't want to lose your frock I'm afraid there's nothing for it. You'll have to come in with me.'

"Now that Vicar was a fool in many ways, as you've probably guessed, and you can just imagine him giving in to Gedling like a lamb. Fancy it—just letting himself be blackmailed like that and putting up his money without a murmur! Anyhow, Pratt was in, and though he never took a very active part, he did what he could to help with the organization. So far, so good. We went on for several years and we were as safe as it's humanly possible to be in that sort of game. But the War came, and that queered our pitch.

"I joined up. But I was the only one. The amount of whiskey Gedling had drunk had broken him up far too much for any regular service. Yeo had a fatty heart. Pratt was safe in his cloth. And besides me, Ridd was the only one who didn't manage to stay at home. He was drafted into the Preventive at Symouth! As you can imagine, the War wasn't very good for trade—and for a time, things were at a standstill. They couldn't do much without Ridd and me, but Gedling (and I suppose this is the first sign of his real craziness coming out) was dead set on carrying on.

"And now I'm coming to the part that's really going to interest you, the part that's directly responsible for our little meeting to-night." The old man was back on his box again. He sighed and paused for some time before he continued.

"You see, although the risk was just about trebled, they had the inestimable advantage of having one of their party in the local Preventive Service, for you see, Ridd was able to tell them what boats were going to be out and where and when. It was desperately risky in war-time like that, but it might just come off once every two or three months. The parson could take my place as go-between and all they needed was somebody else to work the boat with Yeo. That in itself was difficult. All the able-bodied chaps round about Larcombe were out in France like me."

Hannabus began to bite his nails and his voice dropped to little more than a hardly intelligible mumble.

"But Gedling got his man in the end. He got my young brother. The boy was only seventeen. Nice boy, healthy, but no good for the War. He'd got three fingers missing. Well, as I say, Gedling got him. Silly fellow, it was a mistake to have tried it at all in wartime—but it was a bigger mistake still to drag young Ted into it." He looked up quickly. "A tactical mistake I mean, and not at all from my point of view. That's something quite apart. But let me tell you about Ted. After he left school when my father died he did odd jobs about the village, mostly with the boats; but he'd nothing definite. As I say, he was a nice boy, quite a simple sort of lad, easily led and lazy as the devil. I suppose Gedling picked on him first of all because of him being my brother—quite apart from him being one of the very few chaps left in Larcombe. Anyhow, there it was. Gedling got him. Ted was in and in up to the hilt.

"Bert Yeo had dropped me a line, giving me a hint of what was going on. And for some reason I was mad angry. I say, for some reason, because it wasn't as if I had any tremendous sentimental love for Ted. He was my young brother—and it stopped at that. It wasn't as if I even had any objections on moral grounds to him getting mixed up with that sort of game. And although I knew just how dangerous it would be in war-time, it wasn't fear for his safety that made me mad. To tell you the truth, I'd never thought about him very much up till then. Perhaps the War itself had something to do with it. I'd been in some pretty hot stuff and I was all shaken up. I really don't know what it was. I was just mad angry that Gedling had got hold of him.

"A month or two after I got Yeo's letter, I came home on leave." Hannabus was on his feet again.

"Now I want you to remember this very carefully. I was still furious and I'd come down to Larcombe specially to try to put a stop to it. Remember that. No one was expecting me, and when I turned up sudden like that they found it a bit awkward—the gang I mean—telling me that Ted was dead, for it was the first I'd ever heard of it. People like Bowle, who was the first person I met when I got back, as a matter of fact, said it was a great mystery. 'Young Ted he never been seen since he left the Cloven that night. Some say he went out in a boat, but there be no boat missing. There were a bit of a wind blowing up too. It's a fair mystery!' That's what old Bowle said. It was a different matter up at Old Barton. They gave me a party. Gedling, Pratt and Yeo, they were all there except Ridd. It wasn't a very good party. I could see there was something wrong right from the first. Pratt was drinking hard to cover his nervousness. Yeo was just sitting and sulking and saying nothing. And Gedling was far, far too polite, treating me like a national hero or something. There was something wrong somewhere, all right. First thing I said was, 'What's this I hear's happened to young Ted?'

"Gedling licked his lips before he answered me, and it's not for effect I'm saying he licked his lips; he really did. He licked his lips and took a good pull at his whiskey. His nose had started to grow by that time and he was looking very bloated, a very different Gedling from the one who'd first given me a job. Even before he'd said anything, it was as much as I could do to stop myself smashing his face in. The yarn he pitched was this. One of the Circle's French boats was due and as Ridd had got the night off, it was decided that he and Ted should go out to her. They went, but it was too rough to get nearly far enough out, and Ridd decided to put back again. Ridd got back all right.

Young Ted didn't. He went overboard. Ridd himself wasn't too clear about what had happened. It had been very dark, he said. The water was breaking over them, and Ted just went! Gedling finished up: 'John-Thomas is heartbroken, and so are we all. A terrible thing to happen.'

"Pratt was goggling with drink. Bert Yeo was scratching his ear, scowling and looking on the floor. 'A terrible thing,' said Gedling, reaching for the decanter. 'But come on now, let's have a drink. The warrior's home from the war! We've got to celebrate.'

"Well, Mr. Plumper, I made what inquiries I could in the village and I learned one very significant fact—which was that Ted had been behaving in a very strange way just before he disappeared. He seemed, so they said, to have changed completely. For one thing, he'd started drinking, and for another, he was dressed up like you don't know what. People had started talking. The boy seemed to have got money from somewhere. Money! That's what had happened, my friend. A simple lad who'd never had more than pennies in his pocket before, a few pounds just went to his head. I can understand it. I can just see it—him drinking and gadding about and bragging at the Cloven. And Gedling must have seen it too and realized what a big mistake he'd made. He should have known better than to trust a boy like Ted with such business. You can't blame the lad. He'd treat it like a bit of fun, a bit of adventure. I expect Gedling realized pretty quick just how dangerous Ted had become. The sudden change in the boy wasn't going to go unnoticed. There'd be questions asked—and in war-time, questions were dangerous. The trouble was how to repair the damage. But it was repaired all right. Very effectively repaired. Well, I had to leave Larcombe the next day and that was the last I saw of the gang for a long, long time. I was drafted out to Palestine soon after this, slap into the mess out there. But through it all I couldn't get my mind off Ted. I think the sun must have made it worse. You know, the monotony. We used to get so weary and sick, we couldn't even be bothered to talk to one another, sweating through the desert, thinking, thinking. And it got worse with me. I sort of lived inside myself all the time. I know it sounds fantastic—but all the months I was out there, there'd be hours on end when I hardly knew what I was doing. Marching especially. I'd get in my stride and go on brooding till I might as well have been in Scotland as Jerusalem. Fantastic, but it's true. It went on like that for months. I can hardly believe it myself now when I look back on it. The thing grew and grew and pounded away at me till you might have thought Ted had been my own son and they'd butchered him under my own eyes. Then when Armistice came, it all stopped. Quite suddenly. That is to say, I stopped all this brooding. But the effect of the brooding was there. It was there for ever. Without consciously meaning to, I'd come to a decision. A plan was already mapped out. A very vague plan, like something you'd dream about and think how wonderful it would be if it could really happen. Even the very decision was just something planted right away at the back of my mind like a spider asleep. I didn't come back to England after the Armistice. I got in with a Greek trader at Port Said and worked with him for a bit. I was a changed man. I'd lost all my ambition. I didn't even want to come home.

"Well, when I got fed up with Port Said, I worked my way round to India and did more clerking work for a firm in Bombay. I was lucky there. I made a bit of money. But I was restless. I didn't really know what I did want, but I knew I must move on. I moved on. This time to Australia. With the money I'd saved, I set up with a store of my own just outside Perth: a sort of junk shop rather like the one I've had here. And it was in Perth I met Dodson.

"Now this Frank Dodson was one of the Circle's contact-men in London, and it was to him I'd always delivered the stuff in the old days. I'd been pretty lonely out there in Perth and when I saw him in the street one day, like a fool I rushed up to him and made myself known. I'd grown my beard by that time and he didn't recognize me at first. But he soon did when I mentioned the Circle. I took him back with me and made him stay the night. It seemed he'd been fighting out in the East too and that he'd done pretty much like I'd done, except that he hadn't been satisfied with clerking and store-keeping. He'd been mixed up in a lot of shady business and he'd only just managed to steer clear of the police. He'd landed up in Perth broke to the wide, and I think he was as glad to see me as I was to see him. Only for a different reason.

"Again to cut the story short—I let him stay on with me till something turned up for him, and I've wished ever since that I hadn't. To begin with, he called up all the old associations. The question of the Larcombe gang and Ted came back with all its old force and insistence. I might have stayed in Australia, I might have been in Perth at this very minute—if Dodson hadn't turned up. He got money out of me too. And stayed on. I couldn't get rid of him. He used to spend most of his time down at the billiard saloons, gambling, loafing around, and he'd come home soused every night.

"In the end, I got very fed up. I decided to come home. In any case, I was making very little money, and Ted's death had become an obsession again. I couldn't do anything. All day, brooding, brooding all day. I used to dream of Gedling, Ridd, Pratt and Yeo as—as filthy devils—slimy—horrible. I had nightmares and woke up sweating. It got so bad that I just couldn't bear it any longer. I told Dodson that I was clearing out and very foolishly told him that I was going to change my name to Hannabus. Why I chose Hannabus, I don't know, unless it was because there was a big shop in Perth with that name. I sold up, gave Dodson enough money to get him round to Melbourne, and caught the next boat out.

"That's six or seven years ago. I'd changed a lot by then, remember. Out in the East I seemed to have shrivelled up. My nature, mannerisms and so on had changed as much in those twelve, thirteen, fourteen years as my appearance. With a beard, spectacles and a new name, I felt as safe as the Bank. I was safe.

"When I got back I stayed in Setterham for a bit, waited till that shop of mine was empty and then took it. It was weird I can tell you, coming back like that. And at first I found it tremendously difficult not to give myself away. You know, having to pretend to know nothing about the people who I'd been brought up with as a boy and making fresh acquaintance with them. It was most difficult with Bert Yeo, now that he'd taken the Cloven and I was seeing him two or three times every day. It was easier with Ridd, because John-Thomas never expected you to say anything—with him, all you'd got to do was to listen. The other two were easier still. Gedling I hardly ever saw and there was never any need for me to talk to the Vicar. The irony of it all was that now I had come so far in the business, I seemed to have lost all my old loathing and mad hate against the principals. When I first arrived, of course, I told myself that the best thing I could do would be to get a gun and shoot them all down then and there, and get it over and done with. But that mood soon passed. You see, it was such an anti-climax to come back and find them such harmless old chaps—Ridd and Yeo especially. Old Bert, fat and benevolent, doling out drinks with a smile on his face as if he'd never so much as broken the most innocent Bye Law all his life. Comedian Ridd, drinking his rum, the life and soul of the Bar. Gedling a doddering old recluse, and Pratt just a bad-tempered, lazy, normal country clergyman. It was absurd to think that these four had made such a mess of my life, haunted me for years, almost driven me mad. It was absurd! Especially when the thought gradually came to me that perhaps, after all, young Ted really had been washed overboard. It was absurd! But the spider still sat at the back of my mind. They'd been out of the drug business for a long time now, of course. I've never been able to get it really straight—but putting two and two together, as far as I can see there'd been a split after the Ted affair, a big split. Drug-running was one thing, murder was another. It must have given Pratt especially a real shaking. But Bert Yeo was the softest hearted of the lot. I can just imagine him, half-sentimental in a maudlin sort of way, half-worried to death over the possible consequences, losing sleep, going off his feed. You see, Pratt had never been really happy in the outfit, and with Bert sympathizing with him, I should think between them they put further action right out of the question. Ridd, of course, would think no more of it than he would of swatting a fly. And Gedling would be so fuddled with whiskey he'd just never be sober enough to consider it in a detached sort of way. I think that's how the split would come about. Pratt terrified and surly, Yeo terrified and dumb—on one side, and the other two pooh-poohing it but quite unable to carry on by themselves. I'll bet there were one or two interesting parties up at Old Barton before the end did come. Anyhow, that's just my surmises.

"All I know definitely is that the end did come pretty soon after young Ted went. There must have been a share-out of some kind because, you see, Bert Yeo was able to take the Cloven over and Ridd was able to buy his boat—both more or less at the same time. It must have hit Gedling pretty hard. I know for a fact he'd very little money of his own and I'm quite sure he'd done no saving like the others. The amount he drank was phenomenal. I've never seen anything like it—and he used to have them all up there drinking with him. He probably fought them tooth and nail, and then, when he saw it was no use going on, kicked 'em out of the house and told 'em he'd put a bullet in anybody who showed up again! It's just the sort of thing he would do.

"But to get back to me. As I tell you, I settled down in my shop and after the first novelty of pretending to be somebody else had worn off, I was quite happy and contented. I still thought about my plan now and again, but it was more fanciful, more remote than ever. The devilish schemes I had made in the desert seemed very much out of place in Larcombe. However, I never stopped toying with the idea of destroying these four men in as horrible and appropriate a way as possible. And make no mistake about it, these plans of mine—although, as I say, they were fanciful and remote—were nevertheless carefully worked out in great detail. If only I could have hated them as much then as I had done out East, all this would have happened four or five years ago. But, I repeat, out in the street, in the pub, chatting to them, doing things for them in my shop. I didn't hate them. It was only when I went to bed or when I'd been sitting by myself for a long time, that the old feeling would come back. Whenever it did, I used to make excuses to myself. I'd say: 'Oh, but in any case, you must wait. You must wait till Hannabus is well established in Larcombe. If anything happened to these four men, the first person they'd suspect would be a stranger. And so I waited. My plans simmered, modified themselves, grew more daring, more elaborate, sometimes more restrained and sometimes they ceased to simmer at all. Can you understand all this? I don't suppose you can. After what's happened you may well think me crazy. And all this wavering of mine and this twenty-year-old obsession, varying in intensity in the most extraordinary way, combined with what was most certainly a friendship between me, as Hannabus, and Yeo and Ridd, all this must seem quite irreconcilable to you. Don't worry. It does to me. But tell me, before I go any further, from what you know of me and from what I've told you already, do you think of me as an ordinary criminal? Do you think all this has come about because of something conceived in my brain on ordinary lines and for ordinary motives? Do you?"

"Go on," growled Plumper. "Hurry up—I'm getting cold."

Hannabus was growing excited. "You'd call it revenge— just ordinary sordid revenge. Well, I don't, I call it a disease. Something quite beyond me. D'you think, even if my brother had been killed, murdered, that I'd have chosen to have suffered for the best part of my life, to have cut myself off, mentally, spiritually, or whatever you call it, from everybody else in the world? It was a disease, I tell you—something quite beyond my control or anybody else's control. I'm sorry. I'm getting worked up. Forgive me. But I must say this. It was a disease that only became dangerous when it was affected by outside, accidental things. Nothing that I myself ever did or thought influenced it at all. If Dodson hadn't turned up again, nothing of all this might ever have happened. I'd probably have gone down to my grave still wishing that it could happen and without having lifted a little finger against any of them.

"But Dodson did turn up again. He didn't come to Larcombe. But he wrote to me from London. He'd found his way back to England. He was still on with his gambling, still finding it difficult to keep on the right side of the police, still broke, and he wrote to 'Mr. Hannabus, Larcombe,' just on the off chance that I'd be there. He wanted money of course. It was a nasty, half-threatening little letter, breathing blackmail. It had an extraordinary effect on me. I was just as I'd been when I met him in Perth. I was all worked up—and the old bogy was busy again. I replied to him by return of post. I forced myself to do it. I knew that if I once got him down here I should have burned my boats. I should be forced to act. Action, laying the ghost. No more brooding. Action!

"I wrote to him. The game was on. I came back from the post all trembling. I'd done it. As you can imagine, there was a pretty strong reaction to all this. I was terrified. I felt like bolting. For an hour or so, I just sat in my shop and shivered. It wasn't as if I'd been gradually working up to this all those years. It wasn't as if it was the logical carefully-timed outcome of my obsession. Oh no! You see, it was so sudden. It was shattering. You might even call it artificial. And on top of all this there was the question of Dodson. I had to fit him in with my plans.

"I went to the Cloven and had some drink. I felt a lot better. If I was going to kill four men—one more wouldn't make much difference. The drink did me good. I sat in the Bar, within a yard of Bert Yeo, one of the men who was going to die, and I never gave him a thought! That's typical. That just goes to show how I was feeling. It's fantastic—I suppose it sounds inhuman. But believe me, at that moment, I was looking at Yeo as impersonally as I'm looking at you now. I was too busy thinking. A new factor had cropped up, the police. Hitherto, I hadn't given a second's thought to that side of the question. And now, quite suddenly, it had taken the place of everything else. The police and Dodson! If I didn't kill Dodson, he'd give me away. If I did kill him, they'd trace me through him. I wasn't under-estimating them, was I? I started to panic again. How was I to kill him and yet run no risk of being caught through the tracing of my associations with him?

"If it hadn't been for Dodson, you'd have had little difficulty with this case. It would have been simple. I mean, there'd have been none of the bizarre trappings that have developed almost of their own accord. Most likely you'd have caught me. At least I should have had the satisfaction of having made things happen as I wanted them to happen. I shouldn't have bungled it as I have done. It wouldn't have got out of hand. As a criminal, I've been an unqualified failure. Practically every detail of the plan I've been perfecting for twenty years, went astray. The funny thing is, of course, that if everything had gone off according to schedule, you'd have been able to arrest me days ago. But simply because I was changing my plans every minute and acting on sudden impulses, I've been able to get away with it. I set out to kill those four men, and I didn't kill one of them!"

Hannabus sighed and then grinned at Plumper. The latter returned him a stony glare; he gave no sign of any interest in the old man's story. He seemed to be merely angrily preoccupied with the discomfort and humiliation of his position.

"I went back to the shop and wrote another letter to Dodson, telling him I'd got a job for him after his own heart. Easy money and no trouble at all. I gave him precise instructions. He was to take the early morning train to Setterham on the following Sunday, having left his luggage at the Paddington Cloakroom:

once on the train, he was to shave off his moustache. He had a long, droopy one rather like yours only more worn and stained. It's astonishing the difference the loss of a moustache makes to a man. On arrival at Larcombe he was to go straight to Scoutey's in the Orchard, go to church, show himself to Pratt, tell them at the Cloven that he was a detective, station himself conspicuously outside the Vicarage, and report to me at midnight. I told him that this would be worth a thousand pounds or more to him. I knew that would fetch him. I knew he'd do anything for a thousand. By the same post I sent a letter to Pratt and as a precaution I painted it. I'd read in some detective book or other that handwriting experts can't do anything with painting. That's probably rubbish—but that's what I did and that's why I did it. All I said was: 'If you're in Larcombe after midnight next Sunday somebody will tell the police about you know what!'

"It was a good safe bet. If he took it seriously and cleared out before the Sunday, there'd be a search for him, and Pratt knew very well he'd need to do a bit of explaining over a sudden bolt like that. On the other hand, if he didn't take it seriously, the presence of an accredited detective would make him change his ideas. The only risk was that he wouldn't take even Dodson seriously. But I knew my Pratt well enough to have a pretty shrewd idea that he would. As soon as I'd posted the letters, I set to work with enthusiasm. Panic had quite passed off. First of all I came to the cave here. It was going to play a big part in my programme. The old boat had been gone a long time, but there was still this dinghy which Gedling had used for his own purposes up till a few years back. I worked all night setting that right and I also had to spend a lot of time on the gear here: all the pulleys were rusty and the ropes rotten—but I fixed that too.

"Now as you've probably guessed by this time, one of my main ideas was to throw suspicion on everybody—on the old gang particularly. But the more the merrier! Peascod of course was a godsend—and Charnock and Annie Scoutey having bought paint boxes off me, they very nicely put themselves in line for a bit of suspicion as far as my letters were concerned. There was one essential difference though. It was for the benefit of the police that I tried to make Peascod and the rest look suspicious—but throwing suspicion on the gang was scientific terrorism. What I wanted to do was to work on them so much, get them into such a state with blackmail and intimidation and so on, that they'd kill one another out of sheer self-defence.

"Gedling was an ideal subject. I knew he was on the verge of lunacy. I knew there'd been a terrific row between him and the others. If I played on him properly and let him know that something was afoot, once Pratt was killed he'd be liable to do anything. It was as easy as pie to get in and out of his house. He'd no dogs, most of the rooms were empty, he and that fellow Costigan were invariably drunk; planting the fish and Peascod's metronome and the milk, peppering his windows with an airgun and so on, was child's play. Ridd's bungalow was easy to burgle too, with him being away, and I'd very soon taken an impression of his shoe.

"On the Sunday, Dodson arrived and played his part to perfection. As you'll have heard, everybody at the Cloven believed he was a detective and he certainly made an impression on the Vicar. When he came to me at midnight, he very much wanted to know what it was all about. I told him that the Vicar was going to bolt, taking his money with him and that I'd got a foolproof way of getting the money off him. I wasn't at all convinced in my own mind that he would bolt, mind you, but it was worth taking a chance. And in any case, I was determined to get rid of Dodson that night.

"I brought him down here, we got the boat out, we rowed round to the path on Crale Cliffs, and there we waited. We had to wait quite a bit and Dodson began to get impatient. Even I was getting worried and I was trying to think up some excuse for him. Then just as things were getting really awkward, we saw the headlights of a car coming up from Larcombe. It was Pratt all right. We planted ourselves in the middle of the road to stop him—and then things went all wrong. Dodson took charge, treating it as if it was a hold-up pure and simple. He pulled out a gun, yanked Pratt out of the car and ordered him to hand over his money. Matters had been taken completely out of my control and for a minute or two I didn't know what to do. To make things worse, the Vicar showed fight, and when Dodson threatened him with the gun, he backed away towards the edge of the cliff. He made the one gesture of his life. He threw back his head and said in the pompous way he always spoke, 'I defy you to shoot me, you hooligan!'

"I took that as my cue. 'Shoot, Dodson!' I shouted. 'It's part of the plan.'

"He didn't hesitate for a second. Pratt coughed, took a step backwards, doubled up and backed away over the cliff. I think Dodson was almost as unnerved as me. He stood still for a second or two, looking down at his revolver stupidly. My heart was beating as it's never beat before. Then Dodson laughed. 'Well, boy, how was that?'

"I said nothing. Instead I gave him the Ridd footprints and made him stamp them round about the car and where he'd been struggling with Pratt. Lucky for me, he was very flustered and almost hysterical and all he could say was: 'What about the dough, what about the dough?' I just said the first thing that came into my mind. 'We shall have to hurry,' I said; 'it's back there at the Vicarage.'

"You can tell how upset he was because he never questioned that. Actually, he didn't have much time to, because I stuck a knife into him at the bottom of the path."

Hannabus was staring straight in front of him; his eyes were glazed and he was talking very fast.

"My God, it was terrible. It was like killing a pig or something. Shooting's a different matter, but to stab a man in cold blood. No, perhaps it wasn't cold blood. It can't have been. I know I was going mad with excitement and anxiety. He was in front of me, below me. It was a big knife. I got both hands round the handle, shut my eyes and plunged down on him. He fell and I fell on top of him. God, it was awful. You've never sweated cold, have you? No? Well, I did then. You can't believe what it's like to sweat cold. I lay on the rocks for a few minutes, panting. I wanted to be sick. Even if I'd wanted to, I couldn't have made sure whether he was dead or not. Then the nausea passed. I dragged him to the boat, huddled him in and pushed off. Can't you see me there? A full moon, me rowing away there with him lying in the stern, the knife still in his back. I couldn't bring myself to pull it out. I rowed on frantically. For that moment I didn't care what happened. I didn't care at all. I rowed on till I came to the rock in the middle of the creek. I hadn't looked behind me once till then. But the rock gave me an idea. Originally, I'd meant to take him over to the cave but I was in such a state that all I wanted to do was to get rid of him, the quicker the better. I lugged him on to the rock and covered him up with stones. Then I suppose I took the boat back to the cave, and went to bed. But I can't tell you anything about that. I was like a man in a dream and shivering, shivering the whole time. I got to bed and slept like a log.

"I was a changed man when I woke up. From that morning, the Monday morning until this very moment, I've been as cool as a cucumber. I had no more trouble with my nerves and my emotions. The rest has just been commonplace. My subconscious, as they call it, had solved all the immediate problems in my sleep, I suppose. I'd planned out my painted-letter campaign. I'd determined to find out if Pratt had left anything behind at the Vicarage which might put you on to the existence of the smuggling. I'd remembered Peascod's handkerchief that he'd left behind in my shop months ago and that I'd used on my finger when I cut it with a tin-opener. And best of all, I'd decided what to do with Dodson's body. I'd found a way of fitting it in with my original plans. I thanked my lucky stars that I hadn't left him at the bottom of the Crale Cliffs, because what would Gedling, Yeo and Ridd have thought if *two* bodies had been found there? They'd have thought that a common enemy was responsible for both. Now for my purposes that would have been bad. I wanted to dissociate the two, to make Dodson's death seem more mysterious and therefore, to them (since they had got my threatening letters), more alarming. You know—fear of the unknown. For this purpose, it would be specially useful if I could arrange it so that Dodson's body might be found near Gedling's house. So on the Monday night I got the boat out again, rowed over to the rock, stripped him, weighted his clothes and dumped them in the sea. I was as calm then as a surgeon on an appendix case. Then I put him in the boat, rowed round to the Gap, dragged him up through there as best I could and left him in the bushes in front of Old Barton. I realized the mistake

I'd made as soon as I got back to bed—but it was too late to do anything about it then. I didn't sleep much, I can tell you. I was worried. But worried, as it turned out, for no reason at all. You see, it suddenly occurred to me that once you'd found him, you'd be able to trace him—moustache or no moustache. So I decided that the only thing to do was to get rid of the head. I needed the body for Gedling remember, the sooner the better. I'd do it the next afternoon. There'd be nobody about in the Gap. I could hop up the bit of cliff behind my shop, run round through the woods, and it would be a hundred to one against anybody seeing me. If anybody came to the shop while I was away and the police asked for an alibi, I could always say I was busy in my workshop at the back and didn't hear them.

"I went to the Cloven for some drink and I took it as providential when Costigan came in and said they were going to be away for the afternoon. It made things so much easier. But that piece of luck was cancelled out and more than cancelled out when I found Peascod and Rosa sitting there by the pool.

"I'd sawn the head off and, funny enough, it didn't upset me a bit. No more than gutting a bird. And I'd counted on taking it down and chucking it into the sea. Them being there, of course, put a stop to all that. However, I thought if young Peascod was there when the head turned up it would certainly help to lay a false trail—after the handkerchief and the metronome and so on. So I dropped it in the stream, and got back here as quick as I could.

"And that, Mr. Plumper, is all I've had to do with this affair! After that, it was out of my hands.

"Oh no—I beg your pardon! I tried to kill you and I knocked Jack Marsden out. I'm sorry I had to push those rocks down on to you, but you see, I was determined to beat the police and you seemed to be making such progress. Peascod had told me all about it, you know, finding the blood on the rock and all that. The boy seemed so sure that you'd have everything cleared up in no time."

Hannabus chuckled.

"He has an enormous respect for you, that boy. I honestly didn't mean you any harm—as you. But you see, with Gedling, Yeo and Ridd still alive, I simply couldn't afford to be arrested. If I had got you, you'd have had Peascod's eloquence and belief in your own powers to thank for it! It was purely by chance that I came to knock Jack Marsden out. I was up at Old Barton that night, having a look round. As a matter of fact, I was expecting John-Thomas to turn up. Both he and Gedling, knowing that Pratt's death was in some way connected with the old game, and knowing too that someone was trying to get at them both, would want to get together, being the two leading members of the gang. Oh yes, I was expecting John-Thomas to pay a call and I was quite determined, if he did turn up, to throw all my old plans overboard and do for him in the wood with my own hands. Jack Marsden was the hell of a complication. He's a nice boy and I'm sorry I had to hit him like that. But what else could I do?

"D'you know what happened after that? No, I don't expect you do. Oh, it was grand! It was the one part of my whole scheme that went right. I hung about the living-room window, trying to find out what was going on, when suddenly there was a shot. The curtains were drawn and I couldn't see anything. I waited for a little while and I was just thinking of breaking in, when I heard the side door open. I nearly laughed out loud for joy. Gedling and John-Thomas came out—but not as you'd expect two confederates to come out of a side door. Oh no! Gedling was on his hands and knees and balanced across his back was a sack, and in the sack was J-T. Ridd."

Hannabus jerked his thumb in the direction of the bundle that had been worrying Plumper for so long. "That's him. Old Lionel was always a clever devil. He proved it that night. I suppose he thought it was Ridd who was getting at him and got him up to his house on some pretext, and he wasn't going to let you know either, if he could help it. He carried him on his back as slowly and carefully as a snail right across the lawn. Then he stepped into the stream, pulled the sack after him and waded all the way down to the pool. I followed him. He wasn't giving you much chance with your bloodhounds, was he? When he got to the pool, he hauled the sack over the rocks up to the tunnel entrance here—and here it is. Then he went back the same way he'd come. It gave me great satisfaction to see that little comedy. It meant at least that I'd partially succeeded. It made me proud!

"As you've seen for yourself, what happened after that has had nothing to do, directly, with me—and I can assure you, it hasn't given me much satisfaction. But I suppose that's ungrateful of me. Admittedly they're all dead now. My purpose has been achieved—but it isn't me who's achieved it. Satisfyingly and as a whole, I mean."

Hannabus ran his fingers through his hair, sighed, got to his feet and went over to the big doors at the end of the cave. He shot back the bolt and swung them open. The wind blew in cold. He seized hold of a rusty chain hanging from the roof and pulled hard, like a sexton tolling a bell. The great iron bar creaked forward out over the Gap. Hannabus took a length of thin rope, skilfully threw one end over the bar, made a noose with the two ends and pulled the free end tight. Then he made another noose and left it dangling, as a rope dangles from a gibbet.

Plumper, with damp hands and dry throat, still remained silent.

"Good night," said Hannabus, and stepped forward to the very edge of the cave. He placed his head carefully within the noose. "I'm doing this because I can't see what else there is for me to do. I know it's an anti-climax, but the tension of this last week has been more than you can possibly realize. I should certainly go mad if I lived any longer. This afternoon I toyed with the idea of giving myself up in the approved manner and going through with a full-fledged sensational trial. It would have interested me—especially as I've never been in a police court all my life. But I've decided against it. It would probably be so long drawn out. Good night."

He stepped off the edge. The rope tightened with a jerk, swayed and eventually came to rest.

Plumper, icy cold and bound so tight that he could move no part of his body except his head, looked now at the wooden leg protruding from the sack, now at the straight rope that quivered just a very little in the night wind. He said two prayers: first, that there should be oil enough in the lamp to give him light throughout his detestable vigil; second, that Inspector Blutton should not be the one to loose his humiliating bonds.

Daylight would bring a patrolling constable to the Starehole Gap, and however dull this constable might be, he could hardly fail to notice the remains of Sebastian Hannabus dangling on a rope from the mouth of a cave.

But it was a long time to daylight.

Printed in Great Britain
by Amazon

24412323R00143